Resounding Praise for
Dark R̶i̶d̶e̶

"*Dark Ride* is Lou Berney at his best. T̶ at a theme park who finds his purpose̶ dren is both thrilling and heartbreakir̶ story of a man who finally stands for something after a lifetime of falling for anything will haunt you."

—S. A. Cosby, *New York Times* bestselling author of
Razorblade Tears and *Blacktop Wasteland*

"*Dark Ride* is a remarkable book written by Lou Berney, a storyteller I admire as a writer and cherish as a reader. *Dark Ride* effortlessly grabs you and does not let you go until the final page. I didn't want this book to end, and it stayed with me long after I finished reading it. Lou Berney is a magnificent writer with talent to burn."

—Don Winslow, *New York Times* bestselling author of
The Cartel and *City on Fire*

"Poor Hardly Reed! There he is, just peacefully floating through life on a marijuana cloud, working in a rundown amusement park, when he encounters two kids he suspects are being abused. For once in his life he realizes he can't stand by and do nothing. Obsession leads him down a heart-wrenching and twisting path, populated by a richly drawn cast of weird and lovable characters and dangerous scenarios. *Dark Ride* is moving, deeply involving, funny, breathless, and I loved every single page of Hardly's harrowing journey from stoner to sleuth."

—Lisa Unger, *New York Times* bestselling author of
Last Girl Ghosted and *Confessions on the 7:45*

"*Dark Ride* is a brilliant book from a master storyteller. Sometimes the hero you need is the person you least expect and Berney's novel takes you on a remarkable journey where you witness an unlikely stoner become the hero two children in trouble need."

—T. J. Newman, *New York Times* bestselling author of *Falling*

"I've been a Lou Berney fan for years, and *Dark Ride* is a cause for celebration. A suspense novel shot through with heart and soul, it has the feel of an instant classic. Through the journey of Hardly Reed, a lovable pothead turned amateur detective, Berney wrestles with a central existential question: what do we owe our neighbors, and what are we willing to give up to help them?"

—Steph Cha, bestselling author of *Your House Will Pay*,
winner of the Los Angeles Times Book Prize

"*Dark Ride* is a wild, funny, intense, charming, brilliantly written thriller that I couldn't have loved more. From page one to the stunning end, I was under its spell. (If you don't love this book, give me a call so I can tell you what a moron you are.)"

—Lisa Lutz, *New York Times* bestselling author of
The Spellman Files and *The Passenger*

"*Dark Ride* is quite simply dynamite. Lou Berney lights the fuse on the first page and from there, the suspense builds to an utterly explosive climax. Berney offers an endearing and quirky cast of characters, not the least of which is Hardly, the most unusual and likeable protagonist to come along in a great while. This is a story that grabs you by the throat, then reaches deep into your heart. It's a *Dark Ride*, yes, but one well worth the trip."

—William Kent Krueger, *New York Times* bestselling author of
The River We Remember

"Lou Berney is such a talent, and he's at the top of his game here. Hardly Reed is a protagonist to root for—an affable stoner who just might be the one person who can save two children in danger. *Dark Ride* will grab your heart in chapter one and not let go until the final, searing page."

—Alafair Burke, *New York Times* bestselling author of *Find Me*

"Put your to-be-read pile to the side. A new book from Lou Berney should go to the top of your agenda."

—Lori Rader-Day, award-winning author of *The Death of Us*

"Berney's pitch-perfect portrait of the mellowest of dudes on a hero's journey is both hilarious and terrifying."

—*Air Mail* (12 Best Mystery Books of 2023)

"Only Lou Berney could create Hardly, one of the most endearing characters in recent memory. Writing in his Hardly's guileless, hilariously dude-ish narrative voice, Berney is incapable of producing a wrong or unnecessary sentence."

—*Air Mail*

"An insightful look at being an adult, taking responsibility and discovering your inner power."

—*Sun Sentinel*

"Stellar. . . . Hardly is a memorable hero with an extremely satisfying arc, and Berney draws the supporting players with equal care, wringing pathos from their interplay as much as the heartbreaking premise. Few readers will finish this unmoved."

—*Publishers Weekly* (starred review)

"Hardly's trajectory is helped by Berney's superb writing; sometimes self-consciously noir . . . sometimes just colorful . . . it adds both gravity and grace to the protagonist's stubborn, self-destructive path. The whole novel is worth it for the poignant beauty of the final paragraph."

—*Kirkus Reviews*

"[Berney] introduces readers to an immediately unforgettable character: Hardly Reed. . . . Berney brings a compelling human touch to a story that grabs hold of the reader early and never lets go."

—*CrimeReads* (The 10 Best Crime Novels in September 2023)

"Occasionally I'll read a new book that is so exciting, engaging, and beautifully conceived that I cannot wait to write about it and share my latest discovery with readers everywhere. . . . I just found a novel that is so incredible I wanted to tell you about it. The book is *Dark Ride* by Lou Berney. . . . So inspiring, thrilling, and exhilarating, I could not put this book down, devouring it in one sitting."

—*Dayton Daily News*

"*Dark Ride* proves to be one of the most engaging books of the year. Lou Berney gives us a protagonist we root for not only to save the day but to improve his life. The storytelling is crisp and clear with deft, nuanced touches that give it a grounded quality."

—*The Hard Word*

DARK RIDE

DARK RIDE

A Thriller

LOU BERNEY

wm

WILLIAM MORROW

An Imprint of HarperCollins*Publishers*

DARK RIDE. Copyright © 2023 by Lou Berney. All rights reserved. Printed in the United States of America. No part of this book may be used or reproduced in any manner whatsoever without written permission except in the case of brief quotations embodied in critical articles and reviews. For information, address HarperCollins Publishers, 195 Broadway, New York, NY 10007.

HarperCollins books may be purchased for educational, business, or sales promotional use. For information, please email the Special Markets Department at SPsales@harpercollins.com.

A hardcover edition of this book was published in 2023 by William Morrow, an imprint of HarperCollins Publishers.

FIRST WILLIAM MORROW PAPERBACK EDITION PUBLISHED 2024.

The Library of Congress has catalogued a previous edition as follows:
Names: Berney, Louis, author.
Title: Dark ride : a thriller / Lou Berney.
Description: First edition. | New York : William Morrow, an imprint of HarperCollins Publishers, [2023] | Summary: "From Lou Berney, the acclaimed, multi award-winning author of November Road and The Long and Faraway Gone, comes a Dark Ride"—Provided by publisher.
Identifiers: LCCN 2023012570 (print) | LCCN 2023012571 (ebook) | ISBN 9780062663863 (hardcover) | ISBN 9780062663887 (trade paperback) | ISBN 9780062663894 (ebook)
Subjects: LCGFT: Thrillers (Fiction) | Novels.
Classification: LCC PS3552.E73125 D37 2023 (print) | LCC PS3552.E73125 (ebook) | DDC 813/.54—dc23/eng/20230316
LC record available at https://lccn.loc.gov/2023012570
LC ebook record available at https://lccn.loc.gov/2023012571

ISBN 978-0-06-266388-7

24 25 26 27 28 LBC 5 4 3 2 1

For Steve Harrigan

1

I'm lost, wandering, and somewhat stoned. This parking lot, when you're in the middle of it, seems much vaster and more expansive than it does from the street. Or do I just seem much less consequential? That's the question. One for the ages.

It's July, hot as balls. I stare up. The sky, pale and papery, looks like it's about to burst into flame.

How would you describe the sky to someone who has never seen a sky? You'd have to explain how it's different every day. So many shades of blue, of gray. And we're not even talking about sunrise or sunset. Plus the clouds! How would you describe clouds?

"You need some help?"

"What?" I say.

Some dude in a suit is about to climb in his car. He's about my age, probably a couple of years out of college. With the suit and the haircut, though, he's all business. Me, I'm wearing board shorts, flip-flops, and a vintage faded Van Halen T-shirt that I found for five bucks at Goodwill. I haven't cut my hair in almost forever and I'm a minimum-wage scarer at an amusement park fright zone.

Who's happier, though, him or me? I mean, I hope he's happy, but I'm happy too. I don't need much. I don't want much. I have everything I need and want. The perfect balance.

"You're just standing there," the dude in the suit says.

"Yeah. No. I'm good. Thanks."

"Can you move so I can back out?"

"Oh. Yeah. Do you know where the new municipal court administration building is?"

He points to the far end of the parking lot.

"Right on," I say. "Thanks."

The new municipal building isn't actually a new building. It's the old municipal offices inside a different old building. Inside is your standard grim government environment. Low ceilings and dying fluorescent tubes, scuffed floors and dented doors, smudged handprints climbing the walls like vines. People pace up and down the long hallway. One woman is muttering to herself.

"Breathing in, I calm my body," she says as she paces past me. "Breathing in, I calm my body."

I get in line at the parking window. I have a ticket I need to deal with by five o'clock today, which is eleven minutes from now. Waiting will probably take longer than that, but if you're in line by ten till, they usually let you slide.

We inch forward. Down the hallway to my right a guy is kicking a closed door. The woman is still pacing and muttering. Two dudes in line behind me argue loudly and irately first about some quarterback, then about some politician, then about Sonic hamburgers vs. Whataburger hamburgers. It must be exhausting to have so many strong opinions. I only have mild preferences, and usually not even that.

A woman in front of me worries into her phone about a suspicious lump in her armpit. I'm very glad for the bowl I smoked in my car. The weed makes me feel like I'm being gently removed from this moment by a big rubber eraser.

Down the hallway to my left, a couple of kids sit by themselves on a wooden bench. I just now notice them because it's an extra-large bench and they're extra-small. Six or seven years old? A little boy and a little girl. I'm impressed by how well-behaved they are. They're not squirming or wrestling or even swinging their legs. At their age I would have been crawling around, licking the fossilized chewing gum stuck to the bottom of the bench.

We inch forward. Finally, it's my turn at the window.

"Pay or delay?" the clerk asks.

"Delay."

The clerk stamps my parking ticket, authorizing my request for a thirty-day continuation. I step away from the window. While I'm here, I realize, I should go ahead and get a continuation for my ticket due next week. The dude behind me looks anxious, though, so I yield the window to him. A good deed, my mom always said, never hurt anyone.

On my way out, I see those two little kids still sitting all by themselves on the big bench. Is it kind of weird that they're sitting all by themselves? I look around for a likely parent or guardian, but everyone is wrapped up in their own world. Nobody even glances at the kids.

It's none of my business, and I have zero understanding of child development, but the little boy and little girl seem way too young to be on their own—especially in a place like this, with so many sketchy people pacing and muttering and kicking at doors.

I walk over to the bench. I give the kids plenty of space and crouch down so that I'm not looming over them like Godzilla in Tokyo. Technically I'm one of those sketchy people myself, after all.

"Hey, dudes," I say. "What's up?"

The little boy looks past me, over my shoulder. The little girl looks over my other shoulder. They're brother and sister, definitely. Twins? Unclear. They have the same sandy blond hair, the same broad forehead, the same enormous green eyes. They don't seem scared. It's more like they're riding the bus to work, arms folded across their chests and staring out at the same tedious scenery that rolls past every day.

"Is your mom or dad around?" I say.

No reaction. Just: *This bus, this route, so tedious.* I decide, with no scientific basis whatsoever, that the boy is six and the girl is seven. They're wearing miniature sneakers and miniature jeans. The little boy is wearing a miniature striped rugby shirt, blue and yellow. The little girl is wearing a miniature T-shirt with HAPPY! spelled out with sequins. Though some of the sequins are missing, so it's just, *Happy*.

I move my face three inches to the right so the little boy can't miss it. He doesn't even blink. I'm invisible. His eyes are offline, open but empty, just a dim light and lots of shadows.

Same thing with his sister. Very unsettling. They're cute kids. I really wish they'd smile or giggle. I'd get behind even a scowl or a glare.

Should kids be as skinny as these kids? With such narrow, delicate necks and chests, wrists and ankles? They're more like stick figure drawings than actual human children.

I notice the little girl's ankle, the exposed skin between her sock and her jeans—three round dots the size of shirt buttons. Moles? That's my first thought. But the dots are all exactly the same size and too perfectly round. My second thought is: ink? But what kid that age has a tattoo?

From a distance the dots are black, but when I lean closer I see they're actually dark, dark red, just rimmed with black.

Cigarette burns. That's what they are. I can positively identify cigarette burns because in high school some lunatic sophomore dropped acid at a party and thought his skin was made from ballistic nylon fabric. "Watch this," he said, then pressed a cigarette against the inside of his wrist. He screamed and screamed, even after people found some butter to spread on him.

I feel my stomach twist. Cigarette burns? The little boy's socks are pulled up so I can't see his ankles. But then I spot three dots lined neatly along his collarbone, just beneath the collar of his rugby shirt. These cigarette burns are a brighter red than the girl's, with a thinner black edge. More recent.

I stand and take a step backward. One single cigarette burn might, possibly, be an accident. But three on the girl and three on the boy? Arranged in neat lines, evenly spaced? There's no way that's an accident. I'm dizzy. All the noise around me, echoing voices and clattering heels and buzzing fluorescents, drops away and then, a second later, comes roaring back twice as loud. The kids still don't look at me. They just sit and gaze off at nothing.

A woman steps out of an office. She hurries over to the bench. She's the mother. Has to be. She looks just like the kids, with the same sandy hair, the same big eyes. Blouse, skirt. I don't know if she works here or is a citizen with municipal business. The main thing I notice is how sharp she is, her face and her body both, all corners and edges, like origami.

"Let's go, guys," she tells the kids. For the first time they stir. The little girl corkscrews slowly off the bench and slides to the floor. The little boy studies his sister's move, then duplicates it precisely.

The mother is looking at me now. She's suspicious, understandably. As in *Who are you with the long hair and board shorts and why are you staring at my children?* But then I catch movement and glance down. She's tugging at the collar of the little boy's rugby shirt, rearranging it—trying, I realize, to hide the cigarette burns on his collarbone.

What!

The mother eases between me and the kids, blocking my view, and hustles them away. It all happens too fast. My mind drags behind, still three minutes in the past, still processing that first look at the cigarette burns. Down the hallway sunlight flashes as the glass doors of the building slide open. Before I can think or move or even think about moving, the mother and her kids are gone.

I look around for help, but every nearby person is deep into their phone or yawning obliviously. There was a security guard roaming the ground floor earlier—wasn't there? Maybe he's down by the elevators. I jog in that direction, then wonder if I should be following the mother and her kids instead. I wheel around and jog back the other way. The glass doors take forever to slide open wide enough for me to squeeze through sideways.

A couple of vapers lurk outside the building in a cloud of peach-flavored steam. In the parking lot, there's no sign of the mother and her kids. The glare from all the windshields is right in my eyes.

A dark blue car pulls out of a space not far from where I'm standing. A Volvo, I think. The passenger window is down—it's the mother, staring straight ahead. Next to her is a man, driving. I can't get a good look at him. In the backseat I see the tops of two small heads.

Now what? I freeze again. The Volvo is swinging around, heading out. I can chase it across the parking lot. I can probably catch it. What do I do then, though?

License plate. License plate! I start trying to memorize the numbers, but then the little girl lifts her head and turns in her seat and looks out the back window. I'm startled when she looks right at me, right into my eyes. As the car speeds up and speeds away, it's like some strange spell has been lifted and I'm no longer invisible.

2

I go back inside. I need to locate someone, immediately, who is suited to handle this situation. Because I am definitely not someone suited to handle this situation. I have no special skills or talents, and nobody, ever, has put me in charge of anything. Scare acting at an amusement park fright zone doesn't entail much responsibility. Neither does DoorDashing or Grubhubbing, the other jobs on my résumé. In middle school I was second man off the bench for the basketball team. In my one and a half years of college, four years ago, I passed all my courses with flying B-minuses.

All that's fine with me. I like being ordinary. I enjoy the lack of pressure. But I'm getting squeezed hard right now. What am I supposed to do? The dark blue Volvo is gone. The mother and her kids are gone. I try breathing in to calm my body. It works, marginally. There's still no sign of that fucking elusive security guard.

The mother came out of an office. I'll start there. I walk over. The sign on the door says DRIVER IMPROVEMENT VERIFICATION. Ah-ha. I know this place from the old municipal building. It's where I had to show proof I completed traffic school a couple of years ago.

Inside the office, the waiting area is deserted—just empty chairs and a goth chick behind the plexiglassed-in reception desk, flicking through her phone.

"How much do you know about anal warts?" she asks me when I walk over.

"What?"

"The internet is rife with conflicting advice."

She's messing with me. "Hey," I say, "may I talk to someone, please?"

"Sign in."

She nudges a clipboard at me with her elbow, so she doesn't have to put down her phone. Her skin is excessively smooth and white, like it's been freshly poured or ladled, while everything else—her hair, the shadow around her eyes, her lips—is deep, heavy black. She must have to wear civilian attire at work, a vintage dress with flowers, frills around the sleeves, but her silver necklace spells out, in small letters, SATAN LOVES ME, THIS I KNOW.

"I'm not here for an appointment," I say. "Were you here, like, five minutes ago?"

"Sign in."

"Just listen. There was a woman. She was in here five minutes ago. I saw her leave. Sandy hair, maybe thirty-five years old, kind of really . . . sharp. Like origami."

The goth chick looks up from her phone. I have her mild, momentary interest, like she's noticed a dog wearing a hat. "Origami?" she says.

An older woman emerges from a cubicle behind reception. She has the stride of a supervisor, the chin up and out, hair the color of stainless steel. I'm relieved. This is a lady who lives to handle difficult situations.

"How may I be of assistance, sir?" she asks me.

I explain about the kids, the cigarette burns, the mother. The supervisor nods and nods and nods, and then, when I finish talking, she shakes her head.

"Hmm," she says. "The proper authorities should be notified."

I wait for more. That's it, though. The supervisor's eyebrows go up: *So if there's nothing else . . . ?*

"But *you're* the authorities," I say. "I'm notifying *you.*"

"We're city government," she says. "You'll need to speak with the state authorities. The Department of Human Services. Child Services, I would imagine."

I guess that checks out. At least now I know who to call. "What's her name? The mother? So I can report it to Child Services?"

"I'm afraid I can't give you that information," she says. "Our records are strictly confidential. It's a matter of legal liability."

What! "How am I supposed to report the incident to Child Services if you won't give me the mother's name?" I say. It's a genuinely sincere question. I'm not trying to be a dick.

The supervisor blinks slowly. She wants me to appreciate how patient she's remaining. And then she turns, walks away, and disappears back into her cubicle. I stand there in disbelief.

"Sign in," the goth chick says.

"Seriously?" I say.

"*Dude.*" She glances at me, then down at the clipboard. She glances back at me, then back down at the clipboard. "Sign the *sheet.*"

Oh. *Oh.* I get what she's trying to tell me. The sheet clipped to the clipboard is almost full. I scan down to the bottom. A lot of the signatures are just scrawls, but I have no problem making out the very last, most recent name. *Tracy Shaw.*

That's her. The mother. *Tracy Shaw.* The goth chick shows me her phone—a gif of a crowd going wild in the stands of some sporting event, celebrating a victory. I grab the chewed-up ballpoint that's Velcroed to the clipboard and write the mother's name on the heel of my hand.

"Thanks," I tell the goth chick and she shows me another gif—a guy in a race stumbling, falling, skidding on his face across the finish line.

In my car, I look up the Department of Human Services and call the main line. The automated system melts my brain. I press numbers. I return to previous menus. I keep getting dumped for some reason to the voicemail for Angela Prince-Stover, coordinator of Elders, Harmony, and Informatics. Who? Coordinator of what, what, and what?

Finally I get through to Child Protective Services. Because it's after five, I have to leave a message. I explain everything. I state and then spell out Tracy Shaw's name. I state and then spell out my name. I leave my number.

"Call me if you have any questions or, you know, if you need any additional information," I say. "Thank you very much."

I hang up, relieved. My job here is done. Child Protective Services will make sure those kids are okay and once again I don't have a worry in the world.

3

Nobody likes to be the Dead Sheriff. The hassle factor, compared to other jobs, is extreme. Townfolk Ghouls and Zombie Outlaws and Boot Hill Ghosts get to chill most of the night, shooting the shit and eating weed gummies while they wait for the next group to move through. The Dead Sheriff, on the other hand, is always on, always dealing with guests. And then at the end of every loop you get dragged helplessly away by the Outlaw Zombies. You don't even get a big finish.

I've worked at Haunted Frontier for close to two years, so I know how to lie low and avoid unnecessary irritation and labor. Today, though, I'm twenty minutes late. When I slink in, trying to stay invisible, the shift lead spots me and pounces.

"Why, hello, you," Duttweiler says.

A couple of Zombie Outlaws cackle at my misfortune. I pretend I don't hear Duttweiler. I grab a vest and a pair of cowboy boots and take a seat on a defunct bumper car. The scare actors use the park's old tinker shop for a dressing room. Concessions uses it to store fat, sagging bags of surplus Mountain Dew.

Duttweiler tosses me the gold badge. "My hero."

"Duttweiler. *Duttweiler.* My contributions to the team are much better utilized in a different capacity." Like chilling, for example. Like eating weed gummies. "Please."

He walks away. Salvador hops up and volunteers to be my deputy. A couple of Townfolk Ghouls lob plastic water bottles at him. The Zombie Outlaws cackle. Salvador is only sixteen, still in high school. He's too eager, too loud, and looks like a stick insect with braces. For some mysterious reason, and completely against my will, he's appointed himself my loyal and relentless minion.

Duttweiler looks at me. He'll throw me a bone and stick Salvador in a grave if I want. But I know the other Boot Hill Ghosts will just lob dirt clods at him all night. I feel bad for Salvador. Most of the reasons he's annoying aren't really his fault.

"Right on," I tell Salvador. "You're with me. Let's roll."

We pick up our first posse of guests in the central hub of the park. Beautiful America is a knockoff Disneyland that's been teetering on the verge of bankruptcy since the seventies or eighties. Haunted Frontier used to be a part of the park called Frontier America, until Frontier America collapsed into disrepair and somebody in management thought, *Huh, you know what, we can work with that, with collapse and disrepair.*

"Howdy, pardners," I tell the guests. "Ready for a terrifying trip back to the Wild West?"

"Howdy, pardners!" Salvador yells right in my ear.

I go over the rules. A tiny but ferocious-looking woman, like a teacup pit bull, is already grumbling. "I don't know why we have to pay a separate admission for this," she says. "This better be worth the eight extra dollars."

Nope, I could assure her, not even close. But I just tip my Stetson, make sure everybody has a wristband, and lead the way. During the day, Haunted Frontier is just sad and depressing, all the broken windows and sagging balconies and splintered clapboard. After dark, though, the town achieves actual eeriness. Shadows stretch unexpectedly, darkness spills and puddles. There's hardly any lighting—management cuts every corner.

A couple of Townfolk Ghouls stagger out of the General Store, moaning. I tell the tale of Infernal Gulch. Winter storm, massacre, cannibalism, etc. My mind drifts as I go through the spiel. I think about those kids at the municipal building. Do you know how painful a cigarette burn must be? How about three of them?

Those poor kids. I know someone else who'd have a hard time forgetting about them: my mom. She gave money to every homeless person she passed. She stopped for every flat tire and coaxed every lost dog into the backseat of our car. Once, I remember, we saw a dog standing frozen in the middle of the intersection. Traffic whizzed past, nobody slowing down. My mom pulled over and ran out into the street to get the dog. We spent an hour at least, probably more, going block to block in the neighborhood, ringing doorbells until we found the house where the dog lived.

I remind myself that those kids on the bench will be okay. They're in exactly the right hands now. Child Protective Services—it's in the name of the place, their literal reason for being!

More ghouls ahead, popping out of nowhere, shrieking and lunging. Up on Boot Hill: same. The Hanged Prisoner thrashes and gags.

"This is definitely not worth eight dollars so far," the teacup pit bull grumbles.

We wind back down into town. Three drunk high school girls pull smuggled-in bottles of mango White Claw out of their purses and start guzzling.

"Hey, I'm sorry, that's not allowed, please," I say. *No alcoholic beverages* is one of the rules I went over barely ten minutes ago. "You'll have to put those away."

The high school girls ignore me. A guy taking flash photos—*No flash photos at any time* was another one of the rules—ignores me too. There's nothing I can do. My badge is fake and my gun is fake and I have no duly appointed enforcement powers. Officially the Dead Sheriff is supposed to kick out anyone who violates the rules. Unofficially the Dead Sheriff is supposed to absolutely *not* kick anyone out because refunds will be demanded, complaints will be lodged. Officially the park's customer service motto is *Give every guest your best yes!*

Now the drunk high school girls are taking flash selfies. For Instagram or TikTok, I guess? Or something newer than that? I'm not into social media. It takes too much effort. That's my impression.

Here comes the pack of Outlaw Zombies, lurching ominously out of the jail.

"Oh, dang," I say. "This sure don't look good."

"This sure don't look good!" Salvador yells. He swats at a gnat and accidentally slaps himself in the face.

One of the drunk high school girls barfs up hard seltzer and blue cotton candy. The smell is unholy. Her friends squeal with delight. I'm not supposed to, but I slip the barfer a couple of free wristbands for a future visit. I can tell she's not feeling great right now.

A Townfolk Ghoul rips out an eyeball and squishes it in the palm of her hand. It's alarming the first few dozen times you see it.

I can't say I love working at Haunted Frontier. Honestly, though, I don't hate it either. The money isn't great, but it meets my needs. Very little is required of me, zero brainpower. When I leave Haunted Frontier for the night, I forget it exists. Compare that to my brother, Preston, who works for the city planning department and has to bring his work laptop home every night and weekend, who is constantly gnashing his teeth and rending his garments about this deadline or that promotion.

I am content right where I am. The first Outlaw Zombie reaches me and I go down without a fight.

4

Morning. Well, almost still morning. I lie in bed. I like to wake up slowly, gradually, easing into the day. Alarm clocks on phones are an invention sent back from the dystopian future to destroy us. I reach for the one-hitter on my milk-crate nightstand and fire up.

My mom was born in 1972, so the music she loved was from the eighties, her teenage years. She was all about Madonna and Prince, the Go-Go's and U2 and Whitney Houston, the Beastie Boys. Every morning before school she'd blast a song to wake me up, bouncing on my bed and singing along. She had a specific song for every day of the week. "Manic Monday" on Monday, of course. "Vacation" on Friday. That was our unbreakable tradition. Until she died, when I was nine, I don't think we missed a single day.

I try to imagine what waking up is like for those two kids with the cigarette burns. Is there a moment when they're not sure where they are? When they can hope that everything that's happened to them was just a dream?

I check my phone. Is it semi-worrisome that Child Protective Services hasn't called me back? No. It's only been two days since I left the message. Give them a minute, right? And maybe they don't even need to call me back. It's a strong possibility they have all the information they need.

I picture that dark blue Volvo again, the kids in the back. They get home. They pull into their driveway. Maybe the kids can relax while they're in the car. Maybe nothing bad happens to them in the car. Maybe the bad things only happen when they get home.

Is it the mother who's hurting the kids? Or is it the guy who drove the Volvo, the father or the boyfriend? The mother is definitely aware of the cigarette burns. She was definitely trying to hide them from me. Does that mean she feels guilty? Or does it just mean she didn't want to get busted? If she feels guilty, is it because she's responsible for the cigarette burns or because she's responsible for letting the cigarette burns happen?

I roll off my futon and pull on some clothes. I live in a garage apartment that is truly that, a room that used to be a two-car garage. It's fine, very spacious. A big rug covers a fair amount of the concrete floor and I have a portable heater for winter, a fan for summer. I've been meaning for a while to do more decorating. I have one poster taped to the wall above the futon. My friend Mallory gave it to me when I moved in. It's a copy of a famous painting, *The Fall of Icarus*—a farmer is plowing a field while off in the distance, in the ocean, a guy, Icarus presumably, has fallen into the water. He's just two tiny bare legs, kicking. The farmer doesn't notice. That's what grabs me about the painting, how it's composed. I didn't even notice those bare legs myself for a long time.

Why hasn't Child Protective Services called me back yet? I don't have any pressing obligations today, just a hang by the pool with Nguyen and Mallory, and DHS is only a fifteen-minute drive from my house, so I decide to drop by CPS and make one hundred percent sure that everything with those kids is good. What can it hurt?

I search the fridge and grab a leftover slice of pizza that smells viable, then head out. Getting across town takes longer than expected, traffic swallowing my elderly Kia Spectra the way Pompeii was engulfed by lava. The scenery is uninspiring. My city is a midsized metropolitan area in the middle of the middle of the United States. It's flat and sprawling and a lot like a lot of other places, with no distinguishing characteristics geographic or otherwise. If my city was a suspect in a crime, the eyewitnesses would have a tough time describing it. You could probably say the same thing about me.

I find the office for CPS after only a few wrong turns. It's similar to the office for Driver Verification, except the floor of this waiting area is buried under stacks of file folders. I thread my way through the clutter and find a dude down on his hands and knees behind the front counter. He's flipping through folders, sorting one giant teetering stack into two smaller but also teetering ones.

"Hey," I say, leaning over the counter. "Excuse me."

The dude climbs slowly to his feet. His hair puffs out in unique places and the tail of his button-down has pulled loose from his khakis. He looks like either he woke up five minutes ago or he hasn't slept in days.

"Fantastic," he says.

"I'm sorry?"

"Nothing. How can I help you?"

"My name's Hardly Reed. Hardy Reed, officially, but everyone calls me Hardly. I left a voicemail Monday. Two days ago? About a couple of kids I saw?"

"How can I help you?"

I feel like I just explained that to him, but I try again. "I left a voicemail two days ago. Around five-fifteen or so? It was kind of a disturbing situation. I just wanted to find out, I guess, how that's proceeding."

He smiles, then grins, then laughs. "You left the message two days ago?"

"Yeah."

"How rapidly do you think the wheels of justice turn around here?"

"I don't know."

He goes in reverse order this time, from laughing to grinning to smiling to looking once again like he hasn't slept in days. "You can give your statement directly to a caseworker, if you want."

"Sure. Okay."

We walk down a corridor to a small room. He closes the door, takes a seat at the desk, fiddles with an app on his phone.

"Testing, testing, testing," he says, and then plays it back. *Testing, testing, testing.* He opens a desk drawer and pulls out a legal pad. "Okay. Hit me."

"You're the caseworker?" I say.

"Dan. At your service. Hit me."

I go through what happened. He takes notes on the legal pad. Every now and then he lifts a finger to put me on pause and ask a question.

"You said the children were six and seven years old?"

"I think so. But I'm not sure."

"You're confident the marks you observed on the children were cigarette burns?"

"Very confident."

I'm telling him about the Volvo when his ringtone blasts. It's dialogue and sound effects from a submarine movie or video game. *Dive, dive, dive! Ahh-ooga! Ahh-ooga!*

He taps off the recording app and answers the call. "Hello, Richard," he says. "No, Richard. Yes, I would assume so. Respectfully, Richard, that's difficult for me to believe."

After he finishes the call, he apologizes for the interruption and checks his legal pad. "So . . . so we were discussing . . ."

"Do you need to turn that back on?" I say. I point to his phone on the desk.

"Right." He taps the recording app back on. "So . . . right. You said that in the car with the woman and the two children was a male passenger."

"I said he was driving. The male. He wasn't a passenger."

He frowns and crosses out a word on the legal pad. And then he keeps crossing it out—diagonal strokes slanted forward, diagonal strokes slanted backward, tight curlicues—until the word is completely obliterated.

"How many cases do you think I'm assigned right now?" he says.

"What?" I say.

"Ballpark it. I'll give you a hint. It's supposed to be a maximum of twelve at any given time. That's the rule. A *maximum* of twelve cases per caseworker. So how many cases do you think I'm assigned right now?"

I have no idea. I'm not sure why he's asking me. "Well . . ."

He lifts a finger to pause me. "I apologize," he says. "Never mind. Let's continue."

I've just finished answering Dan's follow-up questions when his ringtone blasts again. *Dive, dive, dive! Ahh-ooga!* "I'll be right back," he says. "One minute."

"No worries."

I hear muffled voices from the hallway or another office. Two voices, two guys. One of the voices, louder, says what sounds like, "Really? Really?"

A thud. Footsteps. The door opens. I sit up. It's not Dan, though, but a different guy in a button-down shirt and belted khakis. He's a little older than Dan, with the same frazzled hair but less of it. He slides into Dan's desk chair.

"Excellent." He squares the legal pad of Dan's notes in front of him. "Thank you for your statement. Let me explain how the process works. We'll open an investigation. We'll gather evidence and carefully assess it. I can absolutely, one hundred percent assure you that we treat all allegations of child endangerment with the utmost gravity."

"Excuse me," I say, "where's Dan?"

"Dan has decided to pursue other professional opportunities."

"He decided . . . what?" I was expecting him to say, *Dan has a personal situation at home he has to deal with,* or *Dan is feeling funky from Chipotle and ran to the men's room.* "You mean he quit? Just now?"

The new caseworker has an approach to eye contact that is uncomfortably intense. He reaches across the desk and at first I'm afraid he's going to squeeze my hand or my wrist, maybe pat me on the cheek. Instead he raps his knuckles on the wood laminate.

"Don't worry," he says. "This case will have our full and undivided attention. I can absolutely, one hundred percent assure you."

5

When I finally get to their apartment complex, around three, Nguyen and Mallory haven't made it down to the pool yet. They're taking bong rips and watching an old episode of *The Office*. Nguyen is explaining his theory that Stanley on *The Office* is actually dead and the entire series is set in his own personal hell.

"What about the trip to Tallahassee?" Mallory says. "Explain that, my friend. Stanley is deliriously happy when the Dunder Mifflin team goes down to open the Sabre store. How can he be in hell?"

Nguyen surrenders with a shrug, then clears the bong with superhuman lung power, like a trumpet player holding a note for an entire verse.

"This hybrid is fire," he says. He reloads the bong and hands it to me. "Very CBD forward, but your eyeballs will float out of your head too."

I take a rip. I'm not a connoisseur like Nguyen. You'd think I would be, all the weed I've smoked over the years. I have a general preference for balance and potency, but beyond that I'm down with whatever Nguyen provides.

The commercial ends. *The Office* resumes. We watch Dwight being Dwight. Jim being Jim. It's soothing. The bong rips are soothing. I start to separate slowly from my physical body, a soft silk glove being removed one finger at a time.

Still, my experience at Child Protective Services nags at me. It was kind of a clusterfuck, right? Not just Dan the caseworker quitting his job in the middle of my statement, but also all those stacks and stacks of files. Each file must be a separate case. How many caseworkers does CPS have? Not enough, if Dan was telling the truth. And why did the caseworker who replaced Dan keep reassuring me? That was not reassuring.

Though what do I know? A caseworker quitting in the middle of the day might have been some unusual and rare event. All those files in the waiting area might be completed cases, investigations successfully executed.

My brother, Preston, mover and shaker, might have some inside skinny on CPS since he works in local government. I step outside to give him a call.

"Why haven't you been by lately?" he says. "Come over for dinner this week."

"I'll try. I have to work."

"At the so-called amusement park?"

"How is it so-called? It's literally an amusement park, Preston."

"So-called *amusement*. You know if you had a real job, a career, you'd have normal hours. You could have a normal social life, a girlfriend. Eventually a family."

I resist the urge to hang up. Technically Preston is my former foster brother. When my mom died and I was placed with a family, he was the pre-existing foster kid, two years older than me. We spent the next seven years, until he went off to college, sharing a bedroom. In almost every way we're total opposites. He's black, I'm white. I'm chill, he's uptight. In eighth grade I started smoking weed. In eighth grade he drew elaborate and meticulous plans for efficient metropolises of his own invention.

"What do you know about Child Protective Services?" I say. "The one here in the city?"

"CPS? What do you want with CPS?"

"Never mind. I didn't think you'd know anything. Most people only know about their own branch of government."

Preston prides himself on knowing everything, and he would never consider himself "most people." Still, though, you have to be careful when you play to his ego. He's aware it's his weak spot.

"Off the record," he says, "I wouldn't let most of the dolts at CPS mow my lawn."

"But there are some good ones, right?"

"Sure. There are probably a couple of needles in the haystack, if they last more than a year or two. What do you want with CPS?"

"Nothing."

I go back inside, more unsettled than I was before, which is not the outcome I was hoping for.

Our foster experience, Preston's and mine, was a positive one. We were lucky. Our foster parents weren't exactly the most affectionate or loving or attentive people on earth, but we had enough to eat, we had clean clothes and sheets, we got to school on time. And they never hit us. They yelled a lot, but when we got punished, the punishment was reasonable. No TV for me, curtailed library privileges for Preston. We didn't have to worry about someone burning our skin with cigarettes.

"On the other hand," Mallory is saying, "Stanley *is* eventually forced to leave Tallahassee and return to Scranton. Which makes his eternal torment even more unbearable."

Nguyen concentrates and concentrates. "Exactly," he says. "That's exactly what I'm saying."

"This thing happened to me a couple of days ago," I say. "When I went to deal with this parking ticket."

"What thing?" Mallory says.

I tell her and Nguyen about the kids on the bench. When I describe the cigarette burns, Mallory grabs the remote and mutes *The Office*.

"Fuck, dude," Nguyen says when I finish. "That's heavy."

"Dude," Mallory agrees. "I mean, what the fuck?"

We all sit there in silence for a while, then Mallory shakes her head and unmutes *The Office*. Nguyen reloads the bong.

"Do you think I should do something else?" I say.

"Like what?" Mallory says.

"I don't know."

"What else *can* you do?" Nguyen says.

He's right. I've done everything I can. I could try the police, but they'll just punt me back to CPS.

"We live in a predetermined universe and free will is an illusion," Mallory says. "Our decisions have already been made. We are who we are and nothing will change that—because we are who we are."

She's explained this philosophy before. It's definitely appealing. The absence of free will takes a lot of the stress out of life. Go with the flow because the flow knows where to go. You're where you're supposed to be. The predetermined universe wants me to rip this bong. The predetermined universe requires it.

"Those kids are out of my hands," I say.

"Those kids are out of your hands," Mallory says.

When I get home later that night I smoke more weed and play *Far Cry* on Xbox for a while, liberating outposts with just the socket pipe and smoke grenades. I've played through this individual campaign many times already, so I know every inch of it, every loop of every NPC. My fingers do all the work automatically, mashing away at the buttons without me. It's very meditative and peaceful.

Until it's not.

I toss the controller onto my futon and google "Child Protective Services." After I scroll past a few official government links, the top hit is an article from last year about how child welfare agencies across the country are understaffed and underfunded and overwhelmed. A caseworker in Texas says her caseload is so heavy—twenty-seven families—that she doesn't know if all the kids are safe or not. A director in Ohio says it takes two full years to properly train caseworkers who then leave the job, on average, after only three years. In Nevada the backlog is so bad that it can take weeks to even investigate a hotline call.

A different article, from three months ago, says basically the same thing. Child welfare agencies don't have the resources to gather evidence of abuse. Without sufficient evidence of abuse, they can't step in and protect the children.

Is my eyewitness account of the cigarette burns sufficient evidence? Probably not, I decide. It's enough to *start* the investigation. If the investigation ever gets started. And what if this is one of those times that CPS fucks up? What if these kids end up getting shuffled around, misplaced, forgotten, lost forever?

I click one last link. In 2017 there were 1,720 child abuse and neglect deaths in the United States. More than a quarter of those kids—more than a quarter!—were already in the system, under the so-called protection of a child welfare agency.

I click one more last link. In Kentucky, a five-year-old girl was beaten by her parents, and then beaten some more by her parents, and then pushed out of a moving car. A month before she died, the latest CPS caseworker—her fourth—followed up a hotline call from a nurse. The caseworker went to the wrong house, though, and by the time he finally figured out the right address, a week later, the little girl's bruises had healed. He marked his report: *no evidence of risk.*

A six-year-old boy in Pennsylvania. Two seven-year-old twin sisters in California. A caseworker who was responsible for *thirty-nine* families. A caseworker who suspected abuse but had no way to prove it. Whenever she stopped by for an unannounced visit, the parents didn't answer the door and pretended nobody was home.

Every link I click floods the cracked screen of my phone with the same ugly, stupid, horrifying shit. After a while I can't even comprehend full paragraphs or sentences. I just see individual words and phrases, details that pump through me like poison. Stop clicking, stop reading. But I can't. Before I know it, two hours are gone and my battery is dead.

I google Tracy Shaw. There are more than a dozen Tracy Shaws in the city. It's a common name. No Tracy Shaws I find seem like they might be the mother of the kids.

I gaze up at my poster of *The Fall of Icarus.* Icarus is drowning and nobody pays any attention to those bare legs kicking. The farmer plows his field. A shepherd with his sheep gazes in the wrong direction. So does his sheepdog! There's another guy too, a fisherman I think, at the bottom right corner. He's the closest to Icarus. Icarus is right there in front of him. The fisherman could save Icarus from drowning. All he needs to do is look up and jump in.

These past two days seem like a century or two. Through the mists of time I can barely make out the clerk who stamped my parking ticket, the high school girls with the mango White Claws. The one image that stays sharp is the car driving away, the little girl in the backseat staring straight into my eyes. What if she and her brother have nobody but me?

This is not the plot twist that my life required. I wish I'd never noticed those kids on the bench. I wish I'd never walked over. I wish, most of all, that I existed in a version of the multiverse where hurting kids with the glowing tip of a cigarette falls far beyond the boundaries of the human imagination.

But I don't and it's not.

6

The next morning I'm up early—early for anyone, not just me. Jutta, my landlord's German shepherd, clicks into the bathroom and noses at the plastic shower curtain, baffled by this strange turn of events. I pull back the curtain so I can rub her ears.

"That makes two of us," I say.

I get to the municipal building at seven forty-five. I sit in my car outside the main entrance and hit my one-hitter. I watch a cardinal hop around on the median, a bright drop of blood on the sun-bleached grass.

Cars trickle into the lot. People enter the building. Ten after eight the goth chick receptionist from Driver Verification climbs out of a car. Her car is even more of a disaster than mine, the muffler sagging like a spilled entrail. She's wearing spike-studded Frankenstein boots with her civilian skirt and blouse.

I walk over. She's crouched down, using the broken side-view mirror to touch up her black lipstick. The side-view mirror is ingeniously rigged with chopsticks and duct tape.

"Hey," I say. "Hi. Excuse me."

She straightens up. It takes her a second to compute where she's seen me before. I don't take it personally. I'm not particularly memorable.

"You," she says.

"Me, yeah. The dude from the other day? My name's Hardly."

"Hardly?"

"It's what everybody calls me. Can I talk to you for a second?"

She makes sure I see what she does next: putting a hand into her purse, grabbing I presume a weapon of some sort. But then pretty quickly she determines that I'm not a threat and her posture relaxes.

"What do you want?" she says. "Are you stalking me? Because you should know, I'm strictly into the ladies."

"What?"

"Our love is doomed. Do you have a sister? Preferably one who's cuter than you and doesn't smell so overwhelmingly of ganj?"

She's going to keep messing with me until I get to the point. "I need to talk to you about that woman who was in your office. The one I was asking about? Tracy Shaw?"

"What about her?"

"Is there a way you could get me more info about her? Even just the basic things, like her address."

The goth chick squints at me. I notice a security guard walking toward us. Sure, there he is, now that I'm not desperately in need of a security guard.

"You all right, Eleanor?" he calls.

"I'm just confused," she calls back.

That confuses the security guard, but he's near enough now to also determine that I'm not a threat. He hitches up his pants, lumbers away.

"Didn't you call Child Services?" she asks me. "Why do you need more than her name? Child Services will be able to get whatever they need."

I don't want to get into this with her, but I recognize there's no scenario in which she agreeably hands over the information I want without any explanation.

"I called Child Services and they never called back," I say. "So I went by yesterday and it was kind of a clusterfuck. I'm worried they won't investigate what's happening to those kids I saw. Or they'll start too late. Or mess it up. So I'm thinking maybe I can . . . help."

"Help? How? I'm more confused now than I was before."

So am I, honestly. Last night, three in the morning, the big idea I came up with was a lot sharper, a lot clearer, and made a lot more sense.

"So, what I'm thinking . . . what if I can do some of the, like, grunt work for CPS? What if I can find some evidence that they can use. That would make it easier for them to help those kids. The kids wouldn't fall through the cracks."

"Evidence?"

"I'm not sure yet what exactly that is. I just had the idea last night. But, like, for example, I can try to find out who's actually hurting the kids."

It's not the mother. I'm leaning more and more away from her, a hunch. At the municipal building, when the mother held out her hand for them, the kids didn't flinch. And I remember how she seemed jumpy and anxious before she even saw me. Because of the dude waiting outside for them, behind the wheel of the dark blue Volvo?

"What kind of scam is this?" the goth chick says. "I have to say, it's an original one."

"It's not a scam. I want to help those kids."

She blinks her tarantula lashes very slowly. "*You?*" she says. "*You* are going to *investigate* and look for *evidence*? That is the most delightfully hilarious thing I've heard in ages."

I'm not offended. Believe me, I'm just as dubious about my qualifications as she is. "I'm going to try, at least."

"Why are you so obsessed with helping two kids you don't even know?"

I shrug. I haven't quite figured that out either. "I have this poster on my wall at home. It's some famous painting. *The Fall of Icarus*? A guy has fallen into the ocean and he's drowning and there are all these other people around, on shore, going about their daily business. They must have heard the splash, but they just ignore the drowning guy."

"You're doing all this because of a *poster* on your wall at home?"

"No. That's just a . . . I don't know. If you'd seen those kids, their faces. What if everyone else is ignoring them? What if they don't have anybody but me?"

"Scary thought," she says.

I nod. I agree!

She squints some more at me. "You're actually for real."

"Will you do it?" I say. "Can you get me Tracy Shaw's info?"

"It will cost you. You'll have to do a favor for me."

"Sure."

"Multiple favors. I could get fired for giving you that information."

She doesn't seem too concerned about getting fired. I think she's just squeezing me now. "Okay. What are the favors?"

"I'll let you know."

I'm slightly worried what kind of favors she might ask me to do. I've been assuming her SATAN LOVES ME, THIS I KNOW necklace is ironic. It has to be ironic, right?

"Deal," I say.

She hands me her phone and I put my number in her contacts. I hand the phone back.

Ten minutes later, driving home, my phone dings—a text from an unknown number. It's a photo of a sheet of paper. The photo is crooked and fuzzed, snapped in a hurry. When I tap to enlarge, I see it's a printed form, filled out by hand. The name at the top: *Tracy Paige Shaw.*

I pull into the parking lot of a Cheesecake Factory and scan through the form. The usual basics. Date of birth, home address, phone number. Occupation: *No.* Married? *Yes.* Name of spouse: *Nathan Shaw.* Spouse's occupation: *Self.* Children: *Yes.*

Nathan Shaw. The husband's name rings a bell, but I'm not sure why. I notice a couple of words squeezed sideways into the right margin of the page, next to the line about the spouse's occupation.

Pearl Jack.

I'm trying to work out who or what that is—the name of the husband's company?—when I realize that *Pearl* and *Jack* are Tracy Shaw's children.

The little girl: Pearl. The little boy: Jack. Knowing their names gives me a jolt. They're not just some kids anymore. It's Pearl with her lips pursed like the knot of a balloon. It's Jack with the big head on the skinny neck, studying his sister's dismount from the bench.

My phone dings again. Another text from the goth chick, Eleanor.

go crazy, it says.

7

It's only two o'clock, and I'm not even on tonight, but I head over to Haunted Frontier. The abandoned Abandoned Mine Train dark ride is one of my go-to spots for peace and reflection. The doors to the ride shed are chained shut, but the covered loading platform—the prospector's shack—is still accessible. Pull back a torn flap of nylon mesh fencing, climb over a few crates of fake dynamite, and there you are, far from all foot traffic and protected from the elements. Best of all, nobody knows about the prospector's shack but me. A couple of fellow scarers tipped me off when I first started. They're gone now, so I'm the last slacker standing.

The form the goth chick sent doesn't tell me much about Tracy Paige Shaw. She's thirty-nine years old. She's married to Nathan Shaw. Was Nathan Shaw the dude behind the wheel of the Volvo? I pin her address in Google Maps. I know the general vicinity from my DoorDash and Grubhub days—a lot of new construction, nice houses. Who lives out there? Nobody like me. Anesthesiologists and marketing executives, families with kids in private schools. I shouldn't be surprised, but I am. I'd assumed, without even thinking about it, that the kind of people who abuse their children live in my kind of neighborhood or worse.

I google Nathan Shaw. He's a lawyer who specializes in bankruptcies and disputes with the IRS. That's how I know the name, from the local TV commercials. "Does the IRS have *you* in a corner?" "Do *you* need a fresh start fast?" "Call the law offices of Nathan Shaw and get *your* life back."

I watch a couple of his commercials on my phone. You don't ever actually see Nathan Shaw, just shots of trucks getting repossessed and people at the kitchen table struggling with their bills. On the website for Shaw Law there's a photo. Nathan Shaw smiles sternly. He has wavy hair and piercing eyes, a handsome dude who's not too handsome to trust with the fate of your truck.

Nathan Shaw looks like he's older than Tracy by five or ten years, his hair going gray. Is this the face of a person who hurts his own children? I don't know. You can't just look at someone and know if they're evil or not. Life would be simpler if you could.

I hear scraping, clomping, heavy mouth-breathing. You've got to be kidding me. Sure enough, though, here comes Salvador, barging into the prospector's shack.

"What are you doing here?" I say.

"I followed you!" he yells.

"Salvador! You don't have to be so loud all the time. I'm like three feet away."

"I followed you!" he yells slightly more softly. "I saw you come in and thought you might need me for something."

What could I possibly need him for? What have I ever needed him for? To prove my point, he picks up a heavy prop pickax and almost immediately drops it on his foot.

"It's excellent in here!" he says. "How did you know about it?"

I'm about to tell him to get out, go away, never come back, but then I have an idea.

"Salvador," I say. "Suppose I want to do some research on someone. Like really dig up everything possible. You know?"

He nods. "Yes!"

I've never been into coding or programming or bending the internet to my will. Plus I'm twenty-three, seven years older than Salvador and prehistoric when it comes to the latest technology. "Would you know how to do that?"

Salvador nods again, but it's different this time—a confident lift of the chin instead of the usual vigorous bobble-heading. His expression changes too. There's a sly relaxing of his features, which suddenly seem to fit his face. It's like watching something that lumbers or lurches awkwardly on land, like a seal or a penguin, slide into the water and become suddenly graceful, a sleek shimmering bullet.

"I know exactly how," he says. "Let me see your phone."

I hand my phone over. He taps away, then hands it back. He's smiling with one corner of his mouth. I think it might be an actual smirk.

"All you have to do is type in the name of the person," he says. "Boom."

Boom? This is an unforeseen side of Salvador. I look at my phone and see what he's pulled up. It's Google, of course.

"Seriously?" I say.

He deflates. "You have to put the name you're searching in quotation marks," he says. "A lot of people don't know that trick."

"Every single person on the planet knows that trick, Salvador."

I kick him out. He's crushed, but he'll be fine. One thing you can say about Salvador is that he always rebounds quickly from the adversity that is himself.

I pull up the pinned address again. Nathan and Tracy Shaw live twenty minutes from here, with traffic green all the way. So . . . why not? I still have only a very vague-ish sense of how I might find evidence for Child Services, but this seems like a reasonable first step. I hit the START ROUTE button and here we go.

8

The Shaws live in a subdivision, Meadow Wood Estates, with a stone guard post at the turn-in. It's just ornamental, though, with no actual gate or guard. I breeze through. The houses are more or less what I expected: big, brand new, faintly medieval. A ribbon of uncracked sidewalk rolls past baby trees staked against the wind.

All the houses look alike to me, just the same basic parts rearranged slightly. The arched entryway on *that* side. The picture window trimmed with *dark* red brick instead of *light* red brick. Every winding street is not only a street but also a drive and a lane and a terrace. Meadow Wood Blossom Drive. Meadow Wood Blossom Lane. Meadow Wood Blossom Terrace. I take a couple of wrong turns. My GPS lady sounds miffed with me, sighing under her breath, "Recalculating, *again*."

Finally I find the address I'm looking for. The Shaw house is at the far end of the farthest cul-de-sac in the development. Since this is the newest development in a chain of developments, there's nothing past this point but pasture and sky.

Isn't a wood the same as a forest, full of trees? And isn't a meadow a field *without* trees? Someone should have thought of that when they named this place Meadow Wood Estates. It's like naming a place Prairie Mountain, or Crash Landing.

I loop through and pull to the curb near the top of the cul-de-sac— close enough for a good view of the Shaw house, far enough that nobody inside the house might glance out a window and notice me.

The house. Let's see. It looks, no surprise, like all the other houses in the subdivision. There's a car in the driveway, a dark blue Volvo, that matches exactly the car I watched drive away three days ago at the municipal administration building.

I roll down my windows, turn off the engine, and observe the house. What should I be looking for? I'm not sure, is the problem. I know that evidence I can take to Child Services won't just drop into my lap. If it does drop into my lap, I hope I recognize it.

One potentially interesting thing I notice: all the curtains in the house are shut tight, all the blinds closed, upstairs and downstairs. It's another hot day, a bright and ferocious sun. Keeping cool makes sense. When I check around, though, none of the neighboring houses are buttoned up like that.

Another potentially interesting thing: the wooden stockade fence around the backyard is also taller than the others. If a standard Meadow Wood Estates fence is, I would guess, six feet tall, this one must be eight. Does that mean anything? Is it not nothing?

The cul-de-sac is quiet on a Thursday afternoon, just one older lady across the street, watering her flowerbeds. I think about Pearl and Jack. I wonder if they're inside the house, behind the closed blinds and drawn curtains. Is it a good day or a bad day for them? What does that even mean for them, a good day? When they can almost forget the terrible shit that happened to them yesterday? When they can almost pretend it won't happen to them tomorrow?

It would be so amazing if right now a car from Child Services pulled into the cul-de-sac. A car from Child Services *and* a couple of police cars too. I could sit here and watch the cops drag Nathan Shaw or Tracy Shaw or both of them out of the house in handcuffs. I could watch some brilliant young righteous caseworker with her shit together hug Pearl and Jack, give them stuffed animals, make them understand with her eyes that everything will be much, much better from this moment on. I'd drive away. I wouldn't have to look back.

I wonder if I should come back here tomorrow with, like, snacks and binoculars? I have no clue how real surveillance works, especially when it's this hot. Does a real detective leave the car on and the AC running? Probably a real detective brings a notepad to jot down observations like the drapes and the fence. Is surveillance of the Shaw house even a smart approach in the first place? I'm not sure, and that's still the problem.

I can hear the annoying goth chick in my head. "*You? Investigate?*" She's annoyingly right. I take out my phone and do a search for "surveillance tips." I find some YouTube videos and click on one of them. A guy flips back the lid of an apartment complex Dumpster and peeks inside.

"Today in part three," he says, "we're going to get our hands dirty and have some fun with garbage."

Boom! Something slams into my car. I jump, startled shitless, and fumble my phone. A man has suddenly appeared right in front of me. I have no idea where he's come from. He's big and beefy, with a thick slab of chest and shoulders in a pink golf shirt, a block of a head, a gray military buzz cut. *Boom! Boom!* He pounds the hood of my car with his fist.

"Dude!" I yell. "Dude! Take it easy!"

He stomps around to my open window and bends down to glare at me eye to eye. His jaw juts and flexes and grinds, like he's trying to bite through barbed wire or the tough hide of some animal he's just strangled with his bare hands. He seems extremely, extremely pissed off, especially for someone in a pink golf shirt.

"Get the fuck out of here," he says.

"What?"

"Right fucking now. You've got two seconds."

I don't understand why this dude is so pissed off at me. I'm not someone, in general, people usually have strong feelings about.

"Hey, listen," I say, "I'm sorry, but I think there's been some kind of total misunderstanding here."

The house I'm parked in front of—I notice now that the front door is open. The angry golfer must have come charging across his perfect lawn while I was absorbed by YouTube. Is he pissed off because I'm parked in front of his house? Possible, but he's escalated straight to the climax of the confrontation. He's completely skipped the early stages of, for example, scowling at me from the porch and then coming over to ask, in an unfriendly way, "Can I help you?"

"Two seconds," he says, "and I call the police."

"What? Okay, okay."

The older lady across the street with the flowerbeds is back outside, observing us with a pinched expression. I feel bad for her, that she lives right across the street from this maniac.

"I have your license plate number. If you ever come back, I will call the police."

"Okay!"

I'm trying to turn the key in the ignition and roll up the window and find my phone, all at the same time. The angry golfer, walking back to his house, pauses to pound my hood again. This is ridiculous. I'm relatively positive there's no law against parking on a public street, though I'm also relatively not positive if the streets and drives and terraces of Meadow Brook Estates are officially public.

My engine finally catches. I can't use the angry golfer's driveway to back up, for obvious reasons, so I have to loop through the cul-de-sac again. The angry golfer stands on his lawn, making sure I don't try anything funny. The flowerbed lady gives me the hairy eyeball too. What! *Me?* In my rearview mirror, as I turn out of the cul-de-sac, I see her shake her head with disgust.

9

Driving home, I review the debacle at Meadow Wood Estates. I'm extremely bummed with myself. I don't know why the guy in the pink golf shirt was so angry, but whatever the reason, I should have seen him coming. Or I should have thought to park between houses, and not right in front of his.

On the radio there's an ad for "cloud-based solutions." At first, my speakers are so blown, I hear *clown*-based solutions. And I think, yeah, that's me, I'm a *clown*-based solution. How will I be able to help Pearl and Jack if I can't pull off something as basic as watching a house for five minutes?

I remember the time a couple of years ago, a hot summer like this one, when Nguyen, Mallory, and I borrowed a boat to go tubing on the lake. We had fun until the line got tangled in the propeller and the boat went dead in the water. I had Mallory shut off the engine before I jumped in. I didn't want her or Nguyen accidentally bumping the throttle while I checked out the propeller. I didn't want to get slapped in the face by my own severed hands.

The line was wrapped too tightly to untangle, so I unscrewed the propeller to slide it down the shaft a couple of inches. The propeller wouldn't budge, though, so I climbed back in the boat and we ran the engine for a few seconds to jiggle loose the propeller.

It seemed like an awesome idea in theory. I remember diving down into the brown murk, searching for the lost propeller, groping around for the bottom of the lake. I never found it, the propeller or the bottom.

I'm in over my head. What I need, I decide, is professional advice, right? And not from some random Dumpster-diving guy on YouTube. I need to talk to a genuine private detective.

When I get home, my landlord, Burke, is in the kitchen. He's sitting at the table and taking apart some tiny, intricate component of oily machinery. Jutta heaves herself up and click-click-clicks over to greet me.

"Hey, Burke," I say.

"Buenos nachos, Mr. Reed," he says.

Burke is in his thirties, attends survivalist prepper expositions at the fairgrounds, and has multiple deadbolts on his bedroom door. If you ask him a question, he'll smile enigmatically and refuse to give a straight answer. I've been renting from him for a whole year and I'm still not sure what he does for a living.

"What do you do for a living, Burke?" I'll ask. He'll smile enigmatically and say something like, "What won't I do?"

He wouldn't be my first choice for a roommate and landlord, but he's tidy and my rent is cheap, even by the standards of what used to be a two-car garage.

I rub Jutta's ears. She presses against me and growls softly, from deep down in her chest, like the rumble of a subway. Rubbing Jutta's ears and listening to her bliss out is usually the best part of my day.

"Don't spoil her," Burke says.

"Hey, Burke," I say, "what would you do if you got the rope, like for tubing on the lake, tangled in the propeller of a boat?"

"I'd put myself out of my misery." He doesn't look up from his oily machinery. "I would load a Mark XIX Desert Eagle with 325-grain fifty-caliber ammunition, put it in my mouth, and leave the world a better place."

Okay, so sometimes Burke does give you a straight answer.

I go back to my room to think. Who do I know who might be able to hook me up with a genuine detective? The head of security at Haunted Frontier used to be a cop, but/and he is highly no-nonsense. That's what he'd probably consider all this, and me—nonsense. Burke? No. I'd rather not get mixed up with Burke on this, or in any other way than just living quietly and independently in his garage.

Around seven I drive over to Preston's house. It's small, of shoddy construction, in a neighborhood almost as scruffy as mine. But Preston owns, not rents, which he'll find some opportunity to mention at least twice before the night is over.

"I can't believe you're forty minutes late," he says. "Except, actually, I can believe it."

"It's nice to see you too," I say.

"Take off your shoes before you come in."

"People say you're pretentious, Preston, but I don't see it."

His fiancée, Leah, takes my hand and gives it a long, hard squeeze. "Oh, Hardly. How have you been? Are you doing okay?"

"I'm doing great, Leah," I say. "Thanks."

"Interesting," Preston says. "By what metric does living in a garage constitute 'great'? Or working for minimum wage at a so-called amusement park?"

"Are these floors genuine hardwood?"

"Engineered hardwood is superior to traditional hardwood in almost every way."

"I'm convinced."

"Guys," Leah says gently.

We move to the table. Preston serves his Instant Pot chili, which, huge surprise, is so bland you could feed it to a baby. Leah tries heroically to keep a civil conversation going. Her sisters are her best friends in life, so she's baffled by me and Preston. We both lost our mothers when we were kids. We never knew our dads. We grew up together. Why aren't we best friends? She believes, sweetly but incorrectly, that deep down Preston and I truly are best friends. We're not. We're probably more like real brothers in that way than any other.

"You need to get your life together," Preston says.

Here we go. Right on schedule. "My life is together," I say. "I am extremely content with my life."

"You need to go back to college. You need to *finish* college. Put your head down and set some goals."

"I'm not you, Preston."

"I am well aware of that."

"I have a goal. My goal is to be extremely content with my life."

He groans, but how is that not a sensible goal? I recognize—as an ordinary person, an ordinary young person without financial means in the America of now—that the deck is stacked against me. College is ridiculously expensive. Almost four years later I'm still paying off the debt, bit by merciless bit, from my semester and a half. And what job awaits me when I graduate? An entry-level job that won't pay much more than I make now? That leads nowhere?

Preston might be moving up the ladder, but only because he's extremely smart, with an iron will and outrageous work ethic. And he's still years and years away from his dream of designing cities. He spends his days combing through retail development studies and writing up his thoughts on the use of storefront building materials, appropriate vs. inappropriate.

Good for him! I'd never say so, but I'm proud of Preston. He knows what works for him. I know what works for me.

"You can't be *extremely* content," he says. "That's inane. You're either content or you're not."

"I'm extremely content. So, so extremely content."

"It's a grammatical issue. For God's sake."

"*Guys,*" Leah says.

"It's okay, Leah," I say. I try to think of a way to make her feel better about our family dynamic. Preston, as always, has to have the good idea first.

"I wasn't popular in middle school or high school," Preston tells her. "I was a black nerd. A black nerd at that age has very little social cachet. Hardly was popular."

Preston wasn't just a black nerd. He was a black, brainy, fastidious nerd who refused to suffer fools, an expansive category that included just about everyone but him.

"I wasn't popular," I say. "Not even close."

"Kids didn't beat you up."

"Is that your definition of popular?"

"One day Hardly saw me getting beat up. He came over."

"And we got beat up together," I say.

Preston nods. Leah waits for more. But that's it, that's all there is. I can tell she's not sure what to think or say. Is it a happy, heartwarming story? Or a sad and depressing one? I don't really know the answer myself.

Leah brings out dessert, cherry cobbler.

"This rocks, Leah," I say. "I think this is the best cobbler I've ever had."

"So," Preston says, "why are you looking into CPS?"

"Do you happen to know anybody who might know a private detective?"

"What? Why do you need a private detective? For what inane reason, to be more precise?"

I tell them about Pearl and Jack, about the cigarette burns, about Dan the caseworker. I explain what I'm trying to accomplish. Preston doesn't react. I suppose he's taking the position that nothing inane I do will ever surprise him.

"Hardly!" Leah says, alarmed. "Is that something you should be involved with?"

"Probably not," I admit.

"It might be dangerous. Is it even . . . legal?"

She turns to Preston for his verdict. He finishes his cobbler, sets down his spoon, and folds his napkin. He wants another serving, but mere temptation has never been a match for his iron will.

"Don't worry," he tells Leah. "He won't get far enough for it to be dangerous. As soon as anything requires effort, he gives up."

I push back my chair and stand. The leg of the chair catches on the edge of the rug and topples over, which gives the moment a level of drama I don't intend. Because Preston's assessment of me is accurate. He's not taking a cheap shot.

"Sorry," I say.

"Don't you want some more coffee?" Preston says.

"I've got to go. Will you try to find me the name of a private investigator?"

He sighs. "I'll see what I can do."

"Thanks for having me over, Leah."

"Take care of yourself, Hardly," she says. "Promise?"

10

The next morning I use Salvador's secret, next-level search engine to find private investigators in the city. Google delivers a ton of listings, but when I call the numbers I mostly get voicemail. I talk to a total of three actual human beings. The first guy cuts me off halfway through my story and quotes his rates. I explain I can't actually afford to hire him—I just want to ask a few questions—and he quotes his rates again. The second guy is marginally more friendly, but he doesn't give free advice either, and his rates are even higher. The third guy laughs and hangs up.

Preston texts me around noon. He sends the name and number of a private investigator. Guess what? It's the name and number of the guy who laughed and hung up.

While I'm waiting for the other private investigators to call me back, I do some more research on CPS and child abuse. It's a huge mistake, just absolutely soul-shredding. I don't know what's more horrifying: how much creativity some people put into hurting their own kids, or how some people don't even seem to think twice about it.

Pearl hears the click of the lighter. She smells cigarette smoke. Or does she hear Jack crying first? Does Jack cry? They were both so quiet on the bench. Does it make Nathan Shaw mad when he burns them and they don't cry?

Fuck. *Fuck.* I toss my phone on the futon, get stoned, play some *Far Cry.* I can't focus. I trip the outpost alarms and get killed over and over again.

By five, none of the private investigators I left messages for, explaining what I want, have called me back. None, as in zero. I head to Beautiful America and look for Beckett, the head of security. Depending on which dubious source I ask, he's already gone for the day or hasn't come in yet or is on vacation for a week in Branson. Try the main offices, try Prehistoric America, try Future America.

I finally find him in Colonial America. He's just standing there, silently contemplating the Valley Forge flume logs, the shrieking passengers. I say hey, hello, and ask if he happens to know any private investigators. I tell him I can't afford to hire someone, that I just want to ask a few questions and get some advice.

Beckett looks me over. He knows me but doesn't know me. We've had a couple of brief conversations about nothing much. He knows I've worked at Haunted Frontier for a while, longer than most scarers do or should.

"Nope," he says, and walks away.

Well, that was quick, at least. I turn and see Salvador lurking behind the Liberty Bell.

"Are you following me again?" I say. "Seriously, Salvador, you're driving me crazy. Are you trying to drive me crazy? If that's your diabolical scheme, good work. Nicely done."

He creeps sheepishly out from the shadows. "Why do you need advice from a private investigator?"

"None of your business, Salvador."

I start walking back to the old tinker shop. My shift begins in twenty minutes and I need to get in costume. Salvador hurries to catch up. He runs like he's being chased by stinging wasps. He runs like his body is a car and he's learning how to drive a stick shift.

"My mom works with someone who's a private investigator," he says, panting wetly from the effort. "I heard her say one time."

That news doesn't exactly stop me in my tracks. "I thought your mom is a real estate agent."

"She works with someone who *used* to be a private investigator."

Even better. "That's okay, Salvador. Thanks."

"I can get the contact information from my mom and text it to you."

"No, thanks," I say as we push through the backstage gate.

A couple of Mournful Ghosts are emerging from the old tinker shop. One of them veers over to hip-check Salvador. They both cackle. "Salva*dork!*"

"You have to stand up for yourself," I tell Salvador. "You can't just let them do that shit or they'll keep doing that shit."

He shakes his head. "That doesn't work," he says.

It's true. He's right. I should know better. "Well, just try not to call attention to yourself."

"Okay."

"Lie low. Like, don't talk so loud. Just try to act as normally as possible."

I realize he has his phone out and is taking notes. I sigh.

"This is excellent information!" he says.

We enter the old tinker shop. I search the pile for a pair of cowboy boots that will fit, more or less. In terms of ten-gallon hats, I just want one that doesn't smell like the boots. Salvador brings me a selection of gun belts and holsters to choose from, even though I've asked him a million times to cool it with the valet shit.

"I need advice from a private investigator," I say, "because I know about these two little kids in trouble, and I want to help them out of it."

Salvador sucks in a big, sharp, wet mouth-breath. "Oh," he says.

"Their parents are hurting them. Or one of the parents is."

"Oh."

How am I going to find a private investigator? How am I going to figure out how to help Pearl and Jack? It's a terrible feeling—to want to do something, to *need* to do something, and know you're just not good enough to pull it off, know you're *never* going to be good enough.

Every single one of the gun belts Salvador has brought me is sized for sumo wrestlers, not someone, like me, who weights a hundred and seventy pounds.

"I'll talk to my mom about the private investigator ASAP," Salvador says. "That's as soon as possible. I'll tell her it's top priority and text you the information."

"Please don't," I say.

11

Sunday afternoon Mallory texts me a pineapple and a lion face. That means that she and Nguyen are going to the zoo to get stoned.

Sounds good. Sounds perfect. A day like any other, a return to my previous frictionless existence.

I text back: can't. I'm on the way to my first-ever open house. A three-bedroom, three-bath contemporary with formal living room and custom built-ins, pool and fire pit, in a much-sought-after neighborhood. At a recently reduced price of three hundred and forty thousand dollars, it's approximately three hundred and forty thousand dollars out of my price range.

I park on the street. There's only one other car, in the driveway. Am I late? I don't think so. It's three o'clock and the FOR SALE sign in the yard says the open house runs from two to four. The name on the sign matches the one Salvador sent me. FELICE UPTON.

The front door is open. I step inside. "Hello?" I say.

Nobody answers. I move through the house. It's cleared out, just an empty, freshly painted shell—no furniture, no pictures or decorations on the walls, no sign that any human has ever habitated here. It's eerily silent too, my flip-flops slapping against the polished wood floors. I smell hot apple pie, fresh from the oven. That's eerie too. It's just a sales tactic that real estate agents probably use, but hot apple pie doesn't make any sense in an empty, silent house. Your mind wants to know *Who's baking a pie? Who's going to eat it?*

In the kitchen, I find the ghost pie warming in the oven. There's a spread of sliced cheeses and various fruits on the island, untouched. A bottle of wine, in a bowl of melting ice, hasn't been uncorked.

I open the patio doors and go outside. A woman in sunglasses lounges on a lounger in the shade, sipping from a plastic cup. She's dressed for success, in a skirt and a shimmering blouse, but her feet are bare. Her stacked-heel shoes sit next to a bottle of white wine that's uncorked and half empty.

She's gazing out across the back lawn and hasn't noticed me yet. I make as much noise as I can shutting the patio doors behind me. I don't want her to think I'm trying to creep up on her.

"Hey," I say. "Hi. Excuse me."

She takes a sip from her cup but doesn't turn her head. "You passed on the cheese."

"I'm sorry?"

"I thought you'd have some of the cheese. Maybe a few grapes. It's good cheese. I thought you'd be tempted."

She lowers her sunglasses. I realize she's facing the lawn but not actually gazing at it. She's had her eyes on me this whole time.

"I was tempted," I admit, "but eating the cheese seemed like bad manners since I'm not interested in buying the house."

"Nobody is. The owners have it priced forty thousand too high and won't pay for staging. It's been on the market eight months."

"So you're Ms. Upton? I'm Hardly."

"Hardly?"

"It's a nickname."

"Felice. Do you want some wine?"

"No, thanks."

"Sit."

I take the other lounger, across the cold fire pit from her. She's forty or forty-five years old, I'd say. She's got a vibe—very cool, very together. She reminds me of jazz, which after a second I worry might be a culturally biased thing to think. Even if she wasn't Black, though, she'd remind me of music that goes where it wants, takes its time, doesn't care what the squares think.

"Hardly." She sips her wine and ponders. "Am I supposed to know who you are?"

"No. I mean, yes. Didn't Salvador tell you about me?"

"Am I supposed to know who Salvador is?"

This is going so well. I'm going to kill Salvador. "You're not a former private investigator, are you?"

"A what?" She fills her cup to the top and hands it to me. "Have some wine."

I take a drink. How dumb am I? How could I ever believe that Salvador might actually be accurate or useful? "I'm sorry for wasting your time."

"I'm wasting my own time, as you can see. Why are you looking for a private investigator?"

I tell her. Why not? I don't have any better ideas. She listens to the short, concise, objective version of my story without saying a word. When I finish, she doesn't say a word. I add some details. The way Pearl and Jack gazed past me like they were riding the bus to work. Nathan Shaw's TV commercials. Dan at Child Services quitting in the middle of my interview.

She still doesn't say a word. The silence becomes highly awkward. I tell her, which I wasn't intending to do, about my surveillance disaster and the angry guy in the pink golf shirt. I explain that I dropped out of college after a year and a half, that I work as a scarer at Haunted Frontier, and that I'm honestly the last person you'd want to be your last hope in a situation like this.

"I see," she finally says.

And I finally catch up. "You *were* a private investigator, weren't you?"

"Fourteen years, in California. I'm not licensed here. But I still don't know who Salvador is."

"That was kind of slick."

"What was?"

"How you got me talking. How did you learn how to do that?"

She smooths her skirt and wriggles her bare toes. "So you want some professional advice?"

"I do," I say. "Yes, please. Anything at all."

"Let it go," she says. "That's my professional advice. Playing detective, trying to prove those children are being abused—it's not a good idea."

"I know. But I can't let it go. I don't understand why."

She crooks her finger at me. At first I think she wants me to lean in, lean closer, so she can whisper the secret answer to me. Instead, I realize, she just wants the cup back so she can refill it. I've finished off the wine we're sharing.

I rarely drink alcohol. I feel prickly, like I'm charged with static electricity. This is a strange afternoon, like a cryptic painting you'd see in some museum. Me in my board shorts and my vintage Hoodoo Gurus thrift-store T-shirt on the patio of a deserted open house, next to a cold fire pit, across from a very attractive middle-aged real estate agent. What would the title of the painting be? *Still Life With* . . . what?

"How would you handle this situation if you were me?" I say. "How would you start?"

"I'd let it go, Hardly. I told you."

"How would you find evidence if you were me and you couldn't let it go, Felice? Where would you look? What would you look for?"

She checks her watch. It's three-twenty. She's stuck here till the open house ends. "Go get that other bottle of wine," she says.

I go inside and bring back the wine and some cheese. We split up the cheese on cocktail napkins. We're still sharing the same plastic cup for wine.

"You tell me," she says. "How would I do it? How do you think I'd find evidence?"

I'm fairly sure I know what she *wouldn't* do. She wouldn't rush into anything. She wouldn't drive by the family's house on impulse. She wouldn't let a guy in a pink golf shirt sneak up on her. When I first got here, remember, she was facing the backyard but had an angle on the kitchen too. She saw me coming.

"You'd have a plan," I say.

"True."

"You'd . . ." I think about how, thirty seconds after meeting me, she coaxed me into telling her basically my entire life story. "You'd talk to people? People . . . who've been around the kids and might have noticed something?"

"Which people?"

Neighbors, maybe. In theory, but I'm no longer welcome on the cul-de-sac. What about parents of the kids Pearl and Jack are friends with? The problem is I can't really imagine Pearl and Jack having a lot of friends, going to birthday parties, playing Little League soccer. Remember how Tracy Shaw hustled them out of the building so fast? Remember how she parked them on a bench outside the office before she went in? She doesn't want anyone to know what's happening to her kids.

Felice smiles. "Look at you."

"What?"

"Nothing. Go ahead."

The only time Pearl and Jack are around other people is when they *have* to be. When's that? Doctor, dentist. Church, maybe. School. *School.*

"You'd talk to their teachers," I say.

"See? You don't need my advice, do you?"

"But what if . . ."

"They're homeschooled? They might be."

Felice smooths her skirt again, stretches her legs. They're nice legs. My cheeks get hot. I hope it's just the wine and I'm not blushing. She's very attractive, I note once again. Her mouth finds the world low-key amusing, but her eyes are dead serious. It's an appealing combination.

I take all those thoughts and put them away before they distract me— before Felice reads my mind again.

Even if Pearl and Jack aren't homeschooled, even if they go to an actual elementary school . . . there are dozens of actual elementary schools in the city. How do I find the right one?

"You just have to grind," Felice says. "That's the only real advice I can give you. Grind and grind and grind. There's no magic trick or secret voodoo."

I'm cautiously encouraged. Grinding I can handle, maybe. Grinding seems more about effort than extraordinary natural talent, which works for someone ordinary like me.

"Why did you quit being an investigator?" I say. "Why aren't you still in California? How did you end up here?"

The shade has shifted. Felice dips her fingers into the creeping sunlight at her side, then swings her long legs off the lounger. She corks up what's left of the second bottle of wine.

"Four o'clock," she says. "Time to go."

She walks me back through the house to the front door. I thank her for her advice and she hands me her business card.

"My personal number is on the back," she says.

"I can call you?"

"Remember what I said."

"I need to grind."

"You need to let this go."

And then she closes the door gently in my face.

12

That night I have nightmares. It would be weird if I didn't, given all the research I've been doing. But what's weird is that I don't dream about kids getting hurt. Instead these nightmares are about me needing to get dressed in a hurry but I can't find my shoes, me needing to catch the bus but it's pulling away, me needing to press the right button—or else—but all of the buttons are blinking. And then it's too late, it's over, I've missed the chance forever to do what I was trying to do, I'm alone and nobody is coming back for me.

I jerk awake, sweating. When I drop back to sleep, it just starts all over again.

Monday morning Salvador meets me at the abandoned Abandoned Mine Train. He's loaning me his old MacBook Air, which is speedier and more reliable than my decrepit Dell. He's also brought packs of index cards, boxes of colored pushpins, and Sharpies in multiple colors.

"It's for organizing our case," he says.

Our case? I can't really say anything, though. I need the MacBook and Salvador did help me find Felice. "Okay, but be quiet, okay? I need to concentrate."

"Yes!" he yells.

I map out and make a list of all the elementary schools within a few miles of Meadow Wood Estates. But the next step stumps me. Obviously I can't just call up and ask each place if Pearl and Jack are students there. Nobody is going to release that information to some random dude. The school websites don't list the names of students either. And the photos of kids laughing and learning and playing dodgeball look suspiciously glossy and stock.

I pick the school closest to the Shaw house—Canyon Ridge Elementary—and check Instagram. Canyon Ridge has an account, and the photos posted seem promisingly amateurish and authentic. Good. If I can spot Pearl or Jack in an Instagram post, then I'll know where they go to school.

Yes, good—except there are a lot of possible schools and each school's Insta will have a lot of photos. It will be like looking for a needle in a haystack, with no guarantee there's even a needle.

We need a system. I tell Salvador to put the name of each school on an index card, one school per card, then write down my notes about the school as I dictate them.

He's overly gung-ho, as usual. "And then pin the card on the wall? Or pin it to the wall first?"

"Whatever you decide," I say. "You're the master of the cards."

I start grinding. Canyon Ridge Elementary. A lot of the posts are quick busts: kids older than Pearl and Jack; kids at birthday parties and soccer games, places where Pearl and Jack probably won't be; family photos. But there are also shots of kids the right age in the classroom and on the playground, spilling out of school at the end of the day, going on field trips to the science museum.

I study each of those photos hard. Each face, each slice of a face, the faces on the edge of the frame and in the background. It's slow, slow going, even more than I expected. Canyon Ridge Elementary takes me half an hour. Just one school! I have Salvador jot down a couple of remote possibilities to come back to later, *pumpkin patch* and *giant globe*, but there's no definitive sighting of Pearl or Jack.

Next up: Good Shepherd Elementary. Then Dundee West. I send Salvador out to 7-Eleven for chicken bites and taquitos. Ashford Hills. Morris Brock. My eyes ache. The faces in the photos blur together. Kids at that age, six or seven or eight, love the camera. They light up: big grins, wild giggles, goofy expressions. All that pure joy and uncomplicated nuttiness should put me in a good mood. Instead I feel grimmer and grimmer, thinking about

Pearl and Jack on the bench in the municipal building, their faces blank, their eyes empty.

I'm worried I might not even recognize them. They've been living in my head twenty-four/seven ever since I saw them, but I remember their general vibe more than I do any actual physical details. I had such a brief look at them, just a few minutes. Jack had a rounder face and bigger ears than Pearl, I think? Am I one hundred percent sure they both had sandy blond hair and green eyes?

Saint Cecilia. Spring Creek. So many photos, so many faces. So much Salvador.

"Have you ever tried breathing with your mouth closed?" I ask him. "Like through your actual nostrils?"

"Yeah," he says, but uncertainly.

"Just try it."

He shuts his mouth. The wet wheezing racket ceases. His cheeks flush and his eyes bulge. Salvador doesn't give up, though. He keeps fighting. I feel guilty. The silence is a relief, but I don't want him to suffocate himself.

"Never mind," I say. "I was just kidding. Breathe however you need to breathe."

"Thank you!"

"You can go home, Salvador. You know you don't have to hang around all day."

"It's fine!"

I turn back to the MacBook. A post from last May, Spring Creek Elementary, is a classroom photo—a bunch of kids sitting in a circle, gawking up at a friendly-looking young teacher guy. He's reading to them from a book. I can't see the cover, but whatever book it is has these kids spellbound, on the edges of their tiny chairs.

And there she is—Pearl. I can't believe I was worried I might not recognize her. It's *exactly* her. She's the only kid in the circle not spellbound by the book, the only kid who's noticed that someone in the back of the room is snapping a photo. Her ear is out of focus and her head tilted, like maybe she's just started to duck away, but her eyes are looking directly into the camera.

I'm jolted again back to the parking lot of the municipal building—the car driving away, Pearl watching me through the back window.

"Hardly?" Salvador says.

I look up. "What?"

"Are you okay? I asked if we're all done with Spring Creek and should I pin it."

I read the comments on the photo of Pearl's classroom. The name of the friendly young teacher guy is right there in the first comment: *Story time with Mr. K!* And he's linked. *Camokellr19*. I jump to his Insta. He's Cameron Keller: "Eager learner, aspiring groundbreaker, second-grade educator, lover of cookies. Let your smile change the world, don't let the world change your smile."

Salvador starts to say something.

"Wait," I say. "Quiet."

The DM to Cameron Keller is going to be tricky. If I tell him the truth—what I'm trying to do, why I want to talk to him—he'll probably think I'm crazy. I am, probably, crazy. But I suck at lying. I get nervous that I'll slip up, then I feel guilty about lying in the first place, which makes me even more nervous. "Oh, baby," I remember my mom saying one time, laughing, "everybody is gonna want to play poker with you."

I decide to go with highly vague and sort of truthful. I tell Cameron Keller that I heard about him from one of the parents at Spring Creek (it was a parent who took the photo, so . . . sort of?) and I'd like to discuss teaching with him (yes-ish). Just before I send the DM, I read Cameron Keller's profile again and think about Felice, how she covers every angle. So I google "inspirational quotes" and add one to the bottom of my DM, under my name. *You are more than who you used to be.* It's kind of sneaky of me. I hit send before I can feel too guilty.

Now, I guess, I wait. I'm only around fifty percent hopeful that Cameron Keller will respond to the DM. If he does, he'll probably need me to be less vague and more truthful before he agrees to meet. Which parent did I talk to? Why would I like to discuss teaching with him? This is what I mean about lying. It's exhausting.

Almost immediately I get a DM back from Cameron Keller. Sure thing! Let's chat! Coffee tomorrow? Five o'clock?

Salvador, rearranging the pinned index cards, is watching me. "What's wrong?" he says.

I shake my head. Nothing is wrong. I need a second to let that sink in. This is actually working.

13

Cameron Keller is one upbeat dude. He's fired up to meet me. He's fired up that I like this coffee place, which has the most awesome coffee in town. All this enthusiastic positivity at five o'clock in the afternoon, after a long day of wrangling summer school second-graders. He should be wiped out, right? A smoking crater of blasted rubble? He's not. He's crisp like a brand-new book when you crack it open.

It turns out we went to the same high school. We don't remember each other—he's two years older than me and it's the biggest high school in the city—but he's fired up about the awesome coincidence.

I like him. His energy seems genuine, not an act. I totally get why seven-year-olds would ride or die with a teacher like Cameron.

"So you're thinking about getting into elementary teaching?" he says.

That must be the conclusion he drew from my DM. I stick with the vague and truthful approach. "Education is really crucial at that age," I say.

"It is, Hardly. It's so rewarding to be there at the beginning, in the early grades. We're force multipliers. We make a real difference."

"The early grades," I say. "Definitely."

"Did you take any education classes in college? It's cool if you didn't. You just need to do an alternative accreditation program. I can answer any questions you have."

He sucks up the dregs of his frappe with a straw. I try to think of a question about accreditation. Not happening. I need to get to the point anyway.

"You had a little girl in your class last year," I say. "Pearl Shaw?"

"I did. Pearl. That's right."

"Did you ever happen to notice anything unusual? Anything . . .wrong?"

"Wrong?"

"Like marks or burns. Bruises. Injuries she shouldn't have."

Cameron's facial expressions, I'm learning, are more expressive than those of a standard human being. When he's curious or encouraging, he's *unmistakably* curious or encouraging. When he's confused, like now, he's *unmistakably* confused. It's like he's done one too many story times for children and now he can't kick the habit.

"You mean signs of physical abuse?" he says.

"Right. Have you seen any signs of physical abuse?"

"I don't understand. What does that have to do with . . ." He ponders. He *unmistakably* ponders. "Are you with DHS?"

I move my head in a way that's nod-adjacent. "So did you ever see any signs of physical abuse? With Pearl?"

"No."

"No?" I say, surprised. Cameron was Pearl's teacher. He was with her every school day for an entire school year. He had to have seen *something*.

"No." He shakes his head. "I didn't see any signs of physical abuse."

"Nothing at all?"

"Why are you investigating?"

My hopes—that this might be it, the big breakthrough, the evidence I needed—collapse. Thundering crash, cloud of dust. There's not even any wiggle room here. "No, I didn't see any signs of physical abuse" is about as emphatic as it gets.

Cameron waits for me to answer his question. It's time for me to dip out. But then I stop, slow down, and think. That's what Felice would do. She'd consider every angle.

It occurs to me that he's been answering an unusual amount of my questions with questions of his own.

Me: Did you ever notice anything wrong?

Him: Wrong?

Me: Have you seen any signs of physical abuse?

Him: Are you with DHS?

Yes, he finally gave me a straight answer, but not until after a lot of dodging and weaving. And then right back to answering questions with questions.

Me: Nothing at all?
Him: Why are you investigating?

Is it possible that Cameron isn't telling me everything he knows about Pearl? Is it possible he's an even worse liar than me?

He's still waiting for me to say something. I try the awkward-silence trick that Felice used on me. It doesn't work. I'm the one who starts sweating. I'm the one who fidgets in my chair. Maybe I'm not literally sweating and fidgeting, but it feels that way. I stare at him for too long. I look away for too long. Cameron is wondering what's wrong with me, if I swallowed a bite of my muffin the wrong way and need the Heimlich maneuver.

Even after Felice's advice, I'm still terrible at this, I still have no idea what I'm doing. I remember a Sunday morning when I was nine, not long after my mom died. I was at church with Preston and our foster parents and their four normal kids. We were singing some hymn. "A Mighty Fortress Is Our God," I want to say? Anyway, I'd always been into singing. I loved it. But I must have sucked, because that day my foster mother leaned down and told me I should just move my lips and pretend to sing. She was just being helpful, I think. She didn't want me to embarrass myself, like I'm embarrassing myself now.

"Okay, so, I never saw any *obvious* signs of abuse," Cameron says, the words rushing out like he's been holding his breath this whole time. "I should clarify that. And abuse isn't the word that I'd . . . I don't want to give the wrong impression."

He fiddles with the plastic lid of his empty frappe. On, off. On, off. Wow. He *does* know more about Pearl than he was telling me, and he's telling me now. I start to ask what he means by *obvious* signs of abuse, but then slam my mouth shut in the nick of time.

"I had what I'd call potential *concerns*," he says after some more fiddling. "But it's hard to be sure. Every kid that age, they get so many bruises and scrapes and . . . have you ever watched kids that age on the playground? They're always bouncing and banging around, falling down . . ."

He stops. I count slowly to twenty in my head. I'm getting the hang of inflicting awkward silence.

"With Pearl," he says, "it was a bad bruise on her wrist once. A bruise on her neck another time. I was actually going to call you, DHS, but I didn't want to get anyone in trouble. If I report something like that and it's just a silly misunderstanding . . . I didn't want to get anyone in trouble."

I'm not following. Get who in trouble? And then I realize he's talking about the parents, Nathan and Tracy Shaw. Wait. What! A little girl in his class showed up with bruises, and he was worried about the *parents*?

"Don't worry," he says quickly. He must see the surprise in my face. "I asked Pearl's parents to come in for a conference. And it was exactly like I thought. Her parents told me Pearl got the bruise on her wrist from skateboarding. And the bruise on her neck—she and her brother like to pretend they're wrestlers, like on WWE."

"The parents told you that?"

"Pearl confirmed it. She came to the conference too. When I asked her about the bruises, she confirmed what her parents said."

My mind blows. Cameron asked Pearl if she was being abused by her parents while her parents were in the room, sitting, like, three feet away from her? How could he be that clueless? Even I'm not that clueless, I don't think. Maybe it was human nature. Maybe Cameron was just hearing what he desperately wanted to hear. I try to see the situation from his perspective and give him the benefit of the doubt. It's really not easy.

What matters, though, is that I'm getting important information from him. I'm in slight disbelief that I've been able to pull this off. "So you'll tell Child Services everything you're telling me?" I say.

"Sure," he says. "But I thought . . . isn't that what I'm doing now?"

He's under the impression that I'm a caseworker. Oh, yeah, that slipped my mind. "An official statement, I mean."

"If you think it's important. Yes. Sure."

It's five-thirty. He's meeting his girlfriend at Home Depot. We bus our table and I ask him about Jack. Cameron tells me Jack is a year younger than Pearl. He'd be in Cameron's class this year, but the parents decided last spring to start homeschooling the kids.

After Cameron brought in Pearl's parents to discuss signs of potential abuse, they decided to start homeschooling their kids. I wait to see if Cameron makes *this* connection. Unbelievably, nope.

On the way out of the coffee shop, I think of one last question. "What are the parents like?" I say. "Nathan and Tracy Shaw?"

"Tracy can be a hard nut to crack, but she has a big heart," Cameron says. "You should see her with the kids. She's all about them."

"And Nathan?"

Cameron unlocks his car and reaches for the door handle. "When do you think I'll need to come in? Or can I just give my official statement over the phone?"

I'm too slow. I should have been ready for this and cut off his escape. "What's Nathan like?"

He slides into his car. "I've got to run," he says, pulling the door shut. "It was so awesome to meet you."

14

The next day I'm ready to roll. But roll *where,* exactly? Hence my dilemma. Pearl's teacher was a big win and I learned some crucial new information. It might not be crucial enough, though. I wonder how much a statement from Cameron Keller will help at Child Services. A couple of bruises, an explanation for the bruises, Pearl confirming the explanation. Based on my experience so far with CPS, that might not move the needle much at all.

Nguyen and Mallory want me to come over. They're planning to get stoned and paint Mallory's bedroom, which means they'll get stoned and probably not paint Mallory's bedroom. I tell them I can't, then put a few gallons of gas in my car and just drive around. I'm hoping that driving around will get my creative juices flowing. Every now and then I take out Felice's business card and look at it. I can't call her already, though. It's only been three days and I don't want to wear out my welcome. I need to figure out the next step on my own.

When I get home, Burke is making homemade sausage in the kitchen. He uses a hand-cranked meat grinder because he says electric appliances have sapped the vigor from Western civilization. He's rocking tactical sunglasses, a bandanna on his head, a sleeveless camo T-shirt. It's his usual retired Navy SEAL look—except that Burke is thicker, softer, and paler than I think a retired Navy SEAL would be.

"Don't sneak up on me like that," he says. "I strongly advise against it."

I didn't know I was sneaking. I'm fairly sure I was just walking normally and opening a cabinet to look for Pop-Tarts. "Sorry," I say.

I go to my room to think. And think. And think. One thing I think about but don't want to: how did Pearl really get those bruises? From what Cameron said, it's got to be Nathan who's hurting the kids. My hunch was right.

Bruises are bad, cigarette burns are worse. What comes next? What comes after cigarette burns? While I lie here, this very minute, Nathan might be coming up with a new way to hurt Pearl and Jack, something even more evil.

Around nine o'clock that night my phone dings. It's a text from the goth chick, Eleanor: ready?

Ready for what? Oh, shit. The favor I owe her. I guess I was hoping that if I forgot about it, so would she.

She texts again. hello?

I'm not nervous. Maybe a little. But I don't really believe she wants me to dig up a grave for some goth-Wiccan ritual. She probably just needs help moving furniture and boxes to a new apartment. Simple, easy.

I text back. when?

She sends me an address. now

My map app sends me to a ramshackle old two-story house in a ram-shackle neighborhood. Here, unlike Meadow Wood Estates, my smoking, shuddering Kia fits right in.

Eleanor is waiting out front. She's still wearing her work clothes, a coffee-colored dress with cream-colored polka dots. That, along with her pale, pale skin and black lipstick, her brow piercings and spiked Franken-stein boots, makes her look like a dystopian cannibal warlord who assistant manages a Banana Republic.

"Did you have to work late?" I say.

"No. Why?"

"The dress."

"What's wrong with my dress?"

Her weird style, I realize, is actually her weird style—a choice, not a work-place requirement. "Nothing," I say. "It's fine."

"I'm so relieved that the straggly stoner hippie dude with the manpone approves."

"Wow," I say. "Okay."

What's wrong with my hair? My long hair is my best feature. At least that's what a chick I hooked up with a few years ago told me. Is it sad I still remember that? It is, yes.

"I really am a lesbian, by the way," she says. "I wasn't lying about that. In case you have the idea in your mind that this is some elaborate ploy to seduce you."

Wow, again. I promise, I do not have that idea in my mind whatsoever. But I've already offended her once, so I don't say anything.

"You actually came, you moron," she says. "You know you could have just ignored my text. I don't have any way to find you."

"But we made a deal."

She studies me the way she did that very first time, like I'm a dog wearing a hat.

"Do you live here?" I say.

"With my grandma, yeah. Ever since my uncle died a couple of years ago. You're going to take her car keys away from her. That's the favor."

"I'm going to what?"

"She shouldn't be driving. She's going to kill someone. You're from the police department. Or the DMV. Give me two minutes, then ring the doorbell."

"The—what? Wait."

It's too late. She's already marching up the walkway to the front door. This is crazy. Nobody is going to buy that I'm from the police department or the DMV. Am I supposed to physically subdue some old lady and wrestle away her car keys? No way am I doing that, deal or no deal.

I give Eleanor two minutes, then ring the bell. Eleanor lets me in. She leads me down a hallway, through the living room, upstairs. The old house is dim and creaky and decorated everywhere with—I'm not kidding—aliens dressed in various outfits. Aliens as in little green creatures with giant black eyes and elongated limbs. There is an alien bride and bridegroom, an alien police officer, an alien family of four around the dinner table. There are paintings, ceramic figures, needlepointed pillows.

"Don't ask," Eleanor says before I can ask.

Eleanor's grandma is in the master bedroom. She's sitting in a recliner, wearing a giant pair of padded, over-the-ear headphones. She's approximately a couple hundred years old, with a ton of black eyeliner and shadow, with fading tattoos up and down her arms, with a withering gaze identical to Eleanor's.

She takes off her headphones. She's blasting what sounds like old-school heavy metal. I can hear the crunching and shredding all the way across the room.

"Who are you?" she asks me.

"Grandma," Eleanor says, "he's from the DMV. I don't know what he wants."

Thanks a lot, Eleanor. "Yes, ma'am," I say. "The Department of Motor Vehicles."

"You're not taking my fucking car keys."

Eleanor turns to me. "You're not taking her fucking car keys."

I'd rather be digging up a grave right now. Please, by all means, bring on the Wiccan-goth ritual. I spot the car keys on the table next to the recliner, next to a can of Mr. PiBB and a pill box. Do I make a grab for the keys? Can I make it across the room before the grandma beats me to them? This is nuts.

The one thing I know about old people, from working at Haunted Frontier and DoorDash and my various other customer service gigs, is that they prefer to be treated like regular people. You can't talk to old people like they're loopy, even if that's exactly what they are. Especially if. So I try to think of a question I'd ask anyone in this situation.

The room is hot and stuffy, with an odd concoction of smells. Baby powder, patchouli oil. "What are you listening to?" I say.

She withers me with her gaze for a few seconds. "Sabbath."

"Black Sabbath?"

"No. Green Sabbath."

"Did you ever see them live?"

"Ha. Only half a dozen times."

"Who's the best guitar player of all time?"

"Who do you think?"

"I don't know, honestly. That's why I'm asking."

She looks over at Eleanor. Eleanor shrugs. "You better leave," Eleanor tells me. "You need to get out of here, mister. Go back to the DMV and stay away."

"Not fucking Clapton," the grandma says.

"Not fucking Clapton," I agree. Who is Clapton? I don't have much knowledge or any strong opinions about guitar players, but I trust an old lady blasting Black Sabbath.

"Or Jeff fucking Beck," she says.

"Ha. Jeff Beck."

The grandma points at Eleanor. "Natalie's into that weepy shit. That mopey shit. Makes me want to slash my wrists."

"I'm Eleanor, Grandma," Eleanor says.

"Where do you stand on Eddie Van Halen?" I ask the grandma. "My mom loved him."

"Not my cup of tea, but he could play."

"This person has no right to take your car keys, Grandma," Eleanor says, looking at me like, *Go ahead and hurry up and take her car keys, will you?*

"I have to take your keys, ma'am," I say. I try to find a way to stick to the truth. I'm not a better liar today than I was yesterday. "It's not my choice. I'm truly, sincerely sorry."

The grandma puts her headphones back on. I guess she's finished with this conversation. But then before either Eleanor and I can say anything, the grandma picks up her keys and chunks them at my head. She chunks them *hard*. I barely duck out of the way in time. The keys *thwack* the wall behind me. Eleanor scoops them off the floor and grabs me by the arm.

"Holy shit," she says as she hustles me down the stairs, "she likes you. You actually did it."

15

Eleanor walks me to my car. "That was just the first favor I'll be collecting," she reminds me.

"I know. We had a deal."

"You're a weird dude."

"How am I weird?"

"I bet you haven't even started investigating those kids yet, have you? I bet you're still in the 'stoned musing' stage of things."

"I've started."

"Let's hear it."

I tell her about finding Felice, talking to Felice, grinding through all the Instagram photos, getting information from Cameron Keller. I'm planning to conveniently omit my surveillance debacle, but in the end I tell Eleanor about that too. She already thinks I'm a moron. I'm not going to change her mind.

After I finish, she blinks her tarantula lashes and regards me. She's deliberating, I suspect, how to most savagely ridicule me about the dude in the pink golf shirt. Instead all she says is "Huh."

"Now I have to figure out my next move," I say.

Her phone lights up with a text. She takes a look, then puts it away. "Booty call," she says.

I wonder what genre of chick gets Eleanor going. Other oddball goths like her? Or the opposite—blond and perky sorority sisters, for example? Most of the chicks I've hooked up with, not that many, and my one briefly serious girlfriend, smoke weed and make jewelry and have vague plans to someday become an apprentice tattoo artist. But am I attracted to those chicks because I'm specifically attracted to them, or because I know they're more likely to be specifically attracted to me?

I start to get in my car.

"Wait," she says.

I wait while she seems to weigh the various implications of some momentous matter.

"Are you hungry?" she says.

"Sure."

"As a reward for your service tonight, I'll let you buy me dinner."

Thanks again, Eleanor. We go to a place nearby that's famous for its mediocre but inexpensive tacos. She raids the empty table next to us for extra condiments.

"So is your grandma doing okay?" I say. "Or is she, you know . . ."

She stuffs an astounding amount of taco into her mouth, practically the entire thing. "Demented? No. Her mind's fairly sharp. It's her eyesight that's dogshit. And she has bad sciatica. And cancer."

"Cancer?"

"It's fine. It's like early stages or whatever. She'll probably outlive us all. They give her superb drugs for the sciatica and she shares the extras with me."

"Who's Natalie? Why did your grandma call you that?"

"Who do you think?"

"Natalie is your mom?"

"Was."

"Oh."

"She's not dead, just absent. Last I heard she lives in Florida. Who knows?"

"Do you look like her or is your grandma just really confused?"

"Yes."

A hip couple in their thirties or forties takes the table next to us. They're too sleek and stylish for this joint. Their Urban Eats app must have accidentally pointed them here, instead of the tastier but more expensive taco place a couple of miles away.

"Hey, excuse me," the husband says, smiling at us, "I think that might actually be our pico de gallo."

Eleanor dips her finger in the bowl, stirs the salsa around, and then offers the bowl to the guy. "This?" she says.

The husband freezes like a FaceTime call, with just the occasional twitch of pixels. His wife murmurs softly. Probably something like *Don't escalate, babe*. I grab the salsa from the empty table on the other side of us and hand it to them. I apologize on behalf of Eleanor.

"You're kind of a maniac," I tell her. I kind of appreciate that.

She doesn't answer. She's already ripping into her second taco, using her fingers to scoop up the ground meat that escapes.

"When did your mom take off?" I say. "How old were you?"

"The first time, seven. The second time, ten. Third time's the charm. I was twelve when she left for good. Not that a girl needs a mother at that age. But I had my dad for a while. My grandma."

"My mom died when I was nine."

"Are we BFFs now? Do I need to tell you about my first period?"

I glance over at the hip husband. I think he's been eavesdropping. I think he thinks Eleanor is my girlfriend and feels bad on my behalf. He gives me a sympathetic frown.

"What happened then?" Eleanor says. "After your mom died?"

"Foster care. But it was a positive experience. I was lucky."

"It all makes sense now."

"What does?"

"You're joking, right? It's obvious now why you're so obsessed with helping those kids."

Is it? Maybe it's partially true, now that I think about it, that my mom dying has something to do with why I can't stop thinking about those kids. But that seems like too simple an explanation. Or, no, a too-*complicated* one.

"What I think the question should be," I say, "like, very simple and not complicated, is not *why* do I want to help those kids, but why *wouldn't* I or anyone else want to help those kids?"

She shoves aside the wreckage of her tacos and regards me again. She does an awful lot of that—regarding me. It's somewhat unnerving.

"I'm bored," she says. "Show me."

"Show you what?"

"The house where the family lives. Let's do a drive-by. We'll take my car so your nemesis in the pink golf shirt doesn't recognize you."

I don't see the point of a drive-by. All risk, no potential reward. On the other hand, it's *something*. If I go home now, I'll just lie awake in bed, thinking about all the terrible things that might be happening to Pearl and Jack, thinking about how I'm just lying there, doing *nothing*.

On the ride across town, I experience Eleanor's playlist. Grandma nailed it. Slow, droning guitar and bursts of feedback that are like getting electrocuted. Slow, heavy drums and wailing. But then, every now and then out of nowhere, a Taylor Swift song or the theme to Disney's *Little Einsteins*.

"What's wrong with my music?" Eleanor says, giving me a withering glance.

"I didn't say anything," I say.

We pull into Meadow Wood Estates. All the houses are dark and our headlights seem aggressively bright. I wonder if there's private security—probably some guy like Burke, cruising around and crossing his fingers that one day his dreams will come true and he'll get to gun down a trespasser.

"I thought it would be skeezier," Eleanor says.

"Me too."

"Which is stupid, I'm aware. People with money can be just as horrible as the rest of us."

We enter the cul-de-sac. The houses here are dark too—except for the house where the Shaws live. It's all lit up, every window on the first floor blazing.

"What!" I say.

"That's the one?" Eleanor says.

"Yeah. Wow."

After what I saw last week, the curtains shut tight and no signs of life, a party late on a weekday night is not what I expected. In the driveway I count three cars plus the Volvo. Two more cars are parked out front.

We roll past the house. With the curtains open now, I can see inside. There's not much to see, though. A corner of an empty room, a corner of another empty room. The party must be happening on the other side of the house, or in the backyard.

Eleanor circles out of the cul-de-sac and we head back toward the Meadow Wood Estates entrance. I wonder what's up with all those cars, all those lights. Is it a potential clue? On TV it's relatively easy to spot a clue. There's a close-up shot of it, or the music gives you a nudge, or there's a cutaway to the detective thinking, *Well, well, what do we have here?* Real life lacks all those convenient elements.

"It's weird, right?" I say. "It's not traditional behavior for parents of young children to have a party at eleven o'clock on a Wednesday night."

"What's behind their house?" Eleanor says.

"A backyard. What do you mean?"

"No. What's behind their backyard. More houses? Or a field?"

"Fields. Pasture."

I get what she's getting at and pull up my maps app. I switch it to satellite view. A county highway cuts through the empty space behind the subdivision, about a hundred yards from the Shaw house. We could park on the shoulder. We wouldn't have to sneak through some neighbor's yard. The stockade fence the Shaws have, eight feet tall instead of six, might be an issue. We'd have to peek through instead of over. We'd have to hope for a knothole.

"I don't know," I say. "What if someone sees us?"

"Who's going to see us? Don't be a candy-ass, you candy-ass. You said you wanted to *investigate*. Isn't *investigating* the whole point? Or am I confused?"

"Okay. But we have to be extremely careful."

"No shit?" she says.

16

We exit Meadow Wood Estates and cross over to the county highway. The two narrow lanes are deserted this time of night, fields on both sides of us. One day in the future all this will officially exist, with a Topgolf and an urgent care clinic and a brand-new subdivision (Hilly Flats Estates?), but for now the dark, endless emptiness seems unreal, a dead spot on a video game map where a glitch has dropped you.

The glow from the Shaw house guides us. Eleanor parks on the shoulder and we walk across the field. There's enough moon, half of one, to see where we're going. Which is also enough moon, I can't help thinking, for that private security guard with the itchy trigger finger to see *us*.

But we make it to the stockade fence behind the Shaws' house without any problems. And we luck out: the side of the fence that faces us is the side with the horizontal cross-rails. They're about three feet apart. I can use them like the rungs of a ladder to climb up and look over.

Eleanor beats me to it. She's freakishly agile for a petite goth chick in a dress. I pull myself up next to her.

We've found the party. It's going down in a den or living/dining area separated from the backyard by French doors. Light darts and flickers across the wooden deck as people move around inside. I hear a muffled bass beat *thud-thud-thudding*.

I still can't see anything, though. There's a tree in the yard that's not very large but large enough to block the view. All I can catch through the leaves are random fragments of faces and bodies, of smoke puffs and hair swishes. We need to try a different spot on the fence, with a better angle.

I start to give Eleanor a nudge, but—*fuck!*—she's already hauling herself over the top of the fence. What is she doing? She hangs for a second on the other side, then drops to the ground.

"Hurry up," she whispers to me, then disappears into the shadows around the tree. I haul myself over the top of the fence and drop to the ground too. Why? I'm not thinking. Now we're both illegally trespassing, both trapped on the wrong side of an eight-foot fence.

I slink over to the tree and crouch next to Eleanor. "What are you *doing*?" I whisper. "Someone's going to see us. And how are we supposed to get back over the fence?"

"No one can see us. Calm down. It's dark and the lights are on inside. They can't see out the windows. Haven't you ever been inside a house at night with the lights on? The windows are mirrors."

Okay, yes, but what if someone opens the French doors and comes outside? They'll be close enough to basically smell the taco on our breath. What if . . .

I have a clear line on the party now, and the scene inside stops me cold. Who *are* these people? Earlier Eleanor was surprised the neighborhood was so non-skeezy. Well, here's some legit skeezy for her. Four or five guys you might see stabbing trash by the side of a highway. A couple of women you might see lined up outside the plasma donation center. Bad skin and worse teeth, greasy hair and greasier jeans. Half the people are meth-head scrawny. The other half are hefty as trucks. One hefty dude has a gray steel-wool beard down to his belly. One scrawny drunk dude has a hunting knife on his belt. A woman with an iffy blond dye job tips her head back and bares her teeth when she laughs. She looks like she's howling, or drowning.

I'm probably not one to judge, but this crowd—wow. I wonder if Pearl and Jack are upstairs, trying to sleep. The music thuds. Any normal parent wouldn't want their kids within a mile of this environment, within a mile of these people. Pearl and Jack are probably too scared to sleep. What if they have to pee in the night? They'll have to hold it. They can't leave their beds, can't creep out into the hallway. Who knows what will be out there? Pain and fear. Pearl and Jack live with it every day, but there's always room for more.

"You said the father is a lawyer?" Eleanor frowns because no one at the party comes close to matching that description. "Which one is he?"

Nathan Shaw isn't there. Neither is Tracy. Just as I'm about to tell Eleanor that, a new person enters the den. There he is—Nathan. I recognize him from his website photo. He looks a little rougher in person. He needs a shave and his tie is pulled loose. Compared to everyone else at the party, though, he looks like a movie star in a tuxedo.

"That's him," I tell Eleanor.

I watch Nathan Shaw work his way through the party. He smiles and chats and tops off plastic cups from a handle of vodka. Seeing him in real life, knowing what he's done—I'm expecting to feel a blast of white-hot fury. Instead, though, I feel mostly just numb. Like I'm separated one inch from my own body, like I've been colored in outside the lines. Nathan Shaw just seems so normal. Which means what he does to his kids is just part of a normal life. He brushes his teeth, he files his lawsuits against the IRS, he grinds out cigarettes on a child's collarbone.

"Are you all right?" Eleanor whispers.

I tell myself to concentrate. I'm here for a reason. I study the room and try to take in every detail. Pale hands but a tan face. A denim vest with ghost stitching on the back, where a patch used to be. I don't know what's important and what's not. Is it important that Tracy isn't at the party? The scrawny drunk dude fist-bumps one and all, at every opportunity. He has a mullet with very short bangs. The mullet looks like it's sliding off the back of his head.

The handle of vodka is empty in a minute.

"We can get closer," Eleanor whispers.

"What? No! We're already too close."

The scrawny drunk bumps into the denim vest. The denim vest shoves the scrawny drunk hard. Scrawny drunk reaches for his knife and for a second it looks like shit will get real, but then he spins around and twerks his ass at the denim vest. Everybody laughs.

Who *are* these people? Why would Nathan Shaw let them into his house? His neighbors in Meadow Wood Estates can't be too happy about it. His *neighbors*. It clicks why the man in the pink golf shirt was so pissed off. He saw me loitering on the cul-de-sac in my shitty car and thought *I* was one of these people. I'm distressed that anyone could mistake *me* for one of *them*, but it also tells me this party isn't a special occasion. Skeeziness must abound at Nathan Shaw's house, on a regular basis.

But that's not hard evidence that Pearl and Jack are being abused. A Child Services caseworker would probably just shrug. I can't tell Child Services about this anyway, since I'm breaking the law by being here. My credibility is already dubious.

I pull out my phone, check to make sure the flash is turned off, and take a photo of the party. For some unknown and inexplicable reason—I *swear* I checked first!—the flash fires. Light bounces off the glass panes of the French doors and for a split second the whole backyard blazes.

Eleanor and I freeze. I try not to freak out. It was only a split second. Nobody inside noticed. The backyard is dark again. Nobody inside has even glanced our way.

And then the French doors swing open. Nathan Shaw steps outside. The music follows him, thick and heavy. I can make out pieces of conversations behind him. *Told the asshole that he . . . year or so ago when . . . shitting me. Go get me one of them other . . . No, no, no.*

Nathan Shaw stands on the deck. His back is to the light in the house, his face in the dark, so I don't know if he can see us or not. Eleanor and I could be totally invisible, in the shadows around the tree, or he could be staring right at us.

He doesn't move. He's holding something down by his leg. His phone, probably, not a gun. Why would he have a gun? That's just my adrenaline pumping, my imagination running wild.

Eleanor's elbow presses against my knee. The fence. She wants to make a break for it. But then Nathan Shaw will spot us for sure, if he hasn't already. And I still have no idea how we're getting back over that eight-foot stockade.

Crouched here and barely breathing isn't a long-term solution either. What if Nathan doesn't go back inside for a while? What if the party moves out onto the deck? I wish he would shift a little to his left so I can positively confirm it's just a phone in his hand.

The French doors swing open again. The hefty dude with the big steel-wool beard steps out.

"The fuck you doing out here?" he says.

Nathan answers, too quietly for me to hear what he says.

"Almost time," the big beard says. "C'mon."

They go back inside, closing the French doors behind them. Eleanor and I quickly creep away, back across the yard. I look for something we can drag over to the fence, a lawn chair maybe, or a wooden barrel that you plant flowers in.

"Find something we can stand on," I whisper.

Eleanor ignores me. She leaps and grabs the top of the fence. In practically the same motion, she twists, kicks, scissors a leg over, pulls herself up. It's astonishing, a total ninja move. I stare up at her.

She peers down at me. "What are you waiting for?" she whispers.

"What? I can't do that."

"You can. For God's sake."

I jump and grab the top of the fence. I'm in decent shape. I can do ten or so push-ups every morning when I remember to do them. But it will take more upper-body strength than that to get up and over this fence. I can barely chin-up to the top.

"Use your legs, dumbass," Eleanor whispers. "Do what I did. Turn your hips and hook your heel. It's easy."

Sure, if I weighed practically nothing, like she does. I try anyway. Unbelievably, it works. I swing myself up and over. Eleanor is already running for the car, laughing like a maniac. I take off after her and don't look back.

17

It seems the more information I have, the less I understand. Is that part of the grinding process too? Taking each individual fact and beating on it with your mind until the truth spills out?

What the fuck is up with Nathan Shaw? Who were those skeezy people at his house? Are they his clients? None of those people seem like they're too worried about the IRS. If Nathan Shaw is up to something shady, will that help kick Child Services into action? Probably, right?

What if—

"Yo. Why did we skip the jail?"

"Excuse me?"

I'm the Dead Sheriff again on Thursday. Just when I most need time and space to think, every two minutes I have guests like this guest—an aggravated dude who's cut me off with his mobility scooter—in my face.

"Last time, back in June, the jail was bomb," he says.

The Old Town Jail has never been bomb, trust me, and never part of the tour, not as long as I've worked here. I could show him actual proof that the building is a bare, empty, dust-covered shell, but in my experience actual proof is never a successful strategy with aggravated dudes. So I say I'm sorry he didn't enjoy his experience at Haunted Frontier and give him a voucher for twenty percent off his next visit. He snatches the voucher out of my hand, disgusted at the level of service around here.

In the next group, a lady gives me her daughter's half-eaten box of popcorn and instructs me—telling, not asking—to throw it away for her. In the group after that, a different lady interrupts my spiel, like I'm not even there, to regale the other guests with trivia about the Old West.

Usually I don't mind being treated this way, like an incompetent and inconvenient servant, because that's basically what I am. Tonight is different for some reason. I'm cranky. I'm hot. I just want the shift to end.

I get my one break when the Let Freedom Ring nighttime spectacular explodes over Colonial America and the fireworks lure everyone in the park to the central hub for fifteen minutes. I guzzle a bottle of water and use my phone to search "Nathan Shaw" again. I need the full story on him, but all I keep turning up is the law firm website and a handful of comments on a review site for attorneys. The comments are brief and vague, possibly fake. *Highly recommend. Professional and friendly. Really listened to my problems.*

The *About Nathan* page on his website lists the name of the reputable law school he attended. That's it. Everything else is sales pitch—how he's defended hundreds of clients, how he works tirelessly on behalf of his clients, etc. Free consultations, walk-ins welcome. Reasonable rates are mentioned twice.

There are multiple Nathan Shaws on Facebook, Instagram, and Twitter, but as far as I can tell none are the Nathan Shaw I'm looking for. What else can I try? I don't have a credit card so I can't access the databases that allegedly *Find Out Anything About Anyone!* Those ads are probably scams anyway.

I take Felice's business card out of my wallet. Now or never, right. She's got to know how to find out something about someone. And she might still have helpful connections from her days as a private investigator.

She answers on the fifth ring, right when I'm thinking the call will go to voicemail.

"Felice Upton."

"Hey, yeah, hi. This is Hardly. From the open house last Sunday?"

"Hello, Hardly." She doesn't sound surprised. Probably she never does. "How can I help you?"

I'm a little nervous. If she didn't want me to call, she wouldn't have given me her number. Still, though, this conversation feels like a test. I can't waste her time. One wrong move and she'll be done with me.

"So I took your advice," I say. "And it actually worked."

"Actually? I like to think it was good advice, Hardly."

"I don't mean that. Sorry. I mean I didn't screw it up, believe it or not."

"And now you need more advice?"

"Yeah. Wouldn't you know it. If you don't mind. If you have time."

"Let's have a drink. What are you doing?"

"Right now?" I was hoping for a short conversation on the phone, at best. "A drink?"

"It's only nine o'clock," she says. "How old do you think I am?"

She tells me to meet her in an hour at the bar in one of the high-end hotels downtown. I track down Duttweiler, the shift lead, and tell him I have to leave early because of an emergency. Kind of true! He's not happy, but I pledge to be Dead Sheriff on demand for the rest of the month. That will make his life easier, so he lets me go.

I zoom home and take a quick shower. None of my usual attire is proper enough for a high-end hotel bar, so I scrounge through the back of my closet. I find some hand-me-down clothes Preston forced on me a while ago, hoping I'd have a real job interview someday. A decent shirt with buttons, good jeans.

I get to the hotel a few minutes early. The lobby is swank and sterile, the air-conditioning cranked. The chill plus all the marble, the marble floors and marble columns and slabs of artistically veined marble mounted on the walls, make me think of a morgue, make me think there should be a wisecracking TV coroner eating a sandwich while she rummages around inside a corpse for organs.

The hotel has two bars, one that's more casual, with multiple TVs playing baseball highlights and waitresses dressed as referees, and one that's dark and hushed, with scattered pockets of light created by the candles on each table. I stand halfway between the two bars, uncertain. I feel stiff and awkward in Preston's stiff and awkward clothes. Not only does he iron his jeans, apparently he uses starch too. Or maybe I'm just used to wearing jeans that haven't been washed in a while.

Felice taps me on the shoulder. Where did she come from?

"You didn't get us a table," she says.

"I wasn't sure which bar you meant."

She smiles like I'm joking and leads me into the dark, hushed bar.

18

As soon as we sit down, a waiter glides over to take our order. The waiter takes his shit seriously, you can tell, but I do catch him glancing at Felice, glancing at me, wondering *what do we have here*. All the other couples are either middle-aged men and women doing important business or middle-aged men with much younger women who are probably not their daughters.

Felice orders an old-fashioned made with a special type of rye whiskey. I struggle to think of something that's equally sophisticated. Finally she bails me out and tells the waiter to bring me an old-fashioned too.

"Thanks for meeting up," I say.

"Let's hear it."

"I tracked down Pearl's second-grade teacher from last year. I talked to him. He said he saw bruises on Pearl, a couple of times. But he didn't report it to Child Services. He brought the parents in for a conference instead, then decided everything was fine."

Felice lifts an eyebrow. "You did all that?"

"I didn't really know what I was doing when I talked to him. But it's something. The teacher thinks it's the father hurting the kids. That's not enough for Child Services, though. I can't even count on the teacher. He believes what he wants to believe."

"Don't we all."

The waiter brings over our drinks. I take a sip of my old-fashioned. It's— wow—strong. I hope the light is dim enough in here that Felice doesn't see my eyes water.

"So I think I need to find out what's up with Nathan Shaw." I tell Felice about the late-night party, the skeezy crowd at the house. "He's sketchy, for sure. But I can't find anything about him online."

She's lifting her eyebrow again. "I see."

"What?"

"So that's why you called me. You just want to use me."

"No!" I say. But it's true and I'm busted. "I mean, yes, I thought maybe if there's some way you could . . . I thought you might have resources that I don't have, to get information about him. I'm sorry."

"Don't worry," she says. She seems more amused than annoyed, which is a relief. "I'll consider it."

"Seriously?"

She lifts her glass so I can clink it with mine. Not that she needs it, but the candlelight works for Felice, bringing out a note of gold in her eyes, her skin. She's fifteen years older than me, easy. Do I have a thing for older chicks that I never realized until now? No. It's not that. I have a thing for Felice.

"Getting what you need from a conversation," she says, "it's tricky."

"Okay."

"Because every conversation, every person you talk to, is different. You don't go to France and speak Japanese, do you?"

"No. But how—"

"You have to pay attention. You have to *keep* paying attention. The most dangerous thing in the world is a first impression."

It's a small table. Her hand rests close to mine, our fingers almost touching. I feel guilty all of a sudden. What's wrong with me? At a time like this I shouldn't be crushing on Felice. I should be totally focused on Pearl and Jack, on helping them, on nothing else. Not to mention, there's no way Felice is into me. She has to have a million better options.

"That's good advice," I say.

"It is."

She waves over the waiter and orders us two more old-fashioneds. How much do the drinks in a place like this cost? I have thirty-one dollars with me, which I may have foolishly assumed would be plenty.

"Don't worry," Felice says. "My treat."

"How did you know I was thinking that?"

"You tell me."

"You're paying attention."

"Quick learner. I like that."

At a table not far from us a middle-aged man sits with a younger woman who is definitely not his daughter. He's leaning in, locked in, whispering urgently. She's staring off into space, drumming her cocktail straw against the rim of her glass. He's in a suit. She's wearing a short, shimmery dress, her hair slicked back, like a sexy otter. My first impression is that he's her sugar daddy, pouring out his problems at home or work. She's enduring it, the same way she'll endure the hooking up later on.

Second impression? I pay attention, but . . . he's got to be her sugar daddy, right? He's boring the shit out of her, right? But then she reaches over and thumps him on the sternum with her knuckles. *Oh, c'mon!* It's intimate and good-natured and maybe she actually *is* his daughter.

"It takes time," Felice says. "It takes practice."

"What do you think was going on with the people I saw at Nathan Shaw's house? What's your professional opinion?"

"Finish your drink."

I get the hint. She's given me more of her time and attention than I deserve. I knock down the rest of my second old-fashioned and it spreads through me like glowing molten ore poured into a mold.

"Thanks again, for all your help," I say.

"Hardly," she says.

"What?"

"Let's go back to my place. That's what I'm saying."

What! The flame of the candle dances. Felice hands her credit card to the waiter. I stay cool, thanks partly to the rye whiskey and partly because I'm too shocked to be anything else.

"Okay," I say.

We walk back to her apartment. She lives just a few blocks away, in our midsized city's best approximation of a big-city luxury high-rise. The elevator is thick with the perfume of a recent passenger, the scent of wet leaves and candy. Felice and I stand facing forward, our arms touching. In her heels she's almost as tall as me, six feet tall. We silently watch the numbers over the doors light up and go out, light up and go out. What is happening right now? Three hours ago I was getting accidentally kneed in the junk by an Outlaw Zombie.

Felice's apartment is kind of a mess, the exact opposite of Felice herself. Clothes piled on the sofa, half-unpacked Amazon packages spilling bubble wrap, an empty wine bottle sitting on top of a Sonos speaker. Either she wasn't planning to invite me back to her place or she doesn't care what I think about it.

"Can I move this?" I say, pointing to one of the piles of clothes on the sofa.

"Why?"

"So we can sit down."

"Why would we want to do that?"

She takes me into the bedroom, kicks off her shoes, and arranges the blinds so that we have some moonlight but not too much. We kiss. What makes someone a good kisser? It's hard to quantify. Felice is an excellent kisser. Right away we find our groove. She starts unbuttoning my shirt.

"Don't be nervous," she says.

"I'm not nervous."

"Is this your first time?"

"What? No! Of course not."

"I'm joking. It better not be your first time."

"Now I'm nervous," I say.

Sex with Felice feels familiar—it's sex—but also part of the strange dream I'm having when I'm with her. She's so comfortable with herself, with us, with this. Not like I have a vast range of experience, because I definitely don't, but all the other women I've been with seemed to some degree self-conscious. Not Felice. Nobody is watching her.

During sex I always feel like someone is watching me. A panel of stern Olympic judges from Eastern European countries, finding fault with my every move. Tonight, though, there's no room in my head for anything but Felice. How amazing she feels and tastes and looks. We speed up and slow down, tense and relax, roll over and swing around. I'm unable to hold a coherent thought in my head for more than a second. Her eyes flash, daring me not to come too soon. I have to turn away or I totally will.

Afterward, Felice dispatches me to the kitchen for two cans of passion-fruit LaCroix. I don't get a choice in the matter of hydration options. We lie in bed, sipping in silence, for a few minutes.

"So," I say. "Do you have any, like, brothers or sisters?"

"Do I what?"

"Or . . . I don't know. What do you do for fun? When you're not working?"

She arches an eyebrow at me. "You're nervous again."

"No. Yes. I'm just thinking. I don't know anything about you. You don't really know anything about me."

"That's correct."

"Shouldn't we get to know each other a little more?"

She reaches under the sheet and wraps her hand, cool from the can of LaCroix, around me. She gives me a long, lazy, passion fruit–flavored kiss. "Let's do that," she says.

19

Felice kicks me out around three in the morning. She doesn't bother with excuses. "You understand," she says, without a question mark.

When I wake up a few hours later, my astonishment at what happened—Felice and me, Felice and *me*—has faded. The guilt starts churning again. It's been more than a week since I first saw Pearl and Jack at the municipal building. Why am I allowed to have a good time, to experience joy and pleasure, to drink expensive drinks and hook up with a woman like Felice, when Pearl and Jack are still trapped in their lives? They don't get to take a night off. Why should I?

Burke's not around, which is a relief, and he's left Jutta inside for once, another win. She lies on my feet while I eat some cereal. I can't stop thinking about all the online stories I read about child abuse. It's strange how pain can't be translated into words. Not really. A cut. A bruise. A burn. None of that sounds so terrible when you just read it on the page, does it? But the pain of a single cut or bruise or burn—when it's happening, it feels like it will last forever.

I smoke a bowl, then call Salvador and tell him to meet me in the parking lot at work. He lives twice as far from Beautiful America as me, but somehow he beats me there.

"I'm ready!" he says.

"For what?"

This throws him for a second. "Anything!"

"Can I borrow your car today?" I say. Salvador has the Honda SUV his mom used to drive, only a few years old. He keeps it spectacularly clean. "You can have mine. We'll swap back tonight."

I can tell he's disappointed that I need his car, not him, so I give him instructions to hole up at the Abandoned Mine Train, hit the internet, write up index cards for all the facts I gathered from the party at the Shaw house. Now he's happy again.

Is it smart to return to Meadow Wood Estates? Even in a different, nicer, cleaner car? I don't have a better idea. I want to go back with fresh eyes. I want to pay attention this time.

The subdivision is quiet, as usual. When I swing into the cul-de-sac, I see that one older lady in her yard again, watering her flowers. She doesn't even glance up as I pass. Salvador's SUV fits right in. No sign of the guy in the pink golf shirt. Maybe he's peering out from inside his house. Go right ahead, dude. I'm not going to give him any reason, today, to go apeshit.

The Shaw house is closed back off again, all the curtains drawn and the blinds shut. Midnight-blue Volvo in the driveway, no other cars. I circle out of the cul-de-sac and pull over on the cross street this time. I still have a view of the house, but I'm a lot less conspicuous. After five or so minutes I take off, cruise around the subdivision, then loop back to a different spot. I'm going to make mistakes, but at least I can make sure they're new ones.

I'm watching the house from the second stakeout spot when the front door opens. Out step the two kids, Pearl and Jack, followed by Tracy. If that photo of Pearl at school gave me a jolt, seeing her and Jack in real life again hits me like a bus. There they are. *Right there.* So close I can see the anime fairy on Pearl's T-shirt, the sandy blond bangs in Jack's eyes. Pearl is leading Jack, holding his hand. The two of them look even smaller than I remember. They're so young, so delicately constructed and insubstantial. Tracy straps Jack into the backseat. She gives him a kiss on the forehead.

My brain can't catch up with my eyes. Before I even realize it, the Volvo is turning out of the cul-de-sac and heading away from me, toward the Meadow Wood gatehouse.

I fumble with the gearshift and yank Salvador's SUV into drive. I bust a U and head toward the gatehouse too, catching sight of the Volvo just as it turns left out of the subdivision.

I've never tailed anyone before. It's intense. In movies, this part of the action gets edited down to a bang-bang sequence of shots. Turn, turn, change lanes, then *Uh-oh, we're losing him!* or *Uh-oh, he's spotted us!* In real life there's no montaging. I have to stay focused on the midnight-blue Volvo every second. I can't get too close or fall too far behind.

My head starts to ache. After a few minutes we enter the busy bloodstream of a commercial area. There's a lot of traffic, a lot of blue Volvo-like cars, and people are terrible drivers. In movies no one drifts into your lane because they're putting in AirPods, no one decides at the last minute to slam to a stop for a yellow light. And I'm not familiar with the SUV. It has more power than my car, plus functional brakes, so I do some unnecessary lunging and jerking.

Slowly I get the hang of it, though, and I don't lose the Volvo. After fifteen minutes or so, it turns, turns again, then stops at a neighborhood park. I slide past and pull to the curb on the other side of the street. This way I can watch the Volvo in my side-view mirror.

Tracy unpacks the kids from the Volvo and leads them over to a little playground. Pearl climbs into a swing. Jack studies his sister's moves, the way he does, then duplicates them exactly. I wonder if Pearl notices how Jack always shadows her. Does it bug her? Comfort her? I imagine, for a second, all this working out. I get the evidence I need, CPS moves the kids into a new life . . . maybe when Pearl is seventeen and Jack is sixteen, she'll give him shit about how he used to follow her around like a puppy. Maybe when she's old and in a nursing home, he'll remind her to make her smile.

My mind is unwinding in some strange directions. I'm not even stoned! Tracy takes a swing too. I watch the three of them rock back and forth, barely getting off the ground. It's not a sad scene, though, but kind of peaceful.

What should I pay attention to? The park. Okay. One question I realize I have is: why did Tracy drive the kids fifteen minutes to this park? That's a relatively long way. I guarantee there are parks closer to their house. There's probably a park and a playground *in* Meadow Wood Estates.

One possible answer: because this park is deserted? There's not a single other kid or person around. Maybe Tracy brought Pearl and Jack here for the same reason she pulled them from school, for the same reason she left them on the bench when she went inside to Driver Verification. She doesn't want anyone seeing a bruise or a cigarette burn and getting suspicious.

I can see what Cameron Keller, Pearl's teacher, was talking about. Tracy does seem to love her kids. She's smiling at them, talking to them, giving Jack another kiss on the head when she lifts him from his swing, hugging Pearl close as they spin on the merry-go-round. I don't want to be judgmental, but who's worse? Nathan for hurting his kids or Tracy for protecting him?

When they finish on the merry-go-round, they get back in the Volvo and drive off. I give them a thirty-second head start and follow. We're moving west now, away from the park and Meadow Wood Estates both. A few miles later, Tracy turns into the parking lot of a strip mall. Hair salon, dry cleaners, pho restaurant, Verizon store, and a vacant business at the end. She parks in front of the vacant business.

I pull into a space outside the Verizon store. I'm not sure what the vacant business used to be. A gym, maybe. Before that it might have been a Blockbuster—the cream-colored stucco is trimmed with faded blue and yellow paint. All the windows now are taped over with brown butcher paper.

Tracy off-loads the kids again. Where is she taking them? There are a few other cars parked in front of the former Blockbuster. I wait and watch. More people trickle in. An old memory taps me on the shoulder: my mom taking me to Blockbuster when I was little, when DVDs were still a thing, the two of us drifting up and down the aisles, the colors of the movie box covers popping. I always got to pick what we watched. That could be overwhelming, all the choices. "Don't worry, baby," my mom always said. "You can't go wrong."

People stop trickling into the former Blockbuster. Twenty minutes go by. My maps app gives an address for the place but no other information. I wish I knew what was inside. I wish I knew why Tracy took her kids inside a place with butcher paper blocking the windows. It doesn't make sense . . . or it makes complete sense. My stomach knots, tighter and tighter. I blame all those articles I read about child abuse. I've made myself a promise that I'll stay sharp and not smoke the joint I have in my pocket, but I break down now and fire it up. It's okay, I tell myself. It's okay.

Forty minutes. An hour. Should I go inside and see what's up? That makes my stomach knot again. Just then Tracy and the kids come out. They get back in the Volvo and drive away. I stay where I am. I can't be a candy-ass. I have to find out where Tracy and the kids have been.

More people exit and drive away. A guy in a suit, a lady in yoga pants, a seedy dude who could have been at Nathan Shaw's party. I pay attention. What am I seeing? I'm seeing people who seem to have nothing in common. All colors and ages and types, from what looks like a stripper to what looks like a high school principal.

I wait five minutes, until I'm sure the last person is truly the last person, then get out of the SUV. I walk down to the mysterious former Blockbuster, take a deep breath, and try the door. It's unlocked. I take another deep breath and pull the door open. I'm fairly confident, based on the demographic of people who just left, that whatever is inside can't be too nefarious. I'm not going to be murdered, right? Right?

I step inside. I'm in a narrow hallway with cheap plasterboard walls. To my left is a small room. I peek inside. Toys, a couple of beanbag chairs, a stack of children's books. Okay. Huh. That must be where Tracy parked the kids.

I continue down the hallway, which opens into a big room with sad tan carpet and sad tan walls. A guy is gathering up a circle of folding chairs. On the other side of the room, next to another doorway, a coffee urn sits on a card table, among the scattered ruins of cookies. A lone plant droops in a pot, most of the green drained from its leaves.

The guy with the chairs notices me. He's an old hippie with Willie Nelson braids. "What's shaking, brother?" he says.

"Hey," I say.

He walks over and—before I have a chance to get into a preemptive hand-shake stance—hugs me.

"I'm a hugger, man," he says unnecessarily. He smells like cats. Not ex-actly in a bad way, but also in a way I don't love pressed all over me.

"Okay," I say, peeling myself gently away.

"My name's Charlie. You missed the one o'clock meeting, but we're still glad to have you."

"The one o'clock meeting?"

"NA, brother. But if booze is your struggle, we've got you covered. All addictions welcome."

NA. Narcotics Anonymous. I start putting it together. Tracy was attend-ing the one o'clock meeting. So she must be in recovery. For how long? And what's her specific struggle? I'd love to know, but I'm following Felice's instructions to pay attention. I'm thinking things through. I'm thinking, *Do I have another parking ticket I should defer before I leave this parking ticket window?*

Obviously I can't ask Willie Nelson about Tracy. Narcotics *Anonymous.* He won't spill any beans. He'll stop being so friendly if I start asking questions about another member.

"So there's a meeting here every day at one?" I say.

"Just Mondays, Wednesdays, and Fridays. But I've always got a minute, if you want to grab a cup of coffee."

"That's okay. Not right now. Thanks."

"Keep us in mind, brother. We're here for you."

He moves in for another hug. This time I'm ready and manage to elude.

I walk back to the SUV and sit there, thinking. Tracy Shaw is in recovery. She attends NA meetings. This is potentially important and useful information, but I feel dumb because I don't know how, if at all, to use it.

On the other hand, it's potentially important and useful information. And I was able to dig it up on my own. So I can't be *that* dumb, right?

20

Felice doesn't call or text that night or the next day. I deploy maximum, Preston-level self-control and don't call or text her. Give her time. Don't push. I'm kind of dying to know if she's decided to help me get info on Nathan Shaw. Also, more selfishly and shamefully, I'm kind of dying to know if I'll get to see her bedroom again, or if she's already regretting what happened between us.

What I'm really focused on right now, though, is Tracy Shaw. I've learned a lot. The playground, Narcotics Anonymous. An idea swims up slowly, slowly from the depths and breaks the surface of my mind. Why don't I try talking to Tracy?

If I could convince her, somehow, to come with me to Child Services . . . that would be it, game over, all the evidence a caseworker would ever need. She's their *mother*. Pearl and Jack would be safe, immediately and permanently.

Or talking to Tracy could be totally pointless. I remember how she hustled the kids away from me at the municipal building. How she drives fifteen minutes out of her way to find a deserted playground for Pearl and Jack. She doesn't want anyone to know that Nathan is hurting her kids.

And what if I'm wrong about her? What if she's not just protecting Nathan? What if she's hurting Pearl and Jack too?

I don't really believe that. Not after what I've seen, what I know about her now. Still, though, I don't think I can take the chance. Talking to Tracy could be the most massive mistake I could possibly make.

Sunday I'm driving around when I pass a Supercuts knockoff, Mister Snips, that advertises a $13.99 special. On impulse, I turn in. I want to look a little more respectable for when I ever meet Tracy, or the kids. And it won't hurt to clean myself up for Felice, in the hopes that more hooking up with her is in my future.

Mister Snips closes for the day in twenty minutes, so only one chick is working. She looks like she's about fifteen years old, but she shakes my hand in a firm, professional manner, has a well-organized workspace, and offers me twenty-five percent off the special.

"I just want to tighten it up a tiny, tiny bit," I say. "Just like a very gentle trimming."

"Like this much?" She holds up her fingers, about an inch apart.

"No, no. Even more gentle than that."

"Okay. Got it."

"Got it?"

"A very gentle trim."

She picks up a pair of scissors and goes to work on me. She goes to work for what is a troublingly long time. When she finishes, the two of us study my reflection in the mirror.

"Um," she says.

My hair is short. Not relatively short compared to what it used to be, but *short* short. Now *I* look like I'm about fifteen years old too. My ears seem gigantic.

The stylist chick bites the inside of her cheek. "It looks good," she says. "Don't you think?"

I nod. I don't want to hurt her feelings. And maybe my hair does look better than I think it does? Maybe once the shock wears off I won't want to curl up in the fetal position and weep with embarrassment?

On my way out I notice a glass fishbowl that's filled with business cards. *Win a Year of Free Snips!* The stylist chick has her back to me, sweeping up her station, so I dig around and find a business card with just a name and contact info, nicely embossed. You never know. It might come in handy.

An hour or so later, a little before ten, Felice calls.

"Want to come over and say hi?" she says.

I don't even try to play it cool. "Yes."

"I'll be home in twenty minutes or so."

It takes me fifteen to get there. I'm walking up to her building when I see her walking up from the opposite direction. She kisses me before I can say anything.

"We'll chat later," she says, then kisses me again.

The second time hooking up with Felice is even more mind-altering than the first. I literally leave my body for a second, I'm fairly certain. Her amused lips, her dead-serious eyes. Afterward I fetch cans of LaCroix without having to be told.

Felice runs her fingers through my short hair. "What happened here?"

"How do you like it?"

"I don't mind."

It's hard to tell if she's being wry and ironic, giving me a compliment, or if that's her genuinely neutral position on the subject. "You were on a date tonight, weren't you?" I say, just now realizing why she was coming home at ten-thirty.

"Look at you. Paying attention."

"How was it? Your date?"

She smiles.

"Speaking of paying attention," I say. "I followed Tracy Shaw two days ago. She went to an NA meeting. Narcotics Anonymous. But she took her kids to a park first, a playground."

Felice smiles again. "I have an early showing in the morning. You don't mind?"

I don't, but before I leave I have to ask. "Did you get a chance to, you know, consider it? About maybe checking out Nathan Shaw?"

"I've got to pee."

She slides out of bed and heads to the bathroom. That's my answer, I guess. I take one last swig of the LaCroix and get dressed. I don't know if I should wait until she finishes peeing, so I can say goodbye face-to-face, or if she expects me to be gone when she comes out.

"I had an old friend of mine do some checking," she calls from the bathroom. "Nathan Shaw had a couple of misdemeanor drug charges, but they were both dismissed. And it was a while ago."

I'm over the bed and across the bedroom and at the door of the bathroom so fast I'm like a cartoon character, rings of smoke trailing behind me. "Anything else?" I say.

"Nothing solid."

Nothing solid. That implies *something*, though. I wait.

"He was a person of interest in an assault case," she says. "A woman he was seeing. This was before he got married. The woman switched her story and they dropped the charges."

"An assault case?"

"The woman had been hospitalized twice before. Before she talked to the police. The third time, though, it was even uglier."

"But they dropped the charges?"

"It happens."

"Because she was scared of him."

"Who knows?"

Oh, wow. This information is huge. I try to get my head around it. This information is huge, right?

Felice steps out of the bathroom. "That's it," she says. "That's all I've got."

"It's a lot," I say.

She runs her fingers through my hair again, then gives me a goodnight kiss. "It's not," she says.

21

Felice is right. I still don't have enough evidence for Child Services. But I have enough evidence for *me*—to move forward with the idea I had earlier. I'm going to talk to Tracy Shaw directly. Her husband is, undeniably, a piece of shit. There's a good chance Tracy isn't protecting him from the authorities. She's protecting herself, and her kids, from him.

Monday morning I call Eleanor.

"I was just about to text you," she says.

"About what?"

"You'll never guess."

She gives me the instructions: go to her grandma's house; convince her grandma to get in my car; take her grandma to her two o'clock doctor's appointment; convince her grandma to actually go inside to the doctor's appointment.

Fantastic. "Why can't you do it?" I say.

"Because you're the grandma whisperer. And I don't want to. That's a key factor too."

"How am I going to talk her into doing all that?"

"Whatever. It's not a big deal. It's not her oncologist or anything like that. It's just the ear doctor."

On the drive over to Eleanor's grandma's house, inspiration strikes. I call Salvador and tell him to search "best guitarist ever." It's fucking Clapton, every single list. Number two is either Jimmy Page or Jimi Hendrix. Opinions differ. I flip a coin in my head and tell Salvador to look up Jimmy Page. Salvador reports that Jimmy Page was in Led Zeppelin. Good. I've heard of Led Zeppelin.

I ring the doorbell. After a long time, the time it takes an ancient head-banger to make it down the stairs, Eleanor's grandma opens the door.

"Hi," I say. "I'm going to drive you to the ear doctor."

Her glare lasers straight through my head, turning my eye sockets to ash. "You," she says. "You're the asshole from the DMV."

"I don't really work for the DMV. I'm a friend of Eleanor's."

"Ha! Eleanor doesn't have any friends."

"She doesn't?"

"What do you want?"

"I'm going to drive you to the ear doctor. I've got some good music in my car."

"Bullshit." She starts to shut the door on me, most of the way, and lasers me with one eye through the crack. "You cut your hair."

"What do you think?"

She shuts the door on me, all the way. After a few seconds, though, it opens back up. She steps out, carrying a purse so big she could probably fit inside it herself. Embroidered on the purse is a little green alien in a bonnet, in a baby carriage. I remember Eleanor's instructions and don't ask.

I lead the grandma to my car. She doesn't need any help getting in. I know this because when I touch her arm, she tries to karate chop my Adam's apple.

My elderly Kia only has a cassette player. To connect my phone, I have to use a cassette tape and cable contraption. I plug everything in, then dial up the Led Zeppelin song that seems the most promising. "Rock and Roll." I haven't listened to it yet. Fingers crossed. I crank the volume and hit play.

Drums kick in. Then a squealing guitar. Heavy metal, or whatever this is, is more frantic and aggressive than I prefer, but this song is catchy, no doubt. I'm nodding along to the beat before I realize it.

I glance over at Grandma to see if she approves. She seems annoyed, but then she flaps her hand at the windshield. "Let's go," she says.

From that point on she's more or less cooperative. I wait in the waiting room while she gets the wax in her ears excavated. When she comes out, she informs me that the doctor said she has perfect fucking hearing. I'm going to assume that's a paraphrase.

Heading home, I cautiously slide some of my own music into the heavy Zeppelin rotation. Prince's "Baby I'm a Star," one of my mom's favorites. Also "Money for Nothing" by Dire Straits. The grandma either doesn't mind or doesn't notice.

"Baby I'm a Star" always makes me think about learning to ride a bike. My mom must have brought the boom box out to the driveway. And probably there were lots of songs while I was learning, but that one stuck.

"Yes!" my mom would yell when I made it, like, three wobbly feet without falling over.

My heart was pounding. Learning to ride a bike, if you don't recall, can be a harrowing experience when you're a small kid, when you've never been up that high before, going that fast, all by yourself, yourself in charge.

"I almost crashed!" I said.

"But you didn't!" my mom said.

But you didn't! I heard that a lot growing up. My mom wanted me to expect the best, not the worst. She wanted me to always go for it—whatever I dreamed of doing, no matter how scary and impossible it seemed.

I almost got lost when I went looking for bugs!

But you didn't!

I park at the curb outside the grandma's house and walk her to the front door. "That wasn't so bad," I say.

"Ha," she says. She spelunks down into her gigantic purse and comes up with an extremely crumpled one-dollar bill. She shoves it at me. A tip, I guess.

"Don't worry about it," I say.

"Jimmy Page tossed his guitar pick to me. I was eighteen. Their first-ever tour in the U.S. My friend Marcie and I drove all the way to Memphis for the show. We were ten feet from the stage. The pick bounced off Marcie's head and hit the floor and I never saw it again. Story of my life."

And then, without another word, she goes inside and shuts the door behind her.

Eleanor gets off work at five-thirty. I meet her at a barbecue shack on the scruffy side of downtown. It's hotter today than it was yesterday, which was already way too hot, but we take our food out to a bench so I can smoke a joint.

"You survived," Eleanor says. Today she's wearing a long skirt, a *Little House on the Prairie* blouse, and a choker made from what might be actual rusty barbed wire.

"It was fine. Your grandma is . . . she's something."

"What happened to your hair? Have you filed charges yet?"

"You made fun of it when it was long."

"This is worse."

"It's not that bad."

"As long as you're not planning to get laid in the near future."

I think about Felice and her lips and her collarbone and all the rest of her, naked. I think about her moving slowly, slowly on top of me. Eleanor stares at me. I must be blushing.

"Are you actually getting laid?" she says. "I find that difficult to believe."

"Will you do me another favor? Will you help me with those kids again?"

"Probably not. What is it?"

I fill her in. The playground, the NA meeting, the dirt on Nathan that Felice dug up. "He's the one hurting those kids, not Tracy. I want to try talking to her. If I can get her to go to CPS, that's all the evidence they'll need. They'll be able to protect the kids."

Eleanor snaps her fingers at me. I pass her the joint. She takes a hit and wrinkles her nose, either at the weed or my idea—I'm not sure which.

"She won't go to CPS," she says. "Because why hasn't she gone there already?"

"I don't know. That's why I want to talk to her."

"It's risky. What if she's hurting the kids too? You could be making it worse for them if you talk to her."

I know. There are good reasons for why I feel the way I do. I've seen Tracy with her kids. I've talked to Pearl's teacher. I know about the assault charge against Nathan. But I'm only *almost* positive that I'm right about Tracy. That's another reason I want to talk to her.

"Do you have a better idea?" I hope she does. "It's risky to just do nothing too. I can't let what's happening to those kids keep happening."

"What do you want me for?" she says finally.

"It's better if you break the ice. Because you're a woman. It's less threatening. I don't want to weird her out."

"Some dude popping up out of nowhere with a bad haircut. Definitely weird."

"You catch her right before or right after her NA meeting, the day after tomorrow. On your lunch hour. You explain what's up, then bring her to meet me for coffee or something."

Eleanor doesn't say anything. We finish our food. We finish the joint.

"Your grandma said something today," I said.

"Was it slightly racist, deeply homophobic, or just the usual general batshit?"

"She said you don't have any friends. Is that true?"

She gives me the finger.

"No, that's not what I mean," I say. "I just . . . it got me thinking."

"Take all the time you need. I know it's a struggle."

"I have friends. I have a couple of best friends. I've known them forever and we hang all the time. Like, constantly. But lately . . . I don't know. All we do is stay stoned all day and watch old TV shows. So does that really make us best friends?"

"This is what you're musing about?"

"Sometimes I think Nguyen and Mallory and I are more like coworkers than friends. Like we just happened to have the same job together for ten years."

"Go get us dessert," Eleanor says.

"Pie?"

"Obviously."

I go inside and bring back pie.

"I'm a fundamentally unlikable person," she says. "But I prefer it that way. I also fundamentally don't like other people. Life is so full of bullshit relationships. That's what causes loneliness. Being in some empty, bullshit marriage or friendship or whatever. Being alone doesn't cause loneliness."

She's completely smashed the lemon meringue and half the chocolate before I've managed a second bite.

"So?" I say. "Will you do it?"

"Do what? I wasn't listening to you earlier. I haven't smoked weed in a while. I feel like the top of my head is the lid of a jar."

"Will you do it? Break the ice with Tracy for me?"

She parries my plastic fork with hers and stabs up the last bite of pie. "Whatever," she says.

22

Because of dinner with Eleanor, I'm late for my shift at Haunted Frontier. Salvador has covered for me with Duttweiler.

"I told him you have a toenail fungus," Salvador whispers loudly. We're loitering behind the Last Chance Saloon, getting ready to get our ghoul on for the next posse of guests. "I told him you had to pick up some special medicated toenail polish that the doctor prescribed for you."

"That's oddly specific, Salvador."

He beams. "Thank you!"

I tell him I need to borrow his car again on Wednesday. He begs and begs to be part of the Tracy mission. That's the word he uses: *mission*. Salvador's involvement is not necessary or desirable in any way, but I am exploiting him for his SUV and cheap labor. I'll have to figure out an assignment that keeps him far, far, far from the action.

Tuesday I have a full day to kill. I'm antsy. Because I haven't swapped cars with Salvador yet, I can't drive by the Shaw house. I realize I *can* drive by Nathan Shaw's law office and check that out. I don't know why I didn't think of that sooner.

Shaw Law is located in an upscale-ish office park, with an optometrist on one side and an orthodontist on the other. I circle a couple of times, then set up across the street in a strip mall that's almost identical to the one where Tracy goes to her NA meetings. A hair salon: check. A pho restaurant: check. An Ace Hardware instead of a Verizon store. A Books-A-Million instead of the former Blockbuster.

Half an hour passes. I don't need to move my car. If anyone at Ace

Hardware notices me, which they won't, they'll just think I'm in Books-A-Million. If anyone at Books-A-Million . . . etc.

The only car parked in front of Shaw Law is a sleek little pearl-colored fang of a sports car. No other cars, or people, come or go. It's been an hour now. The optometrist does steady business. The orthodontist does steady business. Not Shaw Law, though.

A beater like mine chugs up to the pho restaurant. Out hops a shaggy DoorDasher or Grubhubber, picking up an order of pho to deliver. He's me, basically, twenty years from now. Board shorts and T-shirt, flip-flops and three-day scruff. He even has my former manpone. It gives me a chill; I don't know why. I've never really imagined myself twenty years in the future. Live in the moment, right?

He glances over and lifts his chin at me and gives me a shaka. *Hey.* It's like he recognizes me the way I recognized him. I'm him, twenty years ago.

I pretend I don't see him. There's that chill again, even though it's ninety-five degrees outside. The shaggy delivery dude goes into the restaurant and comes out with the order. He searches the pockets of his board shorts for his keys or his lighter or his phone, whatever it is he's misplaced.

A week or so ago, before I first saw Pearl and Jack sitting on that bench, I might have been that dude. Not now, though. I'm not floating or drifting or letting the universe determine my next destination.

How do I feel about that? I'm not exactly sure. I feel *awake.* I know that. Big chunks of my life used to vanish into the ether, like texts you start to write and then delete without saving. This past week, though, has had sharpness and shape.

I pull up the website for Shaw Law. I scroll down and find what I'm looking for: *Walk-ins welcome! Free consultations!*

Okay, I know that pretending to be a potential client will probably be a bust. I'm not going to come away with any concrete evidence—Nathan Shaw won't suddenly, while walking me through tax law for dummies, decide to confess that he hurts his children.

But maybe I'll learn something by observing him up close. I can get a feel for him. Is he cold as ice or full of burning rage? Is he shifty or overbearing, a snake or a bully? Anything might help, right? He could slip up, could drop some detail I can use down the line. You never know.

Also, honestly, I want to sit across from Nathan Shaw and just look him in the eye. *I know who you are. I know what you are.* Pearl and Jack are probably too afraid to look him in the eye. I'm not.

I start my engine, then turn it back off. I can't rush into this. I need to be Felice, in the backyard lounger, considering all angles.

I text Nguyen—pick up—then call him. He doesn't pick up. I try Mallory. She picks up and hands her phone to Nguyen.

"Dude," I say, "I told you to pick up."

"Chill," Nguyen says. "What? We're going down to the pool later."

"Remember your friend who had that hustle? Who bought and sold baseball cards or something?"

"Paul. He made like thirty or forty grand in nine months."

I'm highly doubtful about that, but it doesn't matter. "How did he do it? Do you remember, like, the details?"

Nguyen tells me what he knows. Here's how Paul did it: on days that new baseball or basketball or football card sets were released, he'd get to Walmart or Target first thing in the morning, an hour or two before they opened. He'd be the first customer through the door, load a shopping cart with all the stock, then flip it on eBay for a huge profit.

"He made like thirty or forty grand in nine months," Nguyen says.

"You said that already. So why did he quit if it was such a sweet hustle?"

"It was a lot of effort. He was like, 'I could just get a regular job if I wanted to work this hard.' He's all about Bitcoin now. Or one of the other kinds of coin."

"Cool. Thanks."

"Me and Mallory are going down to the pool later."

"I'll catch you."

I smoke a joint to smooth out my nerves, drive across the street to the office park, and pull in next to the pearl-colored sports car. I sit for a minute and go over the cover story in my head, making sure I have it down cold.

The Shaw Law reception area is small but nice, bland and soothing. A couple of chairs, a painting of peaceful mountains, the sharp scent of artificial freshness.

There's no receptionist, just a door that leads to another room. Knock? Wait? Before I can decide, the door opens and Nathan Shaw steps out. He doesn't seem surprised to see me. The opposite, actually. It's like he's been eagerly waiting. When he smiles, his whole face springs into action. Creases, dimples, eyebrows, lots of teeth. It's a smile like a Broadway musical, the big finish at the end, curtains parting and legs kicking.

"Come on in," he says. He's in better shape than he was at the party. Face shaved, wavy hair perfect, tie knotted.

I feel the same numbness as before, in the backyard when I first saw him, but this time there's also a faint tingle, a far-off buzzing. Anger, boiling and building. This . . . *fucker*. How can he do what he does to his children, then come to work and smile at every stranger who comes through the door? I'm glad I smoked the weed. I very rarely get pissed off. I don't have a lot of experience handling it.

He leads me into the interior office. It's bland and soothing too, but more down to business, with oak and brass and imposing bookcases. I take a seat on the sofa. I'm expecting Nathan to move back behind the desk. Instead, though, he takes a seat on the other end of the sofa, like we're just two buds, casually kicking it.

I'm so glad I smoked the weed. My nerves are holding steady, more or less. Nathan introduces himself. He asks me to call him by his first name. "Let's keep it real," he says.

My name. *Shit*. I planned out this elaborate cover story for why I need his services, but I didn't consider if I should give my real name or not. I think fast and give him the name on the business card I stole from Mister Snips.

"Chris Lee," I say. At least I'm smart enough to not hand him the business card. A guy like me isn't going to have a business card.

"Tell me why you're here, Chris."

I explain about my pretend business flipping sports cards, and how I haven't paid any taxes for the past couple of years.

"So, yeah," I say, "I kind of dropped the ball on that. And now I'm stressed."

Nathan shakes his head. "Here's the deal, Chris. Sometimes our problems are bigger than we are. Nobody is perfect. Everybody fucks up. What's important is how we respond. It's not where we start out. It's who we become."

I wonder if he pitches everyone in the exact same way. Or did he read me right away—*He's a fuckup*—and pick this custom approach? All I know for sure is that Nathan Shaw is a *salesman*. He was selling at the party, turning the full force of his personality on every single person. He's selling now.

"What I can offer you, Chris, is my full attention. My *partnership*. I'm in this with you. The Internal Revenue Service is an army. It's ruthless and tenacious and . . ."

And so on. For sure this part of the pitch is one size fits all. Nathan still brings it, though. He *believes* it. I even catch myself—a couple of times, seriously—worrying that I might have actually screwed up my own taxes, not just my pretend ones.

Nathan is a *good* salesman. My heart sinks. Even if a caseworker ever did follow up on my report, I bet Nathan would handle them with ease. The caseworker wouldn't stand a chance. It makes me wonder about what went down at that parent-teacher conference. Why did Cameron Keller have such a negative reaction to Nathan? My guess: Nathan didn't bother trying to win him over. Either Cameron wasn't worth his time or Nathan already knew he'd be pulling the kids from school.

What else makes my heart sink: Nathan using this talent of his to torment Pearl and Jack. I can see it. Nathan pretending he's sorry for what he's done, convincing them that this time he'll change, getting them—even though they know better—to lower their guard. He does it just for fun, just because he can.

He keeps talking. Pay attention, pay attention, pay attention. What else? I steal a look at his hands. Just normal hands. Normal hands that grab Jack by his spindly arm and . . . I hear that faint buzz of anger get a little closer. I feel the tingle get a little stronger.

"So now it's your turn, Chris," Nathan says. "Any questions you might have for me?"

Ha, as Eleanor's grandma would say. I have a lot of questions, none of which I can ask. Awkward silence won't work on this dude, not like it did on

Pearl's teacher. What can I do to bump Nathan Shaw off his script? I want to get a peek at him, if possible, when the camera stops rolling.

"How did you fuck up?" I say.

He keeps smiling. But now I see, or think I see, a very slight crease between his eyebrows. "Pardon me?" he says.

"You said everyone fucks up. That was inspiring. So have you fucked up?"

Nathan moves a hand from his leg to the arm of the sofa. He makes a fist with the hand, then just as quickly relaxes it again.

"Absolutely, Chris," he says. "Sure. I've made mistakes in my life. But I'll tell you the smartest thing I ever did. I did what you're doing right now. I recognized a problem and I took the steps to fix it."

He's back to selling again. But I see that crease between his eyebrows again and I have a feeling that he's actually just told me something true about himself, whether he meant to or not.

What is it, though? What do I do with it? I don't know, unfortunately.

"But Chris," he says. The big-finish smile returns. "I want to know more about your business. I used to collect baseball cards when I was a kid. Tell me more."

"Okay. So, on certain days the new sets go on sale. Baseball cards, different sports. I get there early, before the distributor shows up. Walmart and Target. I buy what's hot, then sell them on eBay for a profit."

"Smart. The early bird and the worm. What were the hot sets last year? Where did you really score?"

I shrug to indicate it's a loaded and complicated question, with nuances a layman can't grasp, and what precisely are we even talking about when we talk about "hot"?

"That's hard to answer," I say. It's hard to answer because I have no idea which cards or sets were hot last year. I realize my cover story is maybe less watertight than I thought.

"Just an example," he says. "I'm curious. Who are the sleepers? The guys nobody knows about who are going to be big?"

I haven't followed sports of any kind since I was eleven years old. I didn't really follow them very much then. I only know a couple of the most obvious players. LeBron James. Tom Brady. There's a Japanese baseball player who pitches *and* hits, I think? What's his name?

Nathan Shaw waits patiently.

"I probably shouldn't," I say. "I don't want to, you know, lead you accidentally astray."

"I appreciate that. But at least tell me where I can get more information about buying cards. Where do you go online to find out about all the new releases?"

Fuck. *Fuck.* I'm in deep shit. I'm a terrible liar. So what do I do? I can't just tell the truth. Or . . . maybe I can.

"Look," I say, "I'm an idiot. I don't know what I'm doing. My friend Nguyen is into sports cards, not me. He texts me a list every week. I go and buy what's on the list. I know LeBron James and Tom Brady. That's the extent of my knowledge. You could ask me two hours later what was on the list Nguyen texts me and I wouldn't know. My other friend Mallory helps me with eBay. You can probably tell by talking to me. I'm an idiot."

Nathan Shaw laughs. It worked. We're cool. The me of old, I realize, the un-upgraded version, would have botched this epically. But I'm such a different person now. This is the first time in my life, I realize, that I'm a different person.

"Honesty," Nathan Shaw says. "I like it. Always the best policy. Now let's talk about my fees, if you decide to come aboard."

"Right on," I say. "Right on."

23

The next day I wait, in Salvador's SUV, down the block from the cul-de-sac. It's ten minutes before Tracy should be leaving for the playground. I'm early, but not so early that I'll sit here for hours and arouse suspicion.

From the playground, I'm expecting that Tracy will head to the Wednesday NA meeting. Eleanor is already there, outside the former Blockbuster. She'll approach Tracy either before the meeting or after. Eleanor will make a judgment call on that. She'll explain to Tracy that I want to help her and the kids. If Tracy agrees to meet me right then, I'll be waiting at a coffee shop not too far away. If she needs time to think about it, Eleanor will give her my contact info.

Is this a solid plan? I hope so. It's the most detailed plan I've ever designed, the most careful. I'm following Tracy so if there are any unexpected developments I can update Eleanor. I've got Salvador standing by in my car, halfway between Meadow Wood Estates and the NA meeting, out of the way but available in case I need him. I can't think of every possibility, but I'm trying.

Already there's been one unexpected development. When I drove past the cul-de-sac, I saw *two* cars in the driveway of the Shaw house—the dark blue Volvo and the pearl-colored sports car. Nathan must be home today. I don't know how or if that will change Tracy's routine.

I remember the first time I staked out the Shaw house, how totally inept I was. It's a miracle the angry dude in the pink golf shirt didn't call the cops on me. I'm somewhat amazed by how far I've come since then, though to be fair I did have a long, long way to come.

I get a text from Salvador. ready!!!

It's the fifth or sixth ready!!! text he's sent already. I text him back yet another thumbs-up emoji. But it's not Salvador I'm worried about—it's actually Eleanor. A woman is much more likely to put Tracy at ease and make her comfortable, but in my experience Eleanor is better at making people *un*comfortable. For example, I asked her this morning what her strategy was going to be.

"My strategy?" she said.

"With Tracy. Breaking the ice with her."

"Fuck off. I know what to do."

Okay! I wonder if I should have asked Mallory to do this instead of Eleanor. Mallory, though, total smoke hound that she is, might have forgotten the time or date or—mid-conversation with Tracy—what she was trying to accomplish. I couldn't ask Felice, obviously. Preston's fiancée, Leah . . . maybe. She's almost *too* nice and sweet, though. She'd make it too easy for Tracy to blow her off.

Anyway, here we are. And here comes the Volvo, turning out of the cul-de-sac, Tracy behind the wheel. Unexpected development number two: no Pearl or Jack in the backseat. That's okay. It's probably even better. Tracy is more likely to meet with me now if the kids aren't with her.

I give the Volvo some slack, then pull out and follow it. I call Eleanor.

"She just left," I say. "But I'm not sure where she's going, so stay on your toes, okay?"

"I'm already on my toes. Fuck off."

Traffic is fairly light. I have no trouble tailing the Volvo. I have the hang of it now, timing the stoplights and reading the cars between me and Tracy, knowing which ones to pass and which ones to tuck in behind. I'm confident enough to stay farther back this time. The last thing I want to do is make Tracy nervous or paranoid right now.

We're headed toward the NA meeting, that general direction, but then Tracy hangs a left. Where is she going? At the next big intersection, half a mile up, she hangs a right. That's where she's going: the mall. I slow down and watch the Volvo enter the parking structure next to Dillard's and the AMC.

"She's at Prairie Square," I tell Eleanor. "Get here as fast as you can."

This isn't a terrible development. Approaching Tracy in a mall is less weird than approaching her outside her NA meeting. It's definitely not *more* weird.

Salvador texts again. ready and waiting!!!

I'm about to ignore it when I consider how huge Prairie Square Mall is. Eleanor will need to *find* Tracy first, before she can approach her.

I call Salvador. "Go to Prairie Square. Right now. Don't ask questions. Let me know when you're inside."

"On it!" Salvador says.

I turn into the parking structure. The only available spots are on the roof. I end up only three cars away from Tracy's midnight-blue Volvo. No sign of her. I take the elevator down and cross over into the mall.

I don't know where to start, so I take a lap around the ground floor, peeking into store windows. Eleanor calls as I'm riding the escalator up to the food court. I have an aerial view of a toddler splayed out by the dancing fountain, throwing a tantrum, losing his mind. Dude, I feel you. I'm not a huge fan of malls. The din, the artificial glare, the pungent whiff from every kiosk.

"This place is hellish," Eleanor says.

"You remember what Tracy looks like, right?"

"More or less."

"I'm going to scope the second level," I say. "I did the ground floor already, but really fast and not Dillard's or Macy's."

Tracy isn't in the food court. I skip Yankee Candle, pop into Aeropostale and Buckle. There's a lot of ground to cover and I have to be selective, only hitting places where I guess she might actually shop. AMC? It's possible she skipped her NA meeting for a matinee, but I can't just go prowling through dark auditoriums.

Salvador calls. "I'm here!"

I tell him to find a woman in her late thirties, sandy blond hair, thin and kind of sharp, pointy. I didn't see much of what Tracy was wearing today. A white top.

"And Salvador, listen, if you find her—listen to me very, very carefully— do not go near her. Just call me. Okay? Do not go anywhere near her."

"Got it!"

"Don't call me or text me until you find her."

"Got it!"

I try Sephora. A thin blonde, white blouse, body type kind of sharp and pointy, has her back to me as she spins a wheel of lipsticks. I edge closer, trying to stay inconspicuous. It's not Tracy. I call Eleanor.

"Anything?"

"You'll be the first to know."

Thirty minutes later—still no trace of Tracy. Has she already come and gone? If she's already come and gone, we're just wasting our time. I decide to see if her car is still here and book it back out to the parking structure. That's when I realize how stupendously stupid I've been. We didn't have to look for Tracy in the mall. Eleanor could have just waited for her at the Volvo, because obviously—*obviously!*—Tracy has to return to her car at some point. I call Eleanor again.

"Parking structure by Dillard's," I tell her. "Top floor. Come to the roof."

"It'll take me a while. I'm over by Macy's."

"It's where she parked."

"What? You're joking. You *saw* where she *parked*?"

"I know, I know, I know."

I jump in the elevator. I'm hoping we're not too late. If Tracy is already gone, I can't just keep watching the house—with Eleanor on call—until she leaves again. I don't want to wait another two days until the next NA meeting. That's two extra endless days Pearl and Jack will have to endure.

"Hold that!"

A woman slips into the elevator. She checks the panel. I've already pressed the button for the top floor, but the woman jabs it anyway. She stares straight ahead at her reflection in the brushed chrome of the doors.

It's Tracy. I stay calm. Wow. Wow, wow, wow. Stay calm. Her shoulder is inches from mine. The elevator slowly rises. I have minor claustrophobia and have never loved elevators. This one is my least favorite kind, shaky and clanky and groaning, like it's about to clutch its chest and crash to the ground floor any second now.

What should I do? Should I go for it and talk to Tracy myself? Eleanor won't get here in time. She's not even close. When the elevator doors slide back open, Tracy will walk directly to the Volvo and be gone in less than a minute.

Third floor. Fourth floor. I keep my eyes straight ahead too. I'm afraid to even glance at Tracy's reflection. Fifth floor. One more to go. I have to decide what I'm going to do now. She sighs.

"I don't love elevators," I say.

She glances over in my general direction with a faint smile. A ding and the doors slide open. She steps out. I step out behind her. It's too creepy if I follow her all the way across the roof to the Volvo. I have to make my move, now or never.

"Excuse me," I say.

She stops and turns, impatient but also nervous, quick-scanning the area for bystanders in case I'm about to rob her.

"Do you remember me?" I say.

"Do I what?"

"You probably don't." I'm already screwing this up. I shouldn't lead with the first time we saw each other. Or should I? Eleanor was going to do this part. I'm not prepared at all.

"Who are you?" she says. "What do you want?"

"At the municipal administration building, a couple of weeks ago? Outside Driver Verification. I had long hair then?"

The light goes on. She remembers me now. She turns and starts walking toward the Volvo. "Sorry," she says over her shoulder. "You're confused. I've never seen you before."

I follow at a respectful distance. "I want to help you," I say. "I want to try to help your kids. I saw what's happening to them. The burns."

"I don't know what you're talking about."

"Just give me like two seconds to explain."

"Leave me alone, please."

"I went to Child Protective Services, but they just—"

She whips around, dropping the act. "You *what*?"

"Can we just sit down somewhere and talk? My name is Hardly, by the way."

"You called CPS?" The triangle of skin at the base of her throat has turned bright red. I'm not sure if she's furious or terrified or some mix of both. "When did you call?"

"Can we just sit down somewhere and talk for a minute?"

"My children are fine. My children are not abused and they're not in danger. You're confused or mistaken or . . . I don't know. Leave me alone."

She hurries the last few yards to the Volvo, beeps the locks, yanks the door open. My only very slim chance right now is some rousing and dramatic speech. Unfortunately I've never made a rousing and dramatic speech in my life.

"I saw you and your kids at the playground the other day," I say.

She's about to duck into the Volvo, but that freezes her. She's definitely more furious now than terrified. "You *what*?"

"I could see that you love your kids. It's obvious. And I talked to Pearl's teacher from last year. Mr. Keller? He said the same thing. I just want to help you and your kids. I just want to try. I'm on your side. I promise. You deserve someone on your side."

She doesn't do or say anything. I wait. I think about the angry dude in the pink golf shirt and wonder why Tracy hasn't threatened to call the police on me. And then it makes sense: of course she doesn't want the police involved.

"Who are you?" she says.

"Can I borrow a pen?"

She blinks. "What?"

"Do you have a pen?"

Without taking her eyes off me, she reaches in her purse, finds a pen, and tosses it my way. I pick it up, then find the receipt from the taco place in my wallet. I don't know why the receipt is still there, or why I kept it in the first place. I write my name and phone number on the back.

I'm on one side of the Volvo, she's on the other. I'm pretty sure she won't take the receipt if I try offering it over the roof of the car. She's left the passenger window cracked an inch, though, because of the heat. I slip the receipt through. It flutters to the seat.

"That's how you can get me," I say. "I just want to sit down and talk to you sometime. Think about it, okay?"

"Leave me alone," she says. "My children are fine and happy and safe. I don't need your help."

She ducks into the car and slams the door behind her.

24

An hour or so later, after I've filled Eleanor in about my conversation with Tracy and I'm driving home, my phone buzzes. It's . . . Salvador. *Shit.* I forgot all about him.

"I found her!" Salvador says.

"You're still at the mall?"

"Yes!"

"Great job. But you didn't find her. Go home. I'll swap cars with you later."

"Okay!"

Burke is sitting on the couch, two laptops and a tablet arrayed on the coffee table in front of him. When I come in, he shuts the lid of one laptop and flips over the tablet. Then he thinks about it and shuts the lid of the other laptop too.

"That's kind of suspicious, Burke," I say.

"Curiosity killed the cat," he says.

"But didn't—something brought it back, right?"

"I doubt that very much."

"I was just kidding, Burke. I'm not curious. I promise. Sorry to bother you."

I start down the hallway to my room.

"Halt." Burke eyes me. "You've changed. I can't put my finger on it."

"I cut my hair."

He slow blinks and does not deign to respond. Obviously I cut my hair. Obviously that's not what he's talking about. "I'll get to the bottom of it eventually," he says.

In my room, I plug in my phone to charge the battery. I'll need to keep it topped off at all times for when Tracy calls. When or if? I'm cautiously optimistic she'll call. Our conversation on the roof of the mall parking structure didn't go perfectly, and Tracy wasn't exactly receptive, but she *listened,* at least.

I'm somewhat amazed by everything I've accomplished so far. How did I get from that first day at the municipal building, scrambling around in search of a security guard, to this and here and now? I think I might be feeling myself a little bit. I've actually been fairly *competent.* I've become fairly competent at something that's challenging and tricky.

It's like climbing a tree. I remember that feeling, from a long time ago. There was a gigantic tree in the front yard of the house where my mom and I lived. Every day or so I'd climb that tree and every day I'd go just a little bit higher. One day I climbed too high. But the view was amazing! *I* was amazing for climbing so high! The branch beneath me, too skinny and bendy, started to give. I started to fall. I barely managed to scramble to a sturdier branch.

When I made it back down, I must have looked like I'd just had a heart attack. Before I could say anything, though, before I could say *I almost fell!,* there was my mom, like she always was.

"But you didn't!" she said.

My foster parents were definitely not bad people. You could probably say that Preston and I won the lottery of foster parents, or at least hit a decent scratch-off. Our foster parents were just busy. They had four normal kids plus the two of us. My foster father stacked frozen meat for a living. When his back gave out . . . he continued to stack frozen meat for a living. My foster mother cooked and cleaned, did laundry and worked a rotation of part-time jobs and never once, to the best of my recollection, sat down. It was our suspicion, Preston's and mine, that our foster parents themselves had been in foster care, or one of them had, once upon a time. They knew life could be a lot worse than it was.

My foster mother was just being realistic when she told me to move my lips and not sing at church. My foster father was just being realistic when he told me one time, out of the blue, "Don't ask for anything and you won't be disappointed." We had, the two of us, maybe four conversations in nine years. Short conversations. I don't know where it came from—*Don't ask for anything and you won't be disappointed.* My mom would have flipped out, but he was just giving me his best advice.

Will Tracy call? When? I can't just sit around all night, staring at my phone. I'll go crazy. I smoke a bowl, then head off to Haunted Frontier.

"Howdy, pardners. Ready for a terrifying trip back to the Wild West?"

"Howdy, pardners!" Salvador yells in my ear.

The shift, as shifts go, isn't terrible. My boots are too tight, but there's an occasional breeze and only a smattering of assholes. For some reason, though, I get more worn down and more quickly than usual. I'm cranky, my skin tight like the boots, squeezing and chafing.

First group after the fireworks, two smirky hipsters are live-tweeting. They annoy everyone by loudly reading their tweets out to each other. This after I've politely asked them like ten times to please, if they don't mind, keep their voices down. They've just ignored me. Big surprise.

The Hanged Prisoner thrashes and gags. Justin is really working it tonight and one of the too-large boots he's wearing—the size I should have—slips off. I see that he's wearing novelty socks.

"Apparently," the male hipster tweets out loud, "*Squid Game* was popular among cattle rustlers in the nineteenth century."

"Hey," I say. "*Please.* Please keep your voices down."

That finally gets the attention of the hipsters. I exist! All they do, though, is roll their eyes at each other. Like, *Who does this loser, who works at a place like this, think he is?*

"Sheriff is fixin' to lay down the law," the female hipster tweets. "Hashtag 'frontier justice.'"

It's nothing. If I had a dollar for every eye rolled at me when I tried to enforce a rule, every dismissive remark, I could probably buy Beautiful America. It's no big deal. *Give every guest your best yes!* But tonight . . . tonight my skin is getting tighter and tighter. And then another guest, a lady digging around in her backpack, tries to hand me what looks like a giant wad of used Kleenex.

"Hold this for a sec," she says.

Seriously? She waits. I do not accept the giant wad of damp used tissue.

She blinks, flummoxed. Salvador clears his throat and points, discreetly he thinks, at the Hanged Prisoner. Justin is just sort of twitching around in his harness, wondering what's up. We should have moved on past by now.

The lady blinks again. I take her stupid wad of Kleenex and drag myself back into character.

"Well, doggone," I say. "We better mosey. Let's take that shortcut through the cemetery."

I survive the rest of my shift and text Felice. She tells me I can stop by. When she opens the door to her apartment, I kiss her before she can say anything. Inside, I take her pajama top off in practically one fell swoop, like a magician whipping a tablecloth out from under the dishes.

She smiles. "What got into you?"

I don't have an answer for that, so I just kiss her again and we fall into bed.

25

The next three days inch past so . . . so . . . slowly. I'm climbing the walls, waiting for Tracy to call, deciding she absolutely will, then changing my mind and deciding there's no chance. What must three days be like for Pearl and Jack? Three days is forever. I try not to imagine all the terrible things that might happen to them in three days.

Here's what I imagine instead: it's three months from now. I've found the evidence I need to find. I've convinced Tracy to go to CPS. Pearl and Jack are safe now. When Tracy takes them to a park, she doesn't have to make sure she finds a deserted one. Pearl and Jack can play with other kids. They're just like other kids now. The horrific part of their life is over, fading slowly but surely into the past.

I'd love to be keeping an eye on Tracy. Who knows what I still might find out? I don't want to spook or rush or pressure her, though, so I stay away from her and the house, the playground and the former Blockbuster.

But Nathan is fair game. I do keep an eye on him. A few times a day, different times, I park in the strip mall lot across the street and watch his office. I've seen a few of his clients enter and exit—normal people, not sketchy. But I know something is up with Nathan. I'm going to get to the bottom of him sooner or later.

What is Tracy thinking? I wish I knew. Is she trying to decide if she should call me or not? Has she already decided not to call? Has she already decided she will, but is waiting for just the right moment?

Sunday I don't have a shift, so I swing by Shaw Law around nine. I'm not expecting to see much on a Sunday night. I don't. Out front, the office park is dark and empty. As I drive past, though, I catch a flash of light in my mirror—headlights, two pairs of them, *behind* Nathan Shaw's building. I circle the block, kill my headlights, and pull into the office park. There are three buildings, the main long one and two short ones, top and bottom, that make a capital *I*. So I'm able to slide in behind one of the short buildings, edge up to the corner, and see what's going on behind Shaw Law.

A pickup truck and Nathan's sports car face each other, their headlights creating a square of light in the middle, like a spotlight on the stage of a theater. In that spotlight stands Nathan Shaw and two of the sketchy dudes from the party. I recognize them right away—the scrawny drunk and the big gray beard.

Jackpot. It might be. Whatever business Nathan has with these sketchy dudes, it's questionable business. Why else would he be meeting with them after hours, in the dark, *behind* his office and not in it?

My windows are rolled down, but I'm too far away to hear what the three of them are saying. From the body language I'm guessing the two sketchy dudes have failed to complete some task and Nathan Shaw isn't having it. He stands still as stone, his arms folded across his chest, while Scrawny Drunk and Big Beard throw their hands around and shake their heads and occasionally point at each other.

After maybe five minutes or so, Nathan shuts off the headlights of his sports car and enters his office through a back door. Big Beard climbs behind the wheel of the pickup truck. Scrawny Drunk gets into the passenger seat. They go rumbling away.

I have to make a quick decision: stay where I am and wait till Nathan Shaw leaves his office, or follow the truck. Easy call. There's a good chance Nathan Shaw will just go home. Big Beard and Scrawny Drunk, though— who knows where they might be headed? If Nathan Shaw is up to some nefarious shit, they might lead me right to it.

The truck turns onto the street. I give it lots of room, pop my headlights back on, fall in behind. Big Beard sticks more or less to the speed limit. That makes my life easier and it's also encouragingly suspicious. Big Beard doesn't look like a dude who worries about the speed limit, not unless he has a good reason why he doesn't want to get pulled over.

We pass a long march of big-box stores, then cross under the interstate.

For a second I think Big Beard and Scrawny Drunk might be on their way to Haunted Frontier, which is only about a mile from here. I'm just being paranoid, though. At the light where they'd need to turn left, they keep going straight.

Seriously, where are they headed? We're in a part of town that's a mixed bag—warehouses and scrapyards that look like the ruins of ancient rusted civilizations, but also brightly lit islands of brand-new development. A health complex, a Mercedes-Benz dealership, a Caribbean-themed restaurant on a man-made pond.

I wonder what Nathan Shaw is involved with. Drugs, most likely. Or money. Or drug money. The specifics don't matter. If I find evidence that he's involved with something illegal, anything illegal, CPS will have to make Pearl and Jack's case a priority. I'm still hoping Tracy will call me, but this is a solid plan B.

My phone lights up. It's a text from Eleanor: grandma doctr nxt week kthxbai

It's too hard to text and tail the truck at the same time, so I call her back. "You remember those sketchy dudes from the party? I'm following two of them right now."

"What? Why?"

"I saw them meeting Nathan Shaw behind his office. *Behind* the office. At night, in the dark, on a Sunday. And now they're out here past Haunted Frontier, where that new hospital is, where all those old scrapyards are. And whatever Tipple and Pickle is."

"Pickle ball is like tennis but you can play when you're drunk."

"How do you know that?"

"Have you eaten yet? I'm not far from there. I had to drop off a package for my grandma at the twenty-four-hour UPS drop box."

The truck turns off the main road, onto a side street that skirts the parking lot of Tipple and Pickle and then winds off between warehouses.

"I have to go," I say, ending the call. I have to be even more careful now since there are no other cars around. I stay as far back from the truck as possible, only speeding up when the taillights disappear around a curve. It's lucky I have experience tailing cars now. If this was my first time, I'd be screwed.

The truck cuts between two warehouses. By the time I pull close, it's already kicking out the other end of the alley. I'm going to lose them. I gun it, bumping like crazy over the rough pavement, trying not to swerve and clip a loading dock. Halfway down the alley the steering wheel jerks itself out of my hands. I hear a very unsettling grinding noise from my front left tire.

I ease off the gas and grind to a stop. *Shit!* This is bad luck at a bad time. That truck was the best lead I'd had so far. I get out of my car and take a look at my tire. Shredded. I ran over a chunk of metal debris, nails bristling from a metal tube. It's still tangled in the shreds of tire rubber. Why was a bristling chunk of metal debris lying in the middle of an alley? Supremely bad luck.

I don't have a spare. This tire, front left, is my spare. It's too late anyway. Big Beard and Scrawny Drunk are already long gone.

I call Eleanor. "You said you're close by? I've got a flat and I don't have a spare."

"I'm shocked. Where are you?"

"Some alley between two warehouses, a few blocks from that Pickle place."

"And then can we eat?"

"Do you hear that?" I say. "Is that happening on your end or mine?"

I move the phone away from my ear. A hissing sound draws me around to the other side of the car. I can't believe it. The front right tire is going flat too. I crouch down and find three, four, five different nails stabbed into the tread.

"What's wrong with this stupid alley?" I say. "My other front tire is blown too."

"That doesn't make sense," Eleanor says.

"Right?"

"No. I mean it doesn't make sense."

I just agreed, didn't I? Before I can wonder what she's talking about, headlights splash the alley and the red truck turns back in. It stops about fifteen feet away from me and the headlights go off. When my eyes readjust to the darkness, I can see Big Beard behind the wheel of the truck, smiling and waggling his fingers at me. It looks like he might be saying, *Coochie coochie coo, coochie coochie coo.*

26

I understand now—why the alley was full of nails and spiked debris, why both my tires are flat. *Shit.*

"Give me your phone, please."

I turn. It's Nathan Shaw, standing behind me. I hand my phone to him. Why do I hand my phone to him? It's so dumb of me. Because he asked politely? I should have bolted instead. Big Beard and Scrawny Drunk are still climbing out of the truck—I hear the squeak of springs and shocks—and I'm a lot younger than Nathan Shaw, I can juke around him, no problem.

But now he has my phone. He taps the screen to end the call with Eleanor. I don't want to bolt without my phone. I'll need to call the police if they chase me.

"So it's you," he says. "I thought it might be you. Nice to see you again, Hardly."

I don't know how he knows my real name. "Can I have my phone back, please?" I say.

"In a minute," he says. "Let's talk first."

The truck's doors slam shut behind me. Footsteps scuff the asphalt. Scrawny Drunk or Big Beard, probably Big Beard, makes a sound like he's smacking his lips.

"Okay," I say.

"Who the fuck are you?" Nathan says.

"Who am I?" I'm not exactly sure what he's asking. Maybe he's asking if I'm, like, undercover CPS. "I'm nobody."

Nathan Shaw gives me his big-finish Broadway smile. I feel surprisingly calm. That's how powerful his smile is, because I have zero reason to feel calm right now.

"Correct," he says. "I checked you out. You are, precisely, nobody. You're not a cop or DHS or . . . anything. You don't have any connections. So tell me why you're all up in my fucking business."

How long has he known that I've been tailing him? A while, obviously. He's had time to plan, to set all this up, to construct the homemade spike strips that took out my front tires. Or maybe Big Beard and Scrawny Drunk already possessed homemade spike strips, which is a thought, finally, that makes me feel not so calm.

Big Beard and Scrawny Drunk are standing right behind me, way too close. They smell, or one of them does, like sweat and cold French fries.

"Let me put it another way, Hardly," Nathan says. "Why the fuck is my business your business?"

How does he know my real name? I wonder that again. He must have had someone tailing me while I was tailing him and got my license plate that way. He reaches into his pocket. I must have flinched because I hear Big Beard or Scrawny Drunk snicker.

Nathan takes a piece of paper out of his pocket. He shows it to me. I recognize my handwriting. There's my name. There's my contact information. It's the receipt I gave Tracy at the mall parking garage.

My stomach clenches. I picture Nathan finding my note. Going through Tracy's purse while she's in the shower, maybe. Grabbing her, yanking her out of the shower, furiously demanding to know what the fuck is going on. Cocking back his fist and . . .

I should have been more careful and just told her my number. I should never have left behind actual evidence. I've put her in an extremely bad spot, and maybe the kids too.

"How did you get that?" I say.

"How did I get it?" He glances at the piece of paper and seems genuinely puzzled by my question. "She gave it to me. My wife. When she told me that some dipshit was stalking her."

What? *What?* He's saying that *Tracy* gave him the note. Tracy *gave* him the note. She *told* him about me. But that can't be possible. I'm trying to help Tracy and the kids. Why would she do that? Unless I'm wrong about her. Unless I've been wrong about everything.

"So that explained why some dipshit was stalking me too," Nathan says. "I wondered what the fuck you were up to when you came to my office."

"But . . . I didn't . . ."

"Shut up. What I want to know is why some dipshit is under the assumption that *my* family is *his* business."

He waits. I'm supposed to explain. Scrawny Drunk shoves me hard between the shoulder blades and I almost lose my balance. I try to decide if it's too late to bolt. I don't care about my phone anymore. I can outrun these dudes, can't I? Unless they have a gun. Dudes who know how to make homemade spike strips and set a trap like this probably, realistically, have a gun.

"I saw what you did to your kids," I tell Nathan.

"You don't know anything about my kids," he says. "And you don't need to know anything about them. My family is *my* business."

I turn to Scrawny Drunk and Big Beard. This might be my only chance to get out of this. I pick Scrawny Drunk because . . . I don't know. It's just a guess. He's younger than Big Beard. He might have kids the same age as Pearl and Jack. He might be mean but not evil. I look him right in the eye.

"Have you?" I ask him. "Have you seen what he does to his kids?"

Scrawny Drunk punches me in the face. It happens so fast I'm on the ground before I even know I'm falling. And then my nose explodes, my eyes, my entire skull, a blast of pain. Everything goes black, then everything is way too bright, then Nathan Shaw is crouched next to me, looking down, smiling again.

"I'm going to make it simple for you," he says. "Stay away from me and from my wife and from my kids. Stay away from my house and my office. Hardly?"

I think he wants me to say "What?" or at least nod, but I can't do either. My face hurts so bad it's making me dizzy. I feel like if I move an inch I'll hornk. My chin is wet. Did I already hornk? No. It's blood from my nose.

"Stay away or you'll regret it," Nathan says. "Because this is nothing. The next fifteen minutes are going to be nothing. The next fifteen minutes are just a little chat. Keep that in mind, Hardly."

He stands up. The next fifteen minutes? What did he mean by that? I wonder if there's anyone else around, like a security guard for one of the warehouses. No. Nathan would have thought of that. I could still yell for help, but I don't know if I can handle getting punched in the face again.

"One more thing, Hardly," Nathan says. "I have friends in the police department. I'm a lawyer. I have friends everywhere. So keep that in mind too. Go to the police, go to anyone, and you'll regret it."

And then he's gone. I listen to him walk away. I'm staring at one of my shredded tires and the side of a warehouse, cinder blocks and corrugated metal. Some words are stenciled above the loading dock. It's too dark, the paint is too faded, and I'm too far away to make out what the words say.

I close my eyes. *Wake up,* I tell myself. *Wake up right now.* I open my eyes. Big Beard kicks me in the ribs and I pop like a balloon. I can't breathe. He kicks me again, same spot. Work boot. Steel toe. I have to get up. I have to fight back. I make it up onto one elbow and take a wild swing at Big Beard with my other arm. You couldn't really call it a swing. Scrawny Drunk moves in behind and kicks the bone at the base of my spine. Big Beard stomps on my ankle.

I still can't breathe. *Wake up.* The human body is a fragile package without bubble wrap. Bones, soft organs. Big Beard and Scrawny Drunk kick and kick and stomp. My cheek scrapes against the asphalt. I see the words again, above the loading dock. I have this crazy, crazed thought. If I could just make out those faded words above the loading dock, all this will stop, all this will end.

"You warmed up yet?" Big Beard says.

"Gettin' there," Scrawny Drunk says.

Big Beard grabs me by a handful of T-shirt and drags me to my feet. He props me up against the side of my car and breathes cold French fries into my face. Why haven't I blacked out yet? Pain like this—aren't you supposed to black out? Aren't you supposed to have a calming, out-of-body experience?

"How 'bout you?" he says. "You warmed up yet? 'Cause we ain't even started yet."

Everything goes too bright again. I hope that means I'm about to black out. But Big Beard and Scrawny Drunk are squinting too. Headlights. A car. A car rips down the alley toward us, horn honking. Scrawny Drunk has to jump out of the way as it blows past.

"What the fuck?" he says.

The car slams to a stop. An old beater. I've seen that beater before. I can't breathe or think. I've seen this chick before, who has leaped out of the beater and is yelling at Big Beard and Scrawny Drunk.

"Get the fuck away from him!" she says. Eleanor. A hundred and ten pounds soaking wet. What is she doing? Big Beard's beard is bigger than her.

"No," I say, or try to say.

Big Beard drops the handful of my T-shirt. I slide down the side of my car and end up on my ass, flopped sideways against the warm rubber of a shredded tire and staring again at the indecipherable letters above the loading dock. I hear Scrawny Drunk laugh. I hear Big Beard say, "You want to play, little girl?" And then Scrawny Drunk is screaming. Big Beard is cussing. My eyes start to water and burn.

"Come on," Eleanor says. Suddenly there she is, kneeling next to me. She slaps my cheek gently, then less gently, then not gently at all. "Get it together. We have to go now."

"Okay."

"Can you stand up?"

I don't have high hopes. But with Eleanor under my arm shoving, and the side mirror of my car to grab on to, I manage to haul myself up.

"Crazy fucking bitch!" Big Beard says. He's staggering away from us, clawing at his face. Scrawny Drunk has staggered off in the other direction and is flailing viciously at some invisible opponent.

Pepper spray. The collateral whiff is what's burning my eyes. Eleanor must have hit Big Beard and Scrawny Drunk with direct shots. I don't know how they're still standing. The second I think that, literally the second, Scrawny Drunk drops to his hands and knees.

"Get in the car," Eleanor says. "Focus."

I collapse into the backseat of her car. She's left the engine running.

27

In the car, Eleanor plays her slogging, mournful, emo music. After a couple of verses, she glances into the backseat at me and changes to a song with synthesizers and a bouncy beat, lyrics sung in German. She slows for a red light.

"You're fine," she says.

I want to say something sarcastic because obviously I'm not fine. I can't think of anything, though. It hurts just to breathe. Each breath I take is like getting kicked again in the ribs by a steel-toed boot.

"You're going to be fine," Eleanor clarifies. "I'm taking you to the ER."

"No." Talking, I find out, hurts even worse than breathing. So does trying and failing to sit up. "No ER."

She snorts.

"I'm," I say. "Serious."

"We're going to the ER, you moron. Don't worry about the insurance. They have to treat you. It's the law."

It's not my lack of insurance I'm worried about, though that too. If I go to the ER, the doctor will observe that I've had the shit beaten out of me. I'm not positive, but I'm pretty sure what a doctor is required to do if you show up in the ER with the shit beaten out of you.

"No cops," I say. "I'm serious. Eleanor. No police."

"Why? What are you talking about?"

Nathan might have been bluffing about his connections. But there's a very good chance he wasn't. Do I want to take that risk? Do I want to think about what would have happened to me tonight if Eleanor hadn't shown up? I definitely don't.

"Trust me. Eleanor. No police. No ER. Just take. Me home. I'm fine." I want to add something like *You said so yourself, that I'm fine,* but the talking doesn't hurt any less the more of it I do.

She glances back at me again. "Whatever."

I lie as still as I can in the backseat, braced for the bumps and sharp turns. I feel oddly relaxed—my mind doesn't know what to do with so much pain, arriving from so many different locations in such a rainbow of varieties. Throbbing, thudding, stabbing, searing. Ribs, tailbone, ankle, nose, and hip. It's like a rhyme for children, a chant for skipping rope. Ribs, tailbone, ankle, nose, and hip. Throbbing, thudding, stabbing, searing. I just want to be home. I'm going to crawl into bed and never crawl out.

But what right do I have to complain? This isn't real pain. Pearl and Jack know about real pain. I deserve to feel a lot more pain than this.

The car slows, then stops. I don't know how much time has gone by. I'm already home? I lift my head and see that we're outside an ER entrance.

"Eleanor. Fuck."

"I'm not sharing my grandma's drugs. You're getting your own drugs."

"I can't talk to the police. I'm serious."

"They won't call the police just because you were in some dumb fight outside a bar or whatever. Unless you die, I suppose. So probably don't do that."

She helps me limp inside. After she parks her car, she sits in the plastic chair next to me and fills out my paperwork. I've never been to an ER before, but I've heard the horror stories about long waits. Tonight, though, there are only four of us in the waiting area. Eleanor, me, the intake nurse, and a slumped sallow chick holding a can of Sprite against her forehead.

That's not a bad idea. I wish I had a can of cold Sprite to hold against my throbbing, thudding, searing, stabbing. I'm still feeling relaxed, though. I don't mind the pain. It keeps me from thinking about what happened tonight, what it means, and how catastrophically I screwed up.

The doctor who examines me is brisk, brusque, and seems to buy my story that I was in a car wreck. The story is sort of truthful. He gives me a couple of painkillers and never mentions the cops. When he gets the X-ray back, he tells me I have a cracked rib. I also have a broken nose, what's probably a torn ligament in my ankle, and lots of bad bruises and contusions. No sign of a concussion.

"Could be worse," the doctor says. I realize how right he is.

There's no fix for a cracked rib. Just rest and ice and pain meds. Same for my nose, plus nasal decongestants if I have trouble breathing. It's a simple break, the doctor says, so no realignment is necessary. He wraps my ankle with an elastic compression bandage. I'll need to treat the ankle with . . . guess what? Rest, ice, pain meds.

In the car, Eleanor checks the prescription the doctor wrote for me. She nods with approval. "Sweet."

I try to look over the rest of the paperwork they gave me when I checked out, but the painkillers have kicked in and I let myself drift. We're on the street with all the big-box stores. The lights smear past. I feel better. I feel pretty good. I'm nine years old again. Recess ends, school resumes. That afternoon I come home, cutting across the yard of our house, pushing open the door. Look! My mom is waiting there! She's okay! She hugs me. We go about our day.

Eleanor gets out of the car. When did she stop the car? I don't remember that. She goes into the Walgreens and comes out with a white paper bag. She drops it in my lap.

"Don't operate a motor vehicle," she says.

"My motor vehicle doesn't have front tires anymore. It has no front tires. There is a lack of front tires necessary for operation."

In the bag is my bottle of pain meds and a can of something called Vamousse. It's for the removal of head lice.

"What?" I say. "Why did you get this?"

"Because it's funny."

It is funny, but I can't laugh because of my rib. Next thing I know we're at my place and Eleanor is helping me limp through the living room. Jutta sticks her head around the corner, peering in from the kitchen, followed by Burke sticking his head around the corner and peering in from the kitchen.

"What have we here?" Burke says.

"I'm fine," I say. "Right as rain."

Eleanor dumps me in my bed. "Ice in the morning. Will you remember that?"

"I will never, ever be able to repay this debt," I say. "Ever, ever."

"I agree."

28

I wake up with sunlight from the garage windows hot on my cheek. My other cheek is cool and wet and tickles. It's Jutta on that side of the bed, nuzzling my face, making sure I'm still breathing.

"I'm not dead," I tell her. She wags her tail, mission accomplished.

My nose aches. It's fine if I breathe through my mouth. My cracked rib aches. Not too bad. Not too bad until I take a deeper breath through my mouth, just testing, and the pain basically impales me from butthole to scalp. No more deep breaths. Lesson learned.

I sit up, very slowly, and reach, also very slowly, for my phone on the nightstand. I have no idea what time it is. Nine forty-nine a.m. There's a big glass of water on the nightstand, next to the bottle of pain meds. I swallow a couple of the pain meds and drink half the water. I pick up the phone again. Definitely mine—a cracked iPhone screen is as unique and individual as a fingerprint or a snowflake. But where did it come from? The last time I saw my phone, Nathan Shaw was holding it.

I drink the rest of the water. I'm feeling better than I did last night. I'm also feeling much, much worse. Because now that my mind's not fogged by pain, now that I have time to go beat by beat through what happened, I can't ignore how badly, how monumentally, everything is fucked. I take a deep breath. *Shit.* A jagged shard of rib pierces my soul.

When I recover from that, I call Eleanor. "Why do I still have my phone?"

"It was just lying there on the ground. So I grabbed it."

While she was pepper-spraying two dudes and dragging me to her car and probably listening to a podcast at the same time. I'm never going to underestimate Eleanor again. "Thanks," I say.

"Are you all right?"

"Hungry."

"I'll come get you. Give me like ten minutes."

I hobble into the kitchen, Jutta following close behind, and drink another glass of water. I don't know if I'm down for the twisting and flexing required to pop ice cubes out of the tray, so instead I just tuck a Trader Joe's frozen orange chicken bowl between my arm and my cracked ribs. I hold the separate frozen packet of sauce against my nose. Jutta observes me with interest and no judgment.

"I'd like to see the other guy," Burke says. He's standing in the doorway, holding two dumbbells and smiling.

"Ha ha," I say.

"Did you give as good as you got? Tell me everything."

It squicks me out, how titillated Burke seems, how delighted to hear a tale of violence. Until now, a full year, he's shown exactly zero interest in the details of my life. I'm not about to tell him anything.

"I've got to bounce, Burke. I'll catch you later."

"I might be able to provide some useful counsel, young Jedi."

"I'll catch you later."

I give Jutta one last pat on the head and hobble outside. I can't put much weight on my ankle. I try not to think about what Big Beard and Scrawny Drunk would have done to me if Eleanor hadn't shown up. My heart, I realize, is pounding. Sweat beads on my forehead. Which part of all this wrecks me the most? That the beating I took could have been, *should* have been, even worse? Or that I tipped off Nathan at his office? Or that I drove right into an ambush? Or that my big idea to trust Tracy completely backfired?

No, what wrecks me most, the thought I can't bear: what if I, just being me, have made things even worse for Pearl and Jack?

Eleanor rolls up. I jockey myself painfully and clumsily into her car. She frowns and points to my nose. "What's that?"

"Orange sauce." By now it's turned from ice to slush to lukewarm goo. I toss the packet onto the floor, on top of all the wrappers and lipstick tissues and other tossed-away crap. "Never mind."

"Have you seen yourself?" She's still inspecting me as we pull away from the curb. "For God's sake."

I made a point to avoid eye contact with myself while brushing my teeth, but now I go ahead and flip down the visor mirror. Let's get this over with. Wow. Both of my eyes are bluish-black, mottled, bloodshot. My nose is swollen and monstrous. One side of my face looks like a skinned knee.

Even more horrifying is a bill from the ER that I must have left behind in Eleanor's car last night.

"Nineteen hundred dollars?" I say. For one X-ray, an elastic compression bandage, a couple of painkillers, maybe fifteen minutes tops with the doctor? "I thought you said it was the law. That they had to treat me even though I couldn't pay."

"I said it's the law they have to treat you if you don't have insurance. They're still going to bill you. But don't worry about it. You can negotiate it down with the ombudsman."

"The who? Down to what? Fifteen hundred dollars?" Fifteen hundred dollars is basically the same to me as nineteen hundred dollars, which is basically the same to me as a million dollars.

"Is that your biggest concern right now? A bill from the ER?"

She has a point. I shut up. We go to the cheap taco place again. After we get our food, I start telling Eleanor all the details that she doesn't already know. I explain that Nathan knows my real name because Tracy told him about the mall and gave him my info.

"I told you it was too risky to trust that bitch," Eleanor says.

I pick at my taco. I still can't get my head around it, why Tracy would sell me out to Nathan. I know she loves her kids. I know she's not hurting them. I also know she was probably aware of what Nathan would do to me.

"You told me," I said.

Eleanor doesn't rub it in. She wants to, I can tell, but instead she goes up to the counter and brings back churros.

"Not your fault," she says. "You had to try."

"Nobody put a gun to my head."

"Listen. Why can't you go to the police? Tell them what this Nathan fucker did to you. Tell Child Services what he did."

"He warned me not to, before you showed up. He said if I go to the cops, he'll . . . whatever. I don't want to find out, not after last night. That was just him *warning* me. And it's just my word against his anyway. He's a lawyer. He knows people. Who am I? I'm some loser nobody who's been stalking him and his family."

Eleanor frowns. She doesn't disagree with my reasoning. "And since he knows your real name," she says, "he can find out where you live, all that."

"I'm sure he already knows where I live."

"So what's next then?"

"What's next?"

I fish a chunk of ice out of my drink, wrap it in a paper napkin, hold it against my nose. I realize I haven't even let myself ask that question yet.

The pain in my rib and nose and elsewhere ebbs away. But that's just so the anger can come flooding in. I'm so mad at myself. Not just because I fucked up in such spectacularly stupid fashion—tipping off Nathan and walking into an ambush and trusting Tracy, etc., etc.—but because I so stupidly *believed*. I believed I could do this. I believed I could help Pearl and Jack.

I'm the kid in the back row, moving his lips and just pretending to sing. I'm the dude with a fake badge and a toy gun. The dumbest thing you can do, if you're someone like me, is believe you can be more than you are.

Don't ask for anything and you won't be disappointed. I should have listened to my foster father. I never should have stopped listening.

Honestly, I'm relieved. Now that I've done everything I can for Pearl and Jack, I can ease back into the gentle current of my old life. My old life was fine! I didn't have to worry about getting murdered. I didn't have to worry about anything important at all.

"You're finished with all this now?" Eleanor says.

"Obviously," I say.

29

I get home and sleep. I sleep some more. The next day, Tuesday, I feel good enough to scan Craigslist. I find a guy who's selling a pair of used tires for seventy-five bucks. Preston doesn't answer my texts, so I call Salvador and have him drive me over to Preston's office. Salvador keeps staring wide-eyed with amazement at my bashed face. He's already taken the bare, sad facts of my beating and shaped them into a daring escapade in which I, somehow, am the hero.

"It was just like in a movie!" he says.

"It wasn't."

"Three against one. You had to fight for your life!"

A guy at Preston's office points me to a cubicle. Preston isn't there, but I hear him a few cubicles down, lecturing some poor trapped victim about project phasing and zoning-code development. He scowls when he sees me. Preston has a long menu of different scowls for when he sees me. Today I get his "Surprised, Exasperated, and Wary" scowl, followed by "Annoyed but Curious Despite Himself."

"What are you doing here?" he says. "What happened to your face?"

"I'm fine, thanks. Can you Venmo me seventy-five dollars, please? I'll pay you back."

"Are you all right?"

"I'm fine. Just a fender bender. I need new tires."

"What fender bender involves the tires? And what happened to your hair? It actually looks good."

Preston approves of my hair? Awesome. This is what I think they call adding insult to injury. "Will you Venmo me the money? As soon as possible."

"Yes." Preston sighs, then turns to the chick he's lecturing. "My brother. His typical Tuesday."

Next Salvador takes me to the guy who's selling the tires. The tread on the tires is mostly nonexistent and one of the rims has what looks like a bullet hole punched in it. What do I expect for seventy-five bucks? Exactly. I sit on a tire and bounce a little. Salvador sits and bounces on the other one. Neither tire bursts. Sold.

The guy helps Salvador load the tires into the back of Salvador's SUV. I'm not any help because of my rib, my ankle, and a swollen elbow I didn't even notice until now.

I direct Salvador past the medical complex, past Tipple and Pickle, past scrapyards and warehouses. As we get closer to the alley where I was jumped, I feel my chest start to tighten, my scalp start to tingle. I know that Big Beard and Scrawny Drunk are long gone. They won't be coming back here. But keeping that in mind isn't so easy when I can still see them standing over me, can still feel the boot cracking my rib, I can suddenly smell again—no joke—cold French fries.

The alley is empty. I relax. In bright daylight, middle of the afternoon, the alley is grubby but not menacing. Other than my car—slumped forward on the blown front tires, looking like a drunk passed out with his head on the bar—there's no sign of what happened last night. I can finally read the faded letters stenciled above the loading dock. It's just part of a sentence, a couple of words: *DO NOT.*

Good advice. I wish I'd seen that warning last night before I turned down the alley. I wish I'd seen it three weeks ago. I wish I hadn't fooled myself into thinking I could be anything but what I am. That's what hurts the most: getting your hopes up, getting them crushed. My foster father was dead-on. Don't ask for anything and you won't be disappointed.

Salvador parks next to my car. He gets the jack and tire tool from my trunk and we go to work, me telling him what to do and him trying to pop off the wheel cover with the wrong end of the tire tool, dropping the nuts, getting his finger trapped in the jack. Eventually, a true Christmas miracle, we get my new old tires on. I tell Salvador he's a beast. He beams and asks if we should meet up at HQ before our shift tomorrow.

"We don't have an HQ, Salvador. We have some index cards on the loading platform of an abandoned dark ride."

"We need to figure out our next move, don't we?"

"There's not a next move."

"What do you mean?"

"I mean we're done. I'm done."

He's stricken. "You're quitting? But why?"

"Look at me, Salvador."

By that I mean look at my bashed face, at the way I'm limping around and how my cracked rib hurts so bad I can't even pick up a tire jack. But I realize I could also mean it in a more general, more powerful sense. *Look at me.* Am I somebody, based on past performance and future potential, who should do anything but quit?

"Thanks for your help," I say. "I'll see you at work tomorrow."

My new old tires get me home. I smoke a bowl and take another couple of pain pills. Quick nap. When I wake up it's already the next morning. What! But that's fine with me, one hundred percent. The quicker I leave behind this whole episode of my life—the quicker it becomes just a vague flicker of a moment and not even an actual episode—the happier I'll be.

I take a shower so long and hot it starts to feel like the meat is coming off my bones. My rib feels a little better. The swelling in my nose and my elbow has gone down some. I dry off and examine the horror show of my face in the mirror. I don't care for bodily harm, I decide. It's definitely not my jam.

I smoke a bowl and replay some *Far Cry* outposts. A couple of hours glide past before I even know it. Nice. Around noon I venture out for some food. In the drive-through lane at Chick-fil-A, waiting for my strips, a car in the other lane pulls up next to me. In the backseat are two kids, a girl and a boy around the same age as Pearl and Jack. Of course these kids *aren't* Jack and Pearl. Other than their age, they're nothing like Jack and Pearl. The little girl is doing some elaborate TikTok dance in her seat. The little boy is leaning forward to show his mom in the front seat a superhero action figure. He's probably relating the origin story or detailing the powers.

I eat my strips on the way over to Nguyen and Mallory's place. Those kids at Chick-fil-A—it's not a big deal. Eventually I'll get it together. Eventually I won't think about Pearl and Jack every time I see kids their age, my stomach won't lurch. Right?

Nguyen and Mallory are watching reruns of *The Office* and doing bong rips. Is it possible they haven't moved from this spot since I last saw them? It might be. They're both so stoned and so into Pretzel Day at Dunder Mifflin that they don't notice my haircut or my bashed face. Or maybe they do notice but it doesn't, here in a universe without free will, merit a comment.

"Are you hungry?" Nguyen asks me. "We ordered a feast."

"I'm good."

Mallory hands me the bong. "What if, okay, bear with me," she says, "dreams are like the connective tissue between all the minds in existence. Think of the weird shit when you dream. You're like, where did that come from? What if it comes from, part of what you dream, from someone else who's dreaming. And vice versa?"

"Wait. What?" Nguyen's eyes swim briefly out of focus. "That's creepy af."

I take a bong rip. This moment is so familiar to me that it could practically be all moments—it's like the last long stretch of my life has been this and only this, chilling with Nguyen and Mallory as my lungs fill with smoke and the world softens around me. For a second that's a nice thought, very Zen, but then I start to feel the weight of all that smoke and all that softness, folds and folds and folds of it on top of me, suffocating.

The doorbell rings. Nguyen gets up. He collects a big grease-stained paper bag of what smells like greasy gyros. I catch a glimpse of the delivery dude in the doorway before he turns away. I'm not sure if he's the delivery dude I saw at the strip mall or not. Close enough not to matter.

"You sure you're not hungry?" Mallory says. "There is ample abundance."

"I have to bounce," I say.

"See you tomorrow," Nguyen says, and Mallory nods, like the future could contain no other possibility.

30

Five o'clock. I wake up from my nap and pop two more pain pills. I suspect these pain pills aren't as good as the ones Eleanor borrows from her grandma. I put ice on my rib and ice on my ankle, then hobble out to the car. I'm not in great shape to work tonight, but maybe a shift at Haunted Frontier will take my mind off my various pains.

Duttweiler sees that I can barely walk and assigns me a stationary role on Boot Hill. I don't need much makeup since I already look so ghoulish. Salvador gets Boot Hill too. He follows me up, not saying a word, shuffling along morosely.

I'm not feeling it either, honestly. I can't shake this heavy mood I'm in. I feel like I'm dragging around a corpse I need to get rid of, but the corpse is actually me and good luck getting rid of that.

"Should be a chill night," I say.

Salvador flops down, his back against a tilting tombstone. *Here lies Dutch. Quick on the trigger, slow on the draw.* He doesn't say anything and I realize he's giving me the silent treatment. Which, I could point out to him but don't, isn't the worst punishment in the world.

After a while, down below, the Main Street ghouls begin to swarm. That's our cue to climb into our open graves, switch on the fog machines, crouch down, and wait. A few minutes later here comes the first group of guests, crunching up the path from town. I hear the clank of Justin's spurs. He's the Dead Sheriff tonight.

"Don't make a peep," Justin says. "You don't want to stir up the spirits around here."

That's our cue to rise up from the graves, hissing and wailing and whatnot.

Boot Hill is dark, each grave equipped with its own personal fog machine. Still, though, it's a fairly weak jump scare. A couple of chicks scream politely. I'm trying not to cough because of the fog.

Justin leads the group back down the hill. We switch off the fog machines. I stay in my grave. It's not deep, the grave, just three feet or so, but what's the point of climbing out if I just have to climb right back in?

I tell myself there's a version of Pearl and Jack's story that's not too terrible. They get past all this. They grow up, leave home, escape Nathan and Tracy. They'll be damaged, but they'll see shrinks, they'll get busy with life. They'll go places and meet people. They'll fall in love. They'll get dumped. They'll fall in love again. They'll like their jobs or hate their jobs. They'll climb a mountain or buy a frozen yogurt franchise. They'll stay best friends with each other until the day they die or they'll drift apart and reconnect decades later by accident, in an airport gate area. They'll hug and barely recognize the people they've become.

Sure, except the difference between them and me is this: I can get on with the rest of my life starting right now, this minute. Pearl and Jack can't. They aren't going anywhere for the next seven or eight or nine years. Seven or eight or nine years! That's forever. *One* year of what they're going through right now is forever.

And what if Pearl and Jack don't even survive another year? Another month? Another week? What if tomorrow is the day when Nathan hurts them just a little more than usual, goes just a little too far.

But that is no longer my responsibility. I did the best I could. I did everything I could. Now I just have to deal with the two small, pale ghosts, standing on the edge of my grave and staring down at me. I remember Pearl and Jack sitting on that bench at the municipal building, how they seemed to be staring off at nothing. Now I understand they were tuned in to the future, watching me here and now, watching me give up on them.

I should feel light, not heavy. I'm my old self again and the responsibility for Pearl and Jack has been lifted from me. I don't have to stress about them anymore. I don't have to stress about getting my ribs kicked in. I don't have to stress about trying to do a job that's too much for me to handle.

This job, at Haunted Frontier, is definitely not too much for me to handle. Stand up, lie down. Even Salvador can handle this job.

That's partly why I'm in a heavy mood, maybe. As much as I sucked at investigating Nathan Shaw, as badly as I crashed and burned, at least I was doing something important with myself, doing something meaningful.

And I didn't *completely* suck, right? I worked harder than I ever have in my life, I got a lot smarter, I truly didn't make the same mistake twice, and I accomplished a genuinely fair amount. Nathan doesn't have his friends beat the shit out of me unless I accomplished, genuinely, a fair amount.

The next posse of guests trudges up the hill. We rise from our graves. Through the artificial fog I see Justin's thousand-yard stare. *Four more hours of this.* Probably I have the same stare. I'm not going to work at Haunted Frontier for the rest of my life, but whatever job I get next won't be much different. *I'm* never going to be much different.

After the posse trudges back down the hill, I climb out of my grave and walk over to Salvador. I poke his leg with the toe of my boot.

"Listen to me for a minute," I say.

He shakes his head.

"Shaking your head means you're listening to me, Salvador. You're responding to my statement."

He starts to shake his head again, but then stops, confused.

"There was nobody to help those kids," I say. "Nobody but me. That's why I got into all this. And now you know what?"

He surrenders. "What?"

"And now there's still nobody to help them but me."

I sit down next to him. It seems like either fork in the path I take right now could lead to my certain doom. It's possible I'm fucked either way. I think about the sign in the alley, the words painted above the loading dock. *DO NOT.* That sign couldn't be more obviously a *sign.* But what exactly is the message? DO NOT . . . *what*?

DO NOT continue to mess with Nathan Shaw. DO NOT continue to swim in water way over your head. That's what I thought yesterday. Today I'm not so sure.

"I don't think I'm going to quit," I say.

"What?"

"I'm not going to quit on those kids."

In greenish-gray ghoul makeup, Salvador's eyes seem extra wide, the whites extra bright and shining. "You're not?"

I can't abandon Pearl and Jack. I'm not a person, anymore, who gives up. Knock me on my ass and I will get back up. And maybe next time you won't knock me on my ass, because, remember, I'm not going to make the same mistake twice.

"No," I say, and Salvador pumps his fist triumphantly.

31

The next day is Thursday. I was ambushed in the alley Sunday night. So that's almost four days I've been out of action, doing nothing, making no progress. But look, the glass is half full: if Nathan has someone watching me, he'll think for sure I've been scared off.

Though I'm guessing he hasn't been watching me. A guy like Nathan, what I've learned about him—he's overconfident, a mastermind in his own mind, so he'll just take for granted that I've been scared off. Why wouldn't he? To him I'm just a nobody. I'm a cockroach that scrambles away at the first flare of light.

On the other hand, a guy like Nathan might be pissed off that Eleanor showed up with pepper spray to interrupt the warning he intended to send. I can definitely see him deciding to address that issue. So, just to be safe, I become fanatic about checking my mirrors for any possible tail, checking the block outside my place for any suspicious vehicles, scanning and studying the faces everywhere I go.

"Burke," I say, "have you seen anything suspicious around the house lately? Any suspicious bystanders, for example?"

If Burke had ears like Jutta, they would flatten back against his head right now. "What did you see?"

"Nothing. Just . . . the guys who jumped me. I don't want them to come around here."

"God help them if they do."

So that's good. I have Burke on full alert. I don't have to worry about anyone creeping around the house.

I borrow Salvador's SUV and decide to swing by Shaw Law. Nathan won't recognize the SUV, and I doubt he's peering out his window and scrutinizing all the traffic pouring by anyway. I'm still tense, though. You never know what lightning strike of bad luck might come crackling down from nowhere.

It's funny, though not really, how far I've come and yet here I remain on square one. I need evidence against Nathan Shaw. How do I get it?

I drive past the office park. The pearl-colored sports car isn't out front, isn't in back. It's the middle of the afternoon, a couple of hours after lunch. Just one more quick pass. I'm curious. Where is Nathan when he should be at work? Is he at home? Why? When will he be back?

Driving by the Shaw house is risky. And what am I going to see? The blinds closed, the eight-foot fence. But I've got to check it out. Because you never know what lightning strike of *good* luck might blaze down, right? Even if there's only a one-tenth-of-one-percent chance I might be able to help Pearl and Jack, I'm taking it.

By now I know Meadow Wood Estates better than my own neighborhood. I turn past the ornamental stone guardhouse and weave without a hitch through the lanes and terraces, the ways and trails. There's hardly anyone else on the road but me. This is good and bad. It's bad because I can't blend in. It's good because anyone following me can't blend in either.

I'm planning to be extra cautious and stick to the cross street. As I roll slowly past the top of the cul-de-sac, though, I spot a car I don't recognize in front of the Shaw house. Not Tracy's Volvo, not Nathan's sports car. A guy I don't recognize—wearing blazer and slacks, definitely not one of Nathan Shaw's sketchy friends—stands in the yard. I feel a kick of hope. Is the guy maybe CPS? A police detective? I can't resist. I cut the wheel and turn into the cul-de-sac.

The guy in the blazer isn't just standing in the yard. As I get closer, I see that he's wrestling with a yard sign, stabbing it into the grass and rocking it into place. FOR LEASE. The blinds and curtains of the house are open. The front door is open too. Have the Shaws moved out? It's like a bomb dropping on me, the possibility that the Shaws have moved out.

I pull to the curb. If the Shaws *haven't* moved out yet, I'm putting myself in a very dicey position since Nathan might show up at any second. I climb out of the SUV anyway. I need to find out what's going on here.

"Hey," I say. "Hi. Excuse me."

The guy in the blazer, the real estate agent, turns. He looks like he's in a shitty mood, like he's squinting into a bright and annoying light. When he remembers to smile, it's not much of a smile.

"Can I help you?" he says.

That's when I realize—it's him, Pink Golf Shirt, the beefy neighbor who pounded on my car that first day because he thought I was one of Nathan Shaw's sketchy friends. The blazer threw me off, and he's only annoyed, not enraged. He doesn't seem to recognize me. I'm in my usual, board shorts and T-shirt, so it must be my respectable new haircut and Salvador's respectable SUV.

"This house is for lease?" I say.

He flares his nostrils. Can I not see the goddamn sign? "Yes," he says, "the house is for lease."

"Are the people who used to live here . . . do you know where they went?"

"No."

"Do you know why they left?"

"The house is currently vacant, but it's not ready to show yet. Give my office a call and they'll put you on the list. We'll be having an open house next week."

He walks away, done with me. I follow him up the brick path. Being this close to the house, in broad daylight, is a deeply strange experience. I've stared at this house from a distance so many times. I've even dreamed about staring at this house from a distance. And now I'm right here, literally three steps from the open front door.

"Hold on," I say. "Can't I just take a quick look inside? I mean, I'm here right now. You're here right now."

"No." He turns and holds up a big, beefy palm to stop me in my tracks. "The house isn't in suitable condition to show."

"That's okay. I don't mind."

"I do."

Either the house is in seriously not suitable condition to show, or Pink Golf Shirt Realtor Neighbor doesn't find me as respectable as I thought.

"It's my parents who are looking for a place," I say, "not me. My dad has me driving around and scouting. They need somewhere to stay while they remodel their house. Their house is over in Zephyrus."

I have his mild interest now. Zephyrus is one of the ritziest gated communities in the city. My imaginary parents are his ideal leasers. But he shakes his head.

"I apologize," he says. "The previous tenant left it a mess. We'll have it back in tip-top shape by next week, though. Give me your number and we can schedule a private showing."

There's no way I'll be able to wait till next week to get inside the house. And if I'm going to learn anything useful, I need to see the house the way the Shaws left it, *before* it's returned to tip-top shape.

I try to think of other cards I can play. "Do you know Felice Upton?"

"No."

"How about . . ." Salvador's mom—what's her name? I can never remember. Valerie, maybe? Vanessa? " . . . Vanessa Velasco?"

He hesitates, his hand on the knob, ready to pull the front door shut. "Your parents are working with Vanessa?"

"She's a family friend. I just need, like, five minutes."

"You have to understand. It's a disaster in there. The previous tenant . . ." He grinds his teeth and tightens his jaw. He might not hate Nathan Shaw as much as I do, but it's probably a close call. "And you're on your own. I've got to get to an appointment across town."

"I understand," I say. "Completely."

"Have we met before?" He studies me. "You look familiar."

"I don't think so. You probably meet a lot of people."

He gives me his card and instructs me to lock the front door when I leave. After he drives away, I step inside.

The foyer. Junk mail piled knee-high in the corner, a water stain spreading across the ceiling. A smell hits me—faint and funky, unpleasantly fruity, unpleasantly peppery.

The real disaster begins in the next room, the living room. Curtains ripped from the hooks and heaped on the floor, brown smears of what I sincerely hope isn't shit on the walls, a tipped-over quart of motor oil that's bled into the carpet. The only piece of furniture left in the room, a coffee table, has been smashed to bits, splintered wood scattered everywhere.

The bad smell is stronger in the kitchen. Flies buzz around the sink. I'm not going over there. The oven door is open, garbage crammed inside, flies buzzing there too. Empty cans and Styrofoam clamshells, coffee grounds and unidentifiable peelings. On one wall next to me is more smearing—in the shape of a giant smiley face, I realize. It's peanut butter, not shit. I'm pretty sure. I'm crossing my fingers.

The rest of the first floor is in the same shape. In the back, in the den that Eleanor and I spied at from behind the tree, each individual glass pane of the French doors has been shattered into cobwebs.

I'm not surprised that Nathan is this nasty and malevolent, that he'd so totally trash a house when he moves out. Maybe he was mad because the rent had gone up. Maybe he was kicked out because of the sketchy friends at all hours of the night. Going from room to room, though, I get more than just nasty and malicious. Nathan Shaw used his imagination to do all this, he took pride in his craft. He *enjoyed* it. I think about the cigarette burns on Jack's collarbone, on Pearl's ankle, how they were lined up perfectly, so lovingly spaced.

I want to get out of here. I force myself to go upstairs, though. Upstairs is better and worse—better because it's not trashed or smelly, just empty, but worse because it's a lot easier to imagine them now, Pearl and Jack, to picture the lives they've been living. Nathan Shaw yelling at them from downstairs. *Come here.* Pearl making her way down the hallway. Jack shadowing her, close behind. The long descent down the stairs that doesn't take long enough.

A master and two smaller bedrooms. The master bath is flooded and the tub is brimming. The taps are off now, but Nathan Shaw must have left the water running. That's what stained the ceiling below.

Off-white walls in every room, the same cream-colored carpet, all the furniture gone. There's no way to tell if Pearl and Jack each had their own bedroom or shared one. Sunlight pours in through the open blinds, and the bare walls and carpets are relatively clean, but still the second floor of the house is grim, sad, depressing. I'm not sure if it's objectively grim, sad, and depressing, or just seems that way because I know what happened here.

I should be looking for evidence. Concentrate, pay attention. Felice and other professional detectives must be good at putting aside all their personal feelings and emotions. I'm not any good at that yet. Probably I never will be.

People always forget something when they move out of a place, right? I check the cabinet under the sink in the master bath. I check the hallway closet, which is just the HVAC system, and the bedroom closets. I check all the corners of all the top shelves in all the bedroom closets. I don't find anything. *Anything.* That seems suspicious. Maybe it's not. In the walk-in master closet there's a trapdoor overhead. The attic.

I hate attics. Me and everyone else. When has anything good ever happened in an attic? My heart starts thudding even before I pull open the trapdoor and a set of rickety wooden steps unfolds. Overhead, a bulb doesn't click on automatically. I try all the switches in the room. No luck.

I turn on my phone's flashlight. I have to do this. I climb the wooden steps. Excessively rickety. The ceiling is too low for me to stand upright, so I stoop as I move deeper into the attic. It's unbelievably hot, as if every single summer of heat since the house was built is still trapped right here.

I aim my flashlight and start searching. There could be rats or spiders, but mostly I'm dreading what else the beam of my flashlight might suddenly flash on. Every news article I read about child abuse is coming back to me, all the specific details, the objects that adults employed to hurt their kids.

I reach the far end of the attic, the brick chimney, and head back. After a full lap, I haven't found anything. Just pink insulation, lots of dust. I point my phone straight down at the floor. The only footprints I see in the thick dust are mine. I want to find evidence, I *need* to find evidence, but it's also a relief to realize that no one has been up here in a long, long time. Jack and Pearl have probably never been up here.

I climb down and flip the trapdoor back up. I'm soaked with sweat, the heat from the attic sticking to me, so I go out into the hallway and dial the thermostat from seventy-four to sixty-eight. The HVAC system rumbles and starts whooshing, which makes me glance over at the closet where it's located. This time I notice something I missed before: a deadbolt lock on the door.

Really? Do people go around stealing HVAC systems? I open the door and take a look inside again. It's possible, I guess, that Nathan Shaw stored valuables of some sort in here, but it would be a strange place to do that. The space is small and cramped, with hardly enough room for the furnace and the blower, for all the tubing and the metal ducts. The concrete floor is wet from dripping condensation.

Concentrate, pay attention. *Think.* I look at the door again. On the inside there's not a thumb latch on the lock. It's a double deadbolt. Which means you could use it to keep someone out of the closet, but you could also use it to keep someone *in.*

I'm not hot anymore. I'm ice cold. I turn on my phone's flashlight and crouch down. There's no way an adult could squeeze into the closet. Even a kid as small as Jack or Pearl would have to tuck their knees up to their chin, squish under the main duct, and flatten their body against the wall. It would be a nightmare in here. Hot and noisy, no room to move or breathe. Pitch black when the door is closed and locked from the outside. My flashlight catches some color in the back corner, under a pipe wrapped in rubber. Red. I stretch my arm out, feel around. It's a small plastic cowboy, swirling his lasso. I'm ice cold but sweating again.

32

I close the door to the utility closet and put the plastic cowboy in my pocket. I need to get out of here. I've seen enough. Too much.

Outside, I suck in the fresh air. Deep, deep breaths. Does the cowboy belong to Jack or to Pearl? The faint, unpleasant smell from the house is baked into my clothes, shellacked onto my skin, inside me.

How often and for how long—how many minutes or hours or even days—were Jack and Pearl kept locked in that nightmare of a closet? Did they take turns? There's only room for one of them at a time. I picture Nathan with his hand on the back of Jack's slender neck, forcing him forward. I picture Pearl secretly slipping the cowboy into Jack's other hand just before Nathan drags him off. Or maybe it was the other way around, Jack slipping the cowboy into Pearl's hand before Tracy drags her off. Being separated like that—it had to be terrible for the one left behind too. Not ever knowing when your brother or sister would come back. Not ever really knowing *if*.

I force myself to stay focused. First thing: I need to find out where the Shaws have moved. I worry about what it means for Pearl and Jack, that the family has moved. I can't imagine any way it might make their lives easier, just lots of ways the opposite of that.

It shouldn't be too hard to find them. I'll wait until Nathan leaves Shaw Law for the day and follow him home. I'll just have to be extremely, extremely careful tailing Nathan this time, and assume that he and/or his thug-ass friends are watching for me.

I'm supposed to give Salvador his car back at four. I meet him at Haunted Frontier and explain I need the SUV a little longer.

"I'm coming with you," he says.

I notice that he's evolved from begging to stating. "You can't come," I say. "It's too dangerous."

"I'm coming with you or you can't use my car."

"What? Salvador. Seriously?"

He seems even more shocked by his rebellion than I am. His cheeks are flushed and his eyes glazed. He's panting more heavily than usual. When he tries to straighten his shoulders, he almost loses his balance and tips over backward.

"Best and final offer," he says, which is something he must have heard his mom say.

"Salvador," I say. Wow. I think it's been a positive experience for him, helping me these past few weeks. Should I be proud or have I created a monster?

"Best and final offer, *please*," he says, softer this time. But he straightens his shoulders again. He's getting the hang of that. He narrows his eyes with stern resolve.

I can win this battle. Eventually Salvador will fold. But it's almost four. Nathan will be leaving work soon. "Fine," I say. "But you have to do what I say, no questions asked. And no questions in general."

We get to the office park at four-fifteen. I can't risk using my regular spot in the strip mall across the street, even with a new car. Luckily there's a 7-Eleven down the street. From there I'll have a good view of Shaw Law. I'll be able to pick Nathan up when he turns out of the parking lot.

I pull into 7-Eleven. Nathan's sports car still isn't out in front of Shaw Law. Did we already miss him? I pull back out and drive past the office park. The sports car isn't parked behind Shaw Law either.

Salvador is vibrating with the violent desire to ask all the questions he is forbidden to ask. Finally he can't stand it anymore and breaks down. "What do we do now?" he says. "The car isn't there. How do we follow the car if the car isn't there? So what do we do? Do you think that—"

"Stop," I say.

"Sorry. But—"

"Let me think, Salvador."

The patient thing, the obvious thing, is to come back tomorrow at four, or earlier, to make sure I catch Nathan when he leaves for the day. I'm getting a weird vibe from this situation, though. A hunch forms. What are the chances there's no connection between the missing sports car and the vacant house? There's probably a connection. I need to find out if Shaw Law is suddenly vacant too. Otherwise I could end up wasting time I can't afford to waste.

It's too risky. It's not too risky. I can't decide. There's a chance Nathan just stepped out, a quick trip to the post office or something, and could be back any second. But . . . a quick check of Shaw Law will take two minutes, at most. It's not too risky. I glance at Salvador. It's not risky for him. Nathan has never seen Salvador. He doesn't even know he exists.

"Salvador," I say. "Are you maybe down for some action?"

I explain what I'm thinking. Salvador will walk a block, cross the street, and enter the dentist's office. He'll ask if they're accepting new patients. Either way, yes or no, Salvador takes a business card and leaves. He strolls all casual past Shaw Law next door. He peeks in the window and sees whatever he sees.

"I'm on it," Salvador says.

"You sure?"

"Yes!"

I go through the plan again. It couldn't be simpler. Salvador can't screw this up, right? He nods along, point by point, and seems to understand everything. When he gets out of the SUV, he heads off in the right direction. So far, so good.

He walks the one block, zigzags across the street during breaks in traffic, cuts through the office park. A pearl-colored sports car blows through the intersection and my heart hiccups between beats. But it's only *a* pearl-colored sports car, not *the* pearl-colored sports car. It speeds past and disappears.

Salvador approaches the dentist. Good job, Salvador, you're crushing it. But then, he veers suddenly left and heads over to the Shaw Law window. I see him practically mash his face against the glass, cupping his eyes with his hands. What is he doing? He's supposed to stroll past casually and *peek* inside.

Nathan could be back at any second. Or what if, even worse, the sports car didn't start this morning and Nathan took an Uber to work? What if he's actually in there right now? No, Nathan doesn't know Salvador, but that won't matter if he glances up and sees some kid mashing his face against the window. He'll know right away that something is up.

Salvador moves from the window to the door. He reaches for the handle and tugs on it. Unbelievable. You know who's to blame for this? Not Salvador—me. Me, for trusting Salvador to not fuck this up. I'm too far away to honk and get Salvador's attention. If Nathan gets his hands on Salvador, if he starts interrogating him, we're busted. Will Salvador be smart enough to lie and say he's looking for the dentist? I'm not counting on it.

I start the engine. I need to get Salvador out of there. But then I see him zigzagging back across the street. I keep my eye on Shaw Law. The door doesn't open. No movement in the window. I relax. A little.

Salvador climbs into the SUV. His cheeks are flushed, due to excitement or all the walking or both. I wait to make extra sure nobody is following him, then hit the gas and go.

"Stroll all casual past the office, then take *a quick peek* in the window," I say. I check the mirrors, making extra *extra* sure nobody is following us. "Remember that part?"

"I didn't need to," he says. The flushing, I can tell now, is definitely due to excitement. "It's closed. The office."

"Closed for the day or . . ."

"No, *closed* closed. For good. There was a sign. I didn't take a picture but I memorized it."

I wait. "Salvador!"

"Oh. 'The law offices of Nathan Shaw have relocated. Please visit our website for further information.'"

This is bad news. At the next light I take out my phone and check the Shaw Law website. There are no updates about any relocation. The office address that's listed, on the *home* page and the *about* page and the *contact us* page, hasn't been changed either. So Nathan has basically disappeared into thin air. Which means Pearl and Jack have basically disappeared into thin air.

I pick up my car at Haunted Frontier and drive home. Here we go again. How am I supposed to track down the Shaw family now? I text Felice a 911, but she doesn't text me back. She must be working, showing a house. Or, equally possible, she's had enough of me.

I lie on my futon, eyes closed, and relax my mind. I open myself to fresh ideas. No fresh ideas are forthcoming. I get out of bed and pace. That doesn't help.

The key to finding the Shaw family might be figuring out *why* they disappeared. Is Nathan on the run from somebody? Because it's definitely suspicious: no new address on the CLOSED sign, no updates to the website. A normal business would hype its new location as much as possible.

First Nathan warns me to stay away from him and his family. Very soon after, the family disappears. That timing seems too perfect to be a coincidence, but I also have a hard time believing that Nathan is on the run from *me.* For all I know he hasn't given me a second thought. That's much more likely.

For all I know, Nathan has been planning this move for weeks or months, for unknown and completely unrelated reasons. Maybe it has to do with whatever sketchy business he's into. Maybe he's been ripping off his tax-problem clients.

I think about that little snippet of a conversation on the back deck that Eleanor and I overheard, Big Beard telling Nathan, "Almost time, c'mon," at two in the morning. Does that factor into any of this?

Pearl and Jack could be anywhere. Another city, another state, even another country. How am I ever going to find them? When my phone dings I dive for it, thinking it's Felice. Instead it's a text from a number I don't recognize.

i'm sorry

33

Tracy Shaw. I don't know how I know, but I know instantly.

i'm sorry

Sorry for what? For selling me out to her husband, so he could have his thug-ass friends beat the shit out of me? I can't think of any other reason. But why is she suddenly sorry about that now?

But no. Of course she's not really sorry. This is some trick, another setup. Nathan's thug-ass friends told him about getting pepper-sprayed, and now he wants to lure me in and finish punishing me. How dumb does he think I am? How dumb is *he,* that he thinks I'll fall for a trap like this?

I stare at my phone. It has to be a trap, right? On the other hand . . . Nathan *isn't* dumb enough to think I'll fall for this. If he wants to ambush me again, I'm almost a hundred percent certain he'll come up with something trickier and more devious than this. The first time he fooled me—that was way trickier and more devious than this.

i'm sorry

It doesn't matter. Even if this isn't a trap, I'm still not texting back. Because Tracy apologizing at this point would be infuriating. Like, maybe she should have thought about the possibility of being sorry *before* she sold me out, *before* her husband's thug-ass friends beat the shit out of me.

But she must feel pretty terrible about it, if she's taking the risk to text me. Because if this isn't a trap, she must be texting without Nathan's permission. It can't hurt to text back, just in case. I type it's ok, but then stop before I hit send. I change the text to something more neutral, to just ok.

I hit send and wait. If this isn't a trap . . . wow. It means I might still have a shot at convincing Tracy to go to CPS. Or at least I might be able to find out where the Shaws have moved.

My trigger finger itches. I want to send another text. I want to send a bunch of texts. I have so many questions. I stop myself again, though. I can't push Tracy. She reached out to me. I need to be smart and let her reach out on her own schedule.

After a long, long, long time, only actually twenty or thirty seconds probably, a text *bloops* to the surface of my screen. are u ok?

I decide to stick with neutral and objective: cracked rib broken nose etc. Then I worry I've veered too far in the opposite direction, too neutral and objective, and I might be making her feel bad. So I add a second text: but fine more or less

Tracy texts back: i didn't want u to get hurt

She could be sincere. She could be not sincere. I have no way of telling just from a text. I have no way of telling, I realize, if this is even Tracy. It could be Nathan, for example, pretending to be Tracy.

I send a text: can u talk?

Right away, almost instantly: no. Which is either suspicious (Nathan, pretending to be Tracy, wouldn't want to talk) or completely understandable (Tracy doesn't want Nathan to overhear her). But all this is pointless unless I can confirm it's really Tracy I'm texting with.

I send a text: can we meet?

no

five minutes, anywhere

i can't

Maybe this isn't Tracy, or maybe Nathan is sitting right next to her, telling Tracy exactly what to write. Still, though, I have to ask the one question that's bugging me most:

why did u tell your husband about me?

i had to i'm sorry

ok thx but why?

i thought he sent u

Who sent me? It takes me a second to realize she means Nathan. But . . . she thought *Nathan* sent me to talk to her at the mall? That doesn't make any sense.

i don't understand

i couldn't take chance

She couldn't take the chance that . . . what? And then I think about Nathan, I picture the way he so meticulously destroyed that house, how deviously he lured me into an ambush, and finally I get it. Tracy was scared that Nathan sent me to test her, to determine if she was trustworthy and loyal. My story, my number, my offer to help her and the kids—she worried all that might be bait.

he didn't send me

i know now

I wonder if Nathan came home that night and bragged about having me stomped in an alley. Maybe he was sending her a message too.

i still want to help

i have to go

can we meet? plz five min anywhere u want

I wait. There's a chance, I'm hoping, that Tracy didn't text just to apologize. Maybe, whether she realizes it or not, she really *does* want my help. It's a stretch, I know. But Tracy didn't really have to keep this conversation going as long as she did. She really didn't have to text me in the first place.

I wait. My phone rings. It's the number Tracy has been texting from.

"Hello?" I say.

"How do I know you're not just some pervert weirdo who happened to see my children that day?" Tracy says.

"I'm not, I promise." But it's a good question and I doubt she'll take my word for it. She shouldn't.

She's quiet. I try to think, think, think. I have a feeling I have literally one second left before I say the right thing or never hear from her again.

"After I saw your kids," I say, "I called CPS. I gave them my name, everything. A couple days later I went back, to make sure CPS followed up. A weirdo pervert wouldn't do that, right?"

The call goes dead. *Fuck.* But then, a few seconds later, a new text *bloops* to the surface of my screen.

five minutes only

34

Tracy says she'll meet me next Wednesday at one. I realize that's when she has an NA meeting. The address she texts me rings a bell too. When I check my maps app, I see it's the former Blockbuster. Tracy, I note, is being super smart and super careful. She's sticking to her exact routine in case Nathan has her followed, or if he's hidden a tracker on her phone or car. I look it up. A four-pack of Apple AirTags costs less than a hundred bucks.

So now I have almost a week to worry that I'm about to walk into another ambush. Should I trust Tracy? It all comes down to that. More specifically, should I trust a person who's already sold me out once? The obvious answer is *No, no way, are you kidding me?* I'm not worried that Tracy is secretly the evil parent or some shocking Netflix twist like that. It's a possibility, I guess, but I've seen her with the kids. I've seen her with them when she doesn't know anybody is watching. I remember how terrified she was on the roof of the mall parking structure—terrified of Nathan, I know now.

Tracy is not a secretly evil parent. I'll take the risk that I'm wrong about that. But I am worried she'll sell me out again, for the same reason as before: because she's terrified of Nathan, because she thinks it's the best way to protect herself and her kids. That wouldn't be a shocking twist at all.

I'm going to need someone, definitely not Salvador, to watch my back. Friday I call Eleanor.

"Have you recuperated enough to take my grandma to the doctor Monday?" she says.

"Again already?"

"Different doctor. 'How many doctors does she have?' you might ask. 'A shit ton of doctors,' I would assure you."

"Sure. I can do it." My cracked rib feels better and I can breathe through my nose again. My bruises look worse—a mottled, decomposing shade of yellow instead of purple—but feel better too. "What time do you get off work today? Do you want to get some food?"

"In an hour and a half. Okay."

I could try to read or nap or just chill, but I'm too preoccupied. I drive over to the municipal building to wait in the parking lot for Eleanor. My mind is working, working. Let's suppose for the sake of argument that I'm not walking into another trap. I still have to convince Tracy to go to CPS. It won't be easy. It might not even be possible. There has to be a reason why she hasn't gone before now. Because she's scared of Nathan Shaw?

That's a very legit concern. Because she's worried CPS is too understaffed or incompetent to do anything? Also very legit.

I check my phone. I would love to discuss all this with Felice, but she still hasn't returned my texts.

It's too hot to wait in the car. Maybe Driver Improvement Verification isn't busy and I can spring Eleanor early. The glass doors of the municipal administration building slide open. I step inside and back in time. For an instant it's three and a half weeks ago and I have nothing important on my mind, nothing important in my future.

"Can I help you?" the security guard says, since I'm just standing there, blocking the doors.

I shake my head and move on. I think about how different everything would be if I'd been able to find the security guard three and a half weeks ago. Why did he disappear at that one specific moment in time? Maybe it's lucky he did. Because if I'd handed off Pearl and Jack to him, he would have handed them off to CPS and never given them a second thought. Probably *I* would've never given them a second thought either. I'd just be trucking along right now, living my old life.

The bench where I first saw Pearl and Jack is vacant. I stop to look at it. The kids are here in front of me, then gone, here then gone—time flipping back and forth so fast I can't follow it, a dealer shuffling cards. At some point the dealer will stop shuffling, I guess. He'll turn over the cards. We'll find out who wins and who loses.

Inside Driver Improvement, a couple of people are sitting in the waiting area, messing around on their phones. Eleanor, at reception, is messing around on her phone.

"Sign in." Then she glances up, sees me, frowns. "Why are you here?"

"It's too hot to wait in the parking lot."

She glances over her shoulder, back into the bowels of the office. "If Denise comes out, I don't know you. You're just some random dude who was going sixty in a forty. I'm already on her shit list."

"Tracy sent me a text."

"*What?*"

"The mother. Tracy."

"I know who Tracy is. You've told me a million times. She sent you a text?"

"To say she was sorry. For what happened."

"*What?* She wanted to say she was sorry for almost killing you?"

"It wasn't her fault. She explained. She's scared of Nathan. She thought he was setting her up. I'm going to meet up with her. That's why I need to talk to you."

Eleanor just keeps staring at me. She can't even manage a *what?* this time. "I know it seems somewhat risky," I say. "But I'm going to take precautions. That why I need you to have my back."

She shakes her head—in a way I think means she can't believe this shit, as opposed to *No fucking way.*

"So here's the deal," I say, "if—"

"Sign in and take a seat, please," she says.

I look over. A woman stands in the doorway to the back office. It's her, the supervisor who blew me off that first day, who told me to remove the problem of two abused kids from her sight, who refused to even give me Tracy's name. She—Denise, I assume—consults her clipboard.

"Mr. Johnson?" she says. "Keith Barent Johnson?"

One of the people in the waiting area stands. "Hallelujah," he grumbles.

"Denise," I say. My voice comes out a little louder than it should but is calm otherwise. "Do you remember me?"

She blinks a couple of times, startled that I know her name. Eleanor, continuing to play the role of bored and disaffected receptionist, goes back to her phone. But I see her eyes slide over at me. *What the fuck?*

I don't know, honestly, what the fuck. I'm even more pissed now than I was when I first saw Nathan Shaw. And suddenly this time, with no warning or reason. It's like I'm standing a few inches from a jet engine and the heat is blasting my hair back, stretching my skin over my skull. Or am I the jet engine? I don't know.

"I beg your pardon, sir?" Denise says.

"I talked to you a few weeks ago."

"I'm afraid I don't recall that."

How many times, in the past three and a half weeks, were Pearl or Jack locked in that dark, hot HVAC closet? How many times did they think that no one would ever come to let them out?

"There were two kids on the bench outside with cigarette burns all over them, and their mother was in here for an appointment, and I asked you for the mother's name so I could report it to CPS. You wouldn't give me her name. Now do you recall that?"

Denise blinks and blinks. Keith Barent Johnson, who's shuffled up and is standing next to me, says, *"Day-um."*

"Sir," Denise says to me, "I have to ask you to—"

"I don't blame you," I tell Denise. "It wasn't your problem, right? Why should you get involved? But let me ask you one thing. Do you ever even think about those kids? Have you ever wondered for, like, one minute how they're doing?"

I walk out of the office before she says anything. Most likely she doesn't say anything, just rolls her eyes and takes Keith Barent Johnson back to her office. In my car I hit my one-hitter. I've already calmed down, though, even before the weed. The hot wind has ceased to blow. What was up with that? I never blow my top.

At five Eleanor comes out and we take our separate cars to a Korean restaurant not far from her grandma's house.

"That was fascinating," she says after we get our food. A spicy pork bowl for her, plus tofu soup and egg rolls. Pancakes for me. "Watching you lose your mind."

"I don't know what was up with that. I'm sorry. I was an asshat."

"Not really."

I check my phone. Still nothing from Felice.

Eleanor, obliterating her spicy pork bowl, pauses to take a breath. "Who's the mystery girl you're obsessed with? Let me guess. She teaches yoga and has an *All who wander are not lost* tattoo. She smokes a lot of weed. No. She *aspires* someday to teach yoga."

"She's a former private investigator in her early forties."

"Oh, right. The real estate chick who taught you the secrets of the detective trade."

"Maybe mid-forties. We hooked up."

"*What?*" Eleanor says. "No."

"Yeah."

"A former private investigator turned real estate agent in her mid-forties?"

"And she's a total babe. Can you believe it?"

"Not at all. Really? If this is truly true, I'm grudgingly impressed."

I've grudgingly impressed Eleanor! But I can't enjoy the moment because I shouldn't be enjoying that part of my life right now. I don't deserve to lose myself in the warmth of Felice's mouth and body—IRL or memory—when I should be thinking every minute of every day about Pearl and Jack.

"What's the problem?" Eleanor says. "I mean, you're probably terrible in bed, but I wouldn't worry about it too much. As long as you're not just lying there like a dead person. You're not just lying there like a dead person, are you?"

"Why should I be happy when they're not? Those kids? I shouldn't be happy in any way until they're safe."

"That's stupid."

"Is it?"

Eleanor finishes her pork bowl. She moves around a few grains of rice with the tips of her chopsticks and stares down into the bowl like she's reading tea leaves.

"It's totally stupid," she says. "It's like if someone sabotaged every relationship she's ever been in because she knows it'll bomb eventually anyway. It's like someone refusing to be happy because down the line she might not be happy, so why not get on with it now?"

"You?"

"How did you guess?"

"After your mom took off?"

"After the third and final time. Well, I didn't learn my lesson right away. Hope stupidly persisted for quite some time."

"Yeah."

"Listen," she says. "Maybe we're looking at this all wrong. Your situation with the babe of advancing years. Maybe you finding happiness every now and then is what you need at the moment."

"What I need?"

"To keep going. To keep helping those kids. It's a boost of . . . I don't know what. Heart, maybe."

I wonder if she's right. My heart at times during all this does feel utterly depleted, stepped on, ground down. It's possible Eleanor is right. Or do I just want to believe that?

I take the toy cowboy out of my pocket and set it between us on the table. An image flashes through my mind. I picture myself kneeling, handing the cowboy back to Jack and Pearl when all this is over, when they're somewhere safe. *Here you go, dudes. This belongs to you.*

"What's that?" Eleanor says.

I tell her where I found it. I explain about the double deadbolt on the door. She pops what I'm guessing is one of her grandma's pills and washes it down with her beer.

"Fucking hell," she says.

"I know."

"I feel sometimes like we're not supposed to be here," she says. "This world. Human beings. We're in the wrong place. We're all just *wrong*. Sometimes I just want to lie down and disappear."

I think I get what she means. "But it's all we have," I say. "It's who we are."

"You're actually going to meet her? This woman who almost got you killed? You actually think that's a nonsuicidal course of action?"

"I hope so."

35

Eleanor's grandma, once you get her talking, once you ease her into a relatively civil mood, is highly entertaining. She's lived a full life. Just in the twenty or so minutes it takes to get from her house to the oncologist, I find out she spent a summer in the 1960s as a driver on the demolition derby circuit and, in the 1970s, was one of the first female paramedics in the country. On the way back home I find out she was once engaged to a zoo plumber who was almost killed, a week before the wedding, when a sarus crane pecked him on top of the head. The button on his baseball cap saved him from a cracked skull, but Eleanor's grandma took it as bad juju and dumped the dude.

"Are you messing with me, Terry?" I say. She does not, under any circumstances, allow me to call her Mrs. O'Loughlin.

"Ha. Why would I make that shit up?"

"Good point."

I help her out of my car and up the walkway to the house. I'm going too slow for her, then I'm going too fast. "For fuck's sake," she says.

"Sorry."

"What's your story?"

"My story?" I say. "I don't really have one. Not yet, I guess."

"I'll give you some advice."

"Okay."

She waits until I've got her settled upstairs, in her La-Z-Boy, headphones in her lap. "Here's my advice," she says.

"Okay."

"Sell everything you have. Buy a one-way plane ticket to India. Start in Delhi and work your way down south. Don't worry about the monsoon season. It's rain! Big deal! Stick to vegetables, not meat, and your stomach will be fine. See the cities, but don't miss the countryside. Trains are terrible but you'll get used to it."

Wow. I was expecting some very general and vague wisdom of the elders. Follow your heart! I should have known better.

I don't have a shift at Haunted Frontier, so I hole up in my room and have imaginary conversations with Tracy. What I'll say to her Wednesday, what she'll say to me. It's like I'm going on a job interview, except that for the first time in my life I care if I get the job or not.

I told Tracy I'd help her. The question I know she's going to ask Wednesday: *How?* I still don't have an answer.

When I need a change of scenery, I go outside. Burke and Jutta are in the backyard, under the floodlights, Jutta watching Burke use wooden stakes and a roll of string to mark out a big rectangle on the grass.

I rub Jutta's ears. We have an understanding. We both wish she was my dog instead of Burke's.

"Hey, Burke," I say. "What's up?"

"Just enjoying a pleasant summer evening." He finishes the rectangle, about fifteen feet long and ten feet wide, and stands back to survey his work. He's wearing a T-shirt that says LEFT WING RIGHT WING WE ALL SCREAM FOR ICE CREAM.

"It looks like you're going to dig up the backyard," I say.

"I can neither confirm nor deny."

Ten by fifteen seems too small for a pool. And Burke isn't really a pool kind of guy. If he's building a bunker in the backyard, I'm finding a new place to live.

He uses a tape measure to measure, then adjusts the stakes and string. I sit on the steps with Jutta. I'm not really going to ask Burke for his opinion, am I? I tell myself it can't hurt. Any port in a storm, right?

"Hey, Burke," I say. "I have kind of a dicey situation I'm dealing with."

"Dicey?"

"Potentially dangerous."

His eyes light up. "I like the sound of that."

Immediately I regret bringing him into this, but it's too late now. I start at the beginning and explain about Tracy and the kids, about Nathan Shaw, about me getting myself stuck in the middle of everything. I tell him I've convinced Tracy to meet up with me.

"Do you think it's a trap?" I say.

"Does it matter?" he says.

Is this a trick question? Knowing Burke, it's a trick question. "No."

"Correct. Whether or not it's a trap, you have to be *prepared* for a trap." He motions me over and positions me inside the rectangle. "I want to get a sense of scale," he says.

"Are you building, like, a bunker?"

"You'll need a firearm. But what's the most suitable choice? That's the question."

Of course a gun is his first suggestion. This was such a mistake, asking him for his opinion. "I don't need a gun, Burke. I don't want a gun."

Hard pass. I've never fired a gun or even held one in my hand. I don't want to shoot anybody or anything or accidentally myself. Guns basically scare the shit out of me. I'm not ashamed to admit it. Being scared of guns is just common sense.

Burke chuckles like I'm joking. "Something lightweight and compact, probably, but with enough punch to finish the job. Let's narrow down the options."

"No gun, Burke. Nope."

"Do you know what nobody ever said? 'I wish I hadn't had a gun handy, just in case.' Nobody ever said that."

I'm fairly sure that's not true. There have to be lots of people who wish, after the fact, they hadn't had a gun handy. I won't win an argument with Burke, though, especially not one about guns.

"I better bounce," I say. "I'll catch you later."

"Make sure you meet in a public place. Make sure you reconnoiter the location beforehand. Identify all potential exfil options."

"Okay."

Burke smiles as he rubs his hands up and down the legs of his jeans. I'm not sure if he's rubbing his hands gleefully or just wiping off some dirt.

"I can't wait to hear all about it," he says.

36

Wednesday arrives. I'm stressed but ready. I borrow Preston's car. I'm not taking any chances with mine, which Nathan knows, or even with Salvador's SUV, which—a slight possibility—he might.

From Preston's office to the strip mall I take a route so convoluted I literally lose my own bearings a couple of times. I hop onto the highway, then back off at the very next exit. I cut across two lanes of traffic at the last second and make three U-turns in a row. I never take my eyes off my mirrors. If someone is following me, they're invisible.

I get to the strip mall twenty minutes early. I park down from the former Blockbuster, outside the Verizon store again. I back into the space so I can see every car that enters the lot.

Eleanor gets there a few minutes later and stations herself at the other end of the strip mall. She's borrowed her grandma's Lincoln Continental. It's massive, a brown battleship with one cracked headlight. Eleanor's face looks tiny in comparison, like she's a dashboard toy and not the actual driver.

I text her a thumbs-up. She texts me back an eye-roll emoji. Her job is to stay alert and let me know if she notices anything sketchy. Nathan or one of his thug-ass friends still might find some way to sneak up on me, but at least Eleanor will make it tougher for them.

Right on time, five minutes before the NA meeting is supposed to start at one, Tracy's Volvo turns into the lot. She parks in front of the former Blockbuster and gets out of her car. She hasn't brought the kids along this time. Is that good or bad? Does it mean this is more or less likely a trap? Either way, I realize, Pearl and Jack are at home alone with Nathan. They're home alone with him because of me. Am I making all this worse?

I wait until I'm sure that nobody followed Tracy, then walk over.

"Hi," I say.

She shakes her head in an *I can't believe I'm doing this* way.

"Do you want to sit down and get some coffee?" I say. "There's a place across the street."

"No. Come on. Inside."

"Here?"

She doesn't bother answering and pushes through the door into the former Blockbuster. I hesitate. I don't understand how we'll have a conversation during an NA meeting. Sit in the back row and whisper? Or is Tracy only giving me the next two minutes before the meeting starts?

Another problem is the guy who runs the meeting, Willie Nelson with the braids and the hugging. If he recognizes me . . . that will remind Tracy that I've been basically stalking her. Not exactly the foot I want to start off on.

I follow Tracy inside. The folding chairs are out. A dozen or so people mill around. There's Willie Nelson, on the far side of the room. Of course he hurries straight over. He gives Tracy a bear hug that she endures. He tries to give me a bear hug but I hold him off.

"Sorry," I say. "Cracked rib."

"Charlie," he says, holding out his hand for me to shake. "Glad to have you."

He doesn't recognize me. Or he recognizes me and honors my anonymity. Either way, I'll take it.

"Can we use the office in back a minute, Charlie?" Tracy says. "He needs some one-on-one before the group thing."

"All yours," he says.

She motions. I follow. Through a door by the coffee urn and cookies, down a short hallway. At the end of the hallway is a fire exit propped open with a cinder block. A small office is to the left. A couple of folding chairs, a file cabinet, the heavy funk of old smoke.

Tracy takes one of the chairs. I take the other one. Back here I can't hear anything going on in the main room, not even a murmur of people talking. What I can hear, through the propped-open fire exit, are the tires of a car crunching over gravel in the alley behind the strip mall. The car doesn't stop, but I don't relax. I'm not loving this location. It's not a public place. It's way too alley-adjacent.

"What's wrong?" Tracy says.

"Nothing." But then I decide to be straight with her. It can't hurt. No, that's not right. It absolutely can hurt, but it also might be the only thing that helps. "I'm worried this could be, like, another trap."

She studies me for what seems like a long time, probably only a couple of seconds. "Yeah. I get that."

I don't know if that's meant to be reassuring. It's not, really. "Thanks for meeting up with me."

"This place is NA. Narcotics Anonymous," she says. "I come to meetings every week. Did you already know that?"

I stick with honesty and nod. "How long have you been coming to meetings?" I say.

"Not long enough."

"It's none of my business."

She laughs. "That's funny."

I nod. "Yeah."

Neither one of us says anything for a long time. I realize it's on me. She's fine to let my five minutes pass and run out the clock. There are so many questions I want to ask her. Do I start at the top of the list or work my way up from the bottom? I decide I better start at the top.

"Why does he do it?" I say. "How can someone hurt their own kids?"

"How can someone hurt anyone's kids?"

"Yeah."

She shrugs. "I used to tell myself . . . I used to tell myself lots of different things. It was just his temper. I just needed to make sure he didn't lose it. He had a bad childhood. He just needed to work through that. It was me he was really mad at. So once I got clean, he'd take it easier on Pearl and Jack."

Another car crunches slowly over the gravel in the alley. Closer and closer, slower and slower. For a second the car sounds like it's stopping right outside the propped-open door.

I tense. I should've had Salvador watch the back of the strip mall. Nathan and his thug-ass friends could come through the back door. Eleanor, out front, would have no idea what's happening to me.

Tracy's expression remains impassive. She's either not concerned that Nathan might show up or resigned that he will. I wish I knew which. The car keeps going. It crunches past and is gone. Tracy's expression, I realize, reminds me of Jack and Pearl sitting on the bench—gazing off at nothing, waiting to get through a lifetime they've already lived a hundred times.

"I've tried to stop him. I've tried everything. Sometimes I just make it worse." She takes a deep breath and checks her phone. "Time's up. How do you think you can help me?"

I still don't have a good answer. Maybe I won't ever have one. Maybe all I can do is pay attention and listen, let Tracy show me the way.

"What is Nathan into?" I say. "Drugs?"

"Of course. And other things. Who knows?"

"Why haven't you reported him to CPS? Because you're scared of him?"

"No." She sighs. She still hasn't, not once, looked me straight in the eye. "I'm scared of him, yes. And you should be scared of him too, a lot more than you are. But that's not why."

"Okay."

She finally looks me straight in the eye. It's a little bit like getting punched in the face again. I even feel my nose throb. I don't know if she's furious at me or Nathan or CPS or everything, the whole world.

"Don't you understand?" she says. "I can't go to CPS. They'll take Jack and Pearl away. I'm a junkie. I've been clean almost two years, but that won't matter. In the eyes of the law, I'll always be a junkie. I won't let them take my children away from me."

In the eyes of the law you'll always be a junkie. I hear Nathan's voice. I hear the threat he's made to Tracy. But I worry it's a valid threat. The best argument I can think of is *Maybe not?* Because the authorities really *might* take Pearl and Jack away from her. Maybe not permanently, maybe not for long, but I doubt that matters to Tracy. She's not going to risk losing her kids for a minute. And I'm not going to suggest it, not the way she's looking at me right now.

I don't blame Tracy. Mostly not. A tiny part of me wonders if she's being selfish. Would it be so terrible for the authorities to take the kids away from Tracy, if it meant getting them away from Nathan? Isn't anywhere else, for Pearl and Jack, better than where they are now?

But I'm not a parent and have no idea what I'd do in Tracy's place. And then she wipes away a tear with the heel of her hand and that tiny part of me shuts up.

"I just can't do it," she says.

"It's okay. Can you leave Nathan? Take the kids with you?"

She wipes away another tear and laughs. "No. *That's* because I'm scared of him. Listen. Do you know what you are to Nathan? You're mildly annoying. A buzzing fly. And look what he did to you. When I told him about you, he didn't even react. He made a mental note, like he needed to remember to pick up dry cleaning. And look what he did to you. What do you think he'll do to me? To Pearl and Jack?"

"Maybe you and the kids can just, like, disappear."

"He'll find us."

"You could go to some other city, some other state. You could go all the way across the country."

"Someone will find us. They're his children too. I'll be kidnapping them. That's what it will be, legally. That's the way he'll make it look."

And if she tries to explain her situation to the authorities . . . they'll bring in CPS, she'll risk losing her kids. "What about a lawyer? While you're lying low, the lawyer gets it all sorted out somehow."

"How am I supposed to get the money for a lawyer? I don't have access to any money. Nathan makes sure of that."

"I don't know. There have to be lawyers who—"

"How am I supposed to get the money to lie low? Where will we live? I don't have family. The friends I had, from my old life, I'm just going to show up out of the blue? Hi, it's me and my two young children and my extremely dangerous, fucked-up situation!"

"Maybe I can get together some money for you." How am *I* supposed to do that? I'm not exactly flush. But at least it's something tangible, a concrete goal I can work on. "That's a start."

She checks her phone again and stands. "I've got to go."

"Wait. Just—"

"Why are you doing this?" she says.

It's the obvious question for her to ask. But what do I say? By now I understand how complicated the answer is. I want to tell Tracy the truth. If I'm going to get her to trust me, I *need* to tell her the truth.

"When I saw those cigarette burns on Pearl and Jack," I say, "when I realized what was happening to them . . . I couldn't just walk away from that. Kids don't have a choice. Kids are just at the, like, mercy of the world, you know? But . . . it's also more than that. It's about me too, not just them."

Tracy watches me. I've finally said something, I think, that's interesting to her. "What?"

I could tell her about my mom, about the afternoon on the school playground when I found out my mom had died. How on that day the earth tore open and I fell in. How something in *me* tore open—a hole that was even bigger the next day, even bigger the day after that. I'm not comparing what I went through to what Pearl and Jack are going through—definitely, definitely not—but Eleanor was right that first time, calling it. I do have extra feelings for those kids because of who I am.

But it's more than that too.

"This is the first time in my life I've done anything that matters," I say. "This is the first time in my life *I've* mattered. I'm a person I want to be. And I will do whatever it takes to help you and your kids."

Tracy is silent for a moment, then laughs again. She sits back down. "Oh, my God," she says. "My life is so fucked. How old are you?"

"Twenty-three. And I know it doesn't make a lot of sense, but—"

"There's one girl I know, from middle school. We were best friends, but her family moved away, to Tucson. We were like sisters. Maybe she's still there, in Tucson."

It takes me a second to process what she's saying. "Good," I say. "Okay. She's somewhere. We can find out where. That's a start too."

"But I have to get us out first. It's impossible. The farm where we're living now, it's ten miles outside the city, in the middle of nowhere."

"It's not impossible."

"Nathan is always around. Someone is always around. Some of the dirtbags he does business with, they live on the property too. One of them owns it. Nathan has them watching me. He never lets me take Pearl and Jack out by myself anymore."

I'm guessing I've had firsthand experience with two of the dirtbags Nathan does business with. Big Beard, Scrawny Drunk.

"You should just leave us alone," she says. "He'll kill you next time. Please. I don't want that on me. You can't help us."

She keeps saying that, how I can't help her, but why did she text me in the first place? Why did she agree to meet me? She might be truly sorry for what happened to me, but there has to be more to it than that.

"Is it getting worse?" I say. "What Nathan is doing to the kids?"

She looks down at her hands like they belong to someone else. She's digging a thumb deeply and what must be painfully into the other palm. "You can't help us," she says, but more softly this time.

"It's not impossible. We can figure out a way to get you out."

"I can't take my car. It's in his name. He'll report it stolen. He'll find us."

"I'll pick you up. I'll drive you to the bus station, the airport. Wherever you want to go. I'll drive you to Arizona if that's safest."

"You're going along, everything's fine," she says, even more softly, her thumb digging and digging. "You're worried about all the little things, the usual things. And then you look up and you don't understand where you are. You don't understand how you got there."

37

S he asked you for money?" Eleanor says. "That's not unsavory at all."
We're at the coffee place down the street from the former Blockbuster.
I'm still trying to get my head around the conversation I just had with Tracy.
It's a lot to absorb.

"She didn't ask me for anything," I say.

"I'm not giving you any money, if that's what you're thinking. I don't have any money."

"Your rearview mirror is attached with chopsticks and duct tape. I'm not thinking you have any money. But you have to help me figure out a plan. To get Tracy and the kids away from Nathan. From those dirtbags at the farm."

"What?"

"I know it'll be tricky. But we can figure it out."

"Tricky? Try ridiculously dangerous. And literally insane."

"It's the only way. I have to get them out."

"You've been to the ER once already. You may recall that?"

"I do, but—"

"I would rather not have to take you to the ER again. Call me lazy. And you could end up worse than the ER."

"I'm not insane. That's why I need a good plan. You have to help me figure out one."

"Are you listening to me? Are you listening to yourself?"

"Yes."

She takes a deep breath. "I have to get back to work."

"We'll figure out a plan. I'll text you later."

She leaves. I drive to Haunted Frontier and make my way to the Abandoned Mine Train. I dig into Salvador's stash of index cards and break a pack open. Preston starts every project by making a list. It is, according to Preston, the secret to success. I'm willing to give it a shot.

First: the money. If I can't scrounge up some money for Tracy—which, again, she never asked me to do—the rest of any plan is pointless. Tracy isn't going to take her kids and just jaunt off across the country without some kind of cushion.

Second: how much money do they need? Tracy didn't say and I didn't think to ask. She and the kids need as much money as possible, basically. How much money can I get? That's the real question. And I don't have much time. Nathan moving the family out to the farm, not letting Tracy go out with the kids—that's disturbing. The life Pearl and Jack have been living has been bad enough. It's not getting better.

At the moment I have two hundred and eighty-four dollars to my name. My rent isn't due for another two weeks, but forget about the rent anyway. Burke might, possibly, give me a onetime grace period. If he doesn't, I can find a place to crash for a few weeks. Forget the rent. The two hundred and eighty-four dollars is what I'm starting with.

Who can I ask for money? Nguyen and Mallory: no. They're just as broke as me. Felice? She still hasn't texted me back. Preston is tapped out too. He and Leah are saving for the wedding, for their first kid. He has a list, I'm sure. He'd come through for me if I ever got in serious personal trouble, but anything short of a life-threatening illness, with a doctor's notarized diagnosis to confirm, will not meet his standards. I can already see his scowl, hear his scoff, when I tell him why I'm asking for money now.

I call him anyway. I explain what's happening with Tracy. I *don't* mention that I'll also have to extract her from a dangerous situation on a secluded farm. Even so, and as expected, Preston scowls (I can tell, even on the phone) and scoffs.

"You asking me for money again?" he says. "Already? I just loaned you seventy-five dollars. And you want money so you can give it away to a complete stranger? I don't have more money to loan you. I definitely don't have more money to loan you for you to give away to a complete stranger."

"However much you can do," I say. "I'll pay you back."

"When? In your next life?"

"It's her chance for one, Preston. For a next life right now. For her and her kids."

"This is exactly what I'm always trying to tell you."

"What are you always exactly trying to tell me, Preston?"

"That you have to get serious! You have to be serious! Do you know why I started calling you Hardly when we were kids?"

"Do I remember?" He won't let me forget. The first thing Preston does, when he introduces me to a new person, is explain why he started calling me Hardly. "Yes, Preston, I remember. Because, according to you, I hardly ever try hard."

"And because you hardly ever use your head! But you know what? I was mistaken. Instead of Hardly, I should have called you Never."

"And you're, like, some paragon of success? *You* should get serious, Preston. You're not going to design the beautiful and elegantly efficient cities of the future. You're going to keep grubbing around in cubicles the rest of your life, complaining about your job and sucking up to sleazy developers."

He goes quiet. He's probably taking his glasses off and cleaning the lenses. He's powering on the warp drive of his self-control and admiring himself for it.

"How much do you need?" Preston knows just how to disarm and disable me, to trot away on his high horse, across the moral high ground. "I really don't have much, unfortunately. I think the most I can come up with is six or seven hundred. Will that help?"

"Yes," I say. "Thank you."

"I'll have it tomorrow. Now bring my car back already."

"Preston."

"What?"

"I take that back. What I said earlier."

"I have no idea what you're talking about," he says, and kills the call.

Okay. I'm up to almost a thousand dollars. I'm making progress. I open a fresh pack of index cards, blue instead of white, and turn my attention to the rest of the plan. How do I get Tracy and the kids away from Nathan?

It seems fairly straightforward. Tracy will pick a time when Nathan is gone and I'll handle any dirtbags left behind. A diversion—that's what I need. Something that moves the dirtbags out of the way so I can drive in, pick up Tracy and the kids, drive back out.

What kind of diversion? I'll have to think about that. I'll have to get more information from Tracy. In the meantime, back to the money question. A thousand dollars won't get Tracy and the kids far.

I hear the sound of distant panting. I hear a stumble and a squawk of pain. A minute later Salvador careens onto the loading platform. He sees me using the index cards and frowns. *He* is master of the cards.

I hand over the Sharpie and the blue cards. I tell him we're making a list of people who might loan me money to help Tracy and the kids.

"Excellent!" He uncaps the Sharpie and prepares to write down the first name.

"I'm ready," Salvador says. "You can start whenever you want."

"I'm thinking," I say, a little testier than I intend.

"Sorry."

"It's okay."

"I have some money you can have."

"Don't worry about it."

"Really!"

I can't take Salvador's money. He can't have much anyway. He's sixteen years old, makes even less per hour than me, and only works a few shifts a week.

"How much do you have?" I say.

"I'm not sure exactly. Around four thousand dollars."

I swivel around. Salvador is sitting cross-legged on a crate of dynamite, Sharpie still poised. "*How* much?" I say.

"Around four thousand dollars. It's my robot fund."

"Your what?"

"For robot club. Not the official-official robot club at my school. The robot club I'm going to start, for people who aren't invited to join the official-official robot club. The club I start is going to be more democratic and anyone who loves robots can join."

Four thousand dollars. Wow. *Wow*. I was hoping, best-case scenario, that Tracy might not laugh in my face when I offered her a thousand. Four thousand dollars! That's a genuine fresh start for Tracy and Pearl and Jack, a genuine shot at a new life. But I can't take a sixteen-year-old kid's robot money, right?

"I'll pay you back," I say.

"You don't have to!" he says.

"No. It's just a loan. I'll pay you back."

He hops off the crate of dynamite and to his feet, one smooth and fluid—for Salvador—motion. "This is excellent! I'll go get it now. I have my own bank account."

"Are you sure about this, Salvador?" I can't believe it's going to be this easy. And then I'm worried that it's going to be so easy. It's suspicious, right? This kind of good fortune? Or maybe the better way to look at it: you have to seize good fortune when you have the chance.

"I'm sure!" Salvador says. He blows out and a second later I hear him tripping and skidding and tumbling happily down the mountain.

38

Tracy told me not to call or text, under no circumstances whatsoever, so I have to sit on the good news about the money. I don't know when she'll get in touch again, which is stressful.

A day goes by. Nothing from Tracy yet. I can't really work on a plan to get her and the kids away from Nathan until I have more specific information about her situation, the logistics of it. I hit up Eleanor to talk through some general ideas, but Driver Verification is digitizing old records and she has to work late every night this week. Nothing from Tracy on Friday. After my shift, though, as I'm walking to the parking lot, Felice finally texts me back.

Come say hi

Felice buzzes me into her building. I ride the elevator up to the top floor. I'm feeling optimistic. Four thousand dollars. This is happening. I'll figure out a way to get Tracy and the kids away from Nathan, then send them off on their fresh start. I'm going to make this happen.

When Felice opens the door of her apartment, she frowns. My face is in a lot better shape than it was a week and a half ago, but it doesn't take a former private investigator to see I've been banged around fairly gravely.

"What do we have here?" she says.

"Nathan knew I was tailing him. He had a couple of his guys jump me in an alley. But I'm good. It was just a warning. I'm good now. Everything is better than good now."

She touches two fingers against my scraped cheek. "You've been to a doctor?"

"Yes. It's just a cracked rib and my nose broke the best way a nose can break. But listen to this. Tracy got in touch with me afterward. We talked, then she agreed to meet up. Wow. I have to catch you up on some major developments."

"Go take a shower."

"Sorry. I just got off work."

"You don't say."

While I'm soaping up, Felice comes into the bathroom to brush her teeth. Her shower is all glass, so I can watch her. She's wearing a flashy black dress, shorter than her usual business skirt, with a glimmer of silver woven through the threads. Flashy heels too, three or four inches high, and a thin chain I've never seen before looped around her ankle.

Maybe I should be crushed that I'm Felice's mere fallback plan when her date doesn't go well. But look at her. I'm honored to be her fallback plan. And I'm also glad to be here for other, more important reasons. She's my secret weapon against Nathan. Anything I might miss, she definitely won't.

"Okay," I say, "so first of all, there's no doubt now that Nathan is an extreme piece of shit. Tracy is scared of him. But that's not why she hasn't gone to CPS before now. Or not the only reason."

Felice swishes and spits. "Are you clean yet?"

I'm just now starting to rinse off. It takes a minute to scrub away the sweat and grime from Haunted Frontier. "Almost done."

"I didn't ask if you were done. I asked if you were clean."

She steps out of her shoes. The black dress slinks to her feet. Then bra, then panties. She slides naked into the shower with me. I've had sex in the shower a few times. It's always less porny and more awkward than you imagine it will be. You have to do it standing up for one thing, which isn't ideal unless the two people are exactly complementary heights, and you're always bumping into knobs and faucets or knocking over shampoo bottles. You're always too hot if you're right under the water and too chilly if you're not.

With Felice, though, the shower sex is amazing. The rainfall head is mounted in the ceiling, which helps. And she's the perfect height for me, or me for her. A few times my rib lets me know it's still cracked, but I don't let a few minor aches and pains slow me down.

Sometimes it's easy to forget Felice is so much older than me. I don't want to forget, though. The fine lines, the texture of her lips. Her skin is more interesting than that of chicks my age. Am I so into her because she's twenty years older than me and smoking hot? Or am I so into her just because she's smoking hot? Either way, it's a win for me.

After a while we dry off, more or less, and finish up in bed. Felice reaches for the water bottle on the nightstand and smiles. "Well," she says.

I start to feel guilty, like before, but then I remember what Eleanor said. I can have an hour like this every now and then. It powers up my heart. It makes me even more committed to helping Pearl and Jack.

"So can I fill you in now about the kids?" I ask Felice. "Get your take?"

"You're not tired?"

"It doesn't matter."

I fill her in. We're facing each other, heads on our pillows, only a few inches apart. Felice's expression is even more inscrutable than usual. A clean page, a blank slate. As she gazes into my eyes I'm not sure if she's searching the depths of my soul or not thinking about me at all, just remembering that she forgot to floss.

"So what are you thinking?" I say when I'm done.

Felice runs a fingernail lightly but sharply, a little painfully, down the center of me, all the way from my throat to just below my belly button. I think about a surgeon drawing a line with a scalpel and then peeling back the patient's skin and flesh, like opening a pair of balcony doors.

She gives me a peck on the lips and slides out of bed. "Now I need a shower."

This is ominous. I didn't expect a burst of wild enthusiasm from Felice, a fist pump like Salvador's, but . . . I've come a long way, I'm so close to actually, legitimately helping Pearl and Jack. Shouldn't Felice be at least a tiny bit impressed?

I follow her into the bathroom. "I know I've got a lot more to figure out," I say. "I was hoping maybe you could, you know, provide some of your usual excellent guidance."

She cranks the hot water and steam billows. She tilts her face up to the rainfall head and closes her eyes.

"Tell me what you're thinking," I say. "I mean, I'd appreciate it."

She breathes out, the faintest of sighs, the first sign of what's happening behind that inscrutable expression. "You remember what I said?" she says. "The very first time we met?"

"You still think this is a bad idea?"

"It's a worse idea now."

"How can you say that? Have you even been listening?"

"Look at you. Broken rib, broken nose. And that was just a warning? Now there's a farm, middle of nowhere. Some kind of drug operation, probably? You think they don't have guns out there?"

"It won't come to that. Not if I have the right plan."

She finishes her shower without saying anything. I hand her a towel, then she smooths on lotion. One variety of lotion for her face, then a different variety for her legs. I follow her back to the bedroom. She pulls on pajama pants and a faded T-shirt. CAL STATE NORTHRIDGE. I feel dumb standing there naked, so back I go to the bathroom for my boxer shorts and T-shirt.

She's in the living room now. I take a seat on the sofa. She pours two shots of some kind of whiskey and brings one to me. I take a sip. Just the fumes are enough to strip paint off a wall. Felice sits and faces me. Without any makeup on, she looks older and younger at the same time, a version of her superimposed on top of a different one, past Felice and future Felice, both of them complete strangers to me.

"I'm not giving up on those kids," I say.

"You want me to be straight with you."

"I do. But—"

"Then I'll be straight with you. You have a fantasy. You're the hero. You're the hero who saves the day all by himself. Men do that, they have that fantasy. They think they're the white knight on the horse, charging in. It's fine, I suppose. If the man understands what's the fantasy and what isn't."

For a second I'm so stunned I legitimately can't form a thought or a sentence. "*What? My fantasy?*"

She sips her drink. We could be having a conversation about the weather. Been hot lately, hasn't it? "Am I wrong?" she says.

"Yes. One hundred percent, you're wrong."

"If you say so."

I remember what I told Tracy. I remember how good it feels to finally be doing something with my life that *matters*. But that doesn't mean this is my *fantasy*.

"Not one hundred percent, maybe," I say, "I admit that. But, like, ninety-five percent. This is very simple. This is about two kids who are getting hurt by their evil fucker of a father and somebody needs to do something to help them. It's that simple."

"You're a good person," Felice says. "You're trying to be a good person. Most people never even bother. But a good person can be a foolish person."

Fifteen minutes ago Felice and I were in bed, smiling and kissing and rolling around. Now she's dead serious, solid ice. It's like when you sit on the remote accidentally and the DVR skips ahead ten or twenty minutes. No, like when it jumps to an entirely different show.

"You're going to get yourself killed," she says. "You're going to get those children and their mother killed. Don't do this. Let it go."

I stand, but then I don't know what to do next. Storm out? Start pacing? Play it cool and refill Felice's drink for her? I'm still spinning. I can do this. I'm so close. I can come up with the right plan. There are risks, but Pearl and Jack are more at risk if I do nothing.

Felice thinks I'm the same person I was when I met her. That's the problem. She doesn't understand who I've become. I'm a long way from that first open house, when I came to her with absolutely no idea what I was doing.

I sit back down. I knock back the rest of the whiskey. It detonates like a bomb. "Thank you for being straight with me, Felice," I say.

The warmth returns to her eyes. Some of it, at least. She puts a hand on my leg. "Let me tell you a story."

"Okay."

"When I was young, I . . ." She pauses. "I wasn't that young. An opportunity was presented to me. I should have known better. I did. I did know better. But I was a hardheaded girl. Can you imagine that?"

I'm supposed to smile, so I do. I know where she's going with this.

"And I didn't have anyone who cared enough to give me a good hard shake. To wake me up."

"I'm not giving up on those kids."

"Listen to me. You need to go back to Child Services. Tell them what you know."

"CPS? They're hopeless. I told you that."

"Mostly they are, maybe. But the right person is there. The right person at the right desk. There always is. You want to keep pushing? Push there. You'll get some traction eventually. It's a lot safer, for everyone."

For the second time in a few days, after years and years of never letting my feathers get ruffled, I'm pissed off. I'm pissed off because Felice, I'm realizing, is like every other person in the world who sees a problem and just wants to walk the other way.

Pearl and Jack are basically in *hell* right now. He's six. She's seven. What in their life have they done to deserve this? And it's not getting any better for them. Tracy told me that without telling me that. She's desperate. Why else would she even consider the possibility that someone like me could be her way out? And Felice wants to talk about *desks*.

"How long will that take, do you think?" I say. "For me to get some traction at CPS?"

"I don't know that."

"And you can guarantee a happy ending? You're sure it all works out?"

"Of course not."

"They'll take her kids away from her. That's the best-case scenario."

"Maybe they should take her kids away from her."

"What matters, I guess, is that I can feel good about myself. I can say I've done everything I can, right?"

"You have done everything you can."

"That's not true."

She smiles and takes my hand. She kisses my palm and presses it against her cheek. Her eyes are fully warm again. I can feel the beat of my heart rippling through my cracked rib, the mild pain like the *tap tap tap* of a hammer against a nail. It doesn't take a genius to recognize where this is going.

"I'm going to bed," Felice says. "We should say goodbye now."

39

It's close to two in the morning when the elevator drops me at the bottom of Felice's building. I get in my car and hit my one-hitter. Already, though, I'm cooling down. I'm not mad at Felice anymore. I never really was. She's doing what she has to do. I'm doing what I have to do. I'm not too brokenhearted either. Face it, sooner or later she was going to dump my ass. I handled it well and didn't make a scene. I kissed her on the cheek and departed with my dignity intact. My only regret: I didn't think to thank her, sincerely, for helping me, for wanting to help me. Without Felice, where would I be now?

I start the car and get moving. Last thing I need is for a cop to roll up on me and ask what I'm doing out here at two in the morning. It makes me laugh, the story I could tell. I'd have to start at the beginning. *So I had this parking ticket I needed to deal with . . . no, let me back up. I was just living my life, extremely content, then . . .*

I drive home. What if Felice is right? I allow myself to ask that question once and only once. I answer that question once and only once: *No.* The previous me would waffle, would let doubt wish and wash him back and forth. And then finally he'd do nothing. He'd keep on keeping on. But that's not me anymore.

When I get home, I flop into bed. I try to sleep but I'm wondering when Tracy will get in touch with me. She's probably just waiting for the perfect time, being careful that Nathan doesn't find out she's talking to me. It's possible, of course, that he *has* found out about me. I don't want to think about what he might do to her, to the kids. What he might already have done.

Later that morning I'm in the kitchen, scrounging for breakfast, when my phone buzzes with Tracy's number. I bolt back to my room and close the door behind me.

"Tracy?"

"I can't do this. It's too dangerous."

"I found some money for you. Four thousand dollars."

"He'll find us."

"You have to get out of there. You have to get your kids out of there."

Silence. Then: "Four thousand dollars?"

I can't tell if she thinks that's a lot or not a lot. "Yes."

"How long will that last us?"

"I don't know. A while, at least, right? Until you can figure out the next step."

More silence. I know she hasn't hung up only because I can hear her breathing. "Thank you," she says. "I'm a bitch. Thank you for getting the money. I don't know why you're doing this."

It's not a question this time, I notice. It's not *Why are you doing this?* My heart pumps faster. She's made the leap.

"Do you know in advance when Nathan will be gone?" I say.

"Sometimes. It depends. Yes. But I told you. The others are always around. You can't just drive up and honk your horn. Someone is always watching me."

"How many of them are there? I need to know exactly."

"It depends. Three, four. Always two. Two at a minimum."

"Is there ever a time when Nathan's gone and there are just the minimum two left?"

"Maybe. Yes."

Okay. It's not ideal. Ideal would be Nathan and his dirtbags absent from the farm for a long period of time. But I can work with this. I'll just need to come up with a diversion—something foolproof that distracts the dirtbags long enough for me to dart in and pick up Tracy and the kids.

"They'll hurt you," Tracy says. "You don't understand what kind of people they are."

After what happened in the alley, I have a fairly good idea. "I'm going to avoid that. I'm going to avoid them."

"You don't understand. A couple of days ago, some teenagers were playing paintball, trespassing on the edge of the property. Three of Nathan's guys went after them. It was like rabid dogs. They would have killed those teenagers if they'd caught them. They would have killed them for fun. That's what Nathan said."

Obviously I don't love the challenge of avoiding hair-trigger dirtbags who'd murder teenage paintballers for fun. But murderous and hair-trigger might work to my advantage, might be the key to a successful diversion.

"Tell me about the farm," I say. "Like, how many buildings? Where are you and the kids?"

"We're in the main house. There's a barn. A couple of sheds. Oh. An old double-wide too. One of Nathan's guys lives there."

"Can you text me the address so I can check it out on Google?"

"Yes. But—"

"I'm going to figure this out. When's the next time Nathan will be gone? Do you know? And when just the two guys are around."

"I don't know. It could be tomorrow. It could be a week from now. I won't know till the last minute."

"Call me," I say. "As soon as you know."

"I don't understand why you're doing this," she says again, then the call goes dead.

40

On the drive to work that afternoon—checking my mirrors every two seconds to make sure I'm not being followed, brainstorming ways to rescue a woman and her abused kids from a compound filled with murderous drug dealers—I'm suddenly blown away by how all this feels so . . . *normal*. Like, you know, just another Saturday for Hardly Reed.

Why am I so calm? Is it good or bad that I'm so calm? I know what Felice would say, but she's wrong. She's wrong. That's becoming clearer and clearer to me. Or I'm thinking about it less and less. Same difference, right?

My phone *bloops*. Tracy has sent me the pin—the farm's address. I hang a hard right into a Best Buy parking lot and click on Google satellite view. I scroll around. The farm really is in the middle of nowhere. Fields on three sides, woods and a pond on the fourth. I see it's going to be tougher than I imagined to sweep up Tracy and the kids without being spotted. The main house sits at the end of a long, long driveway, and the driveway breaks off from a long, long private road. The distance from the public road to the house is close to half a mile.

Barn. Sheds. I don't see the double-wide. It must have arrived after the most recent shot from the satellite. The woods to the west of the compound spread all the way out to a county highway. The teenagers must have been paintballing out there, in the woods on the opposite side of the pond. That's the spot for the diversion. It's roughly half a mile from the main house to the western edge of the property. If I can draw the dirtbags out there, it should give me enough time. Maybe I should tell Tracy to slip out of the house and meet me at the end of the driveway. I don't want the dirtbags to hear my car. But I worry about Pearl and Jack. They're such little dudes. Will they be able to make it that far, fast enough? I hope so. I'll make sure Tracy travels light. No suitcases. She can carry Jack if she has to.

I'm tempted to blow off work— I can call Duttweiler and inform him that my toenail fungus is spreading—and scope out the farm in person. But it's too secluded and I can't take the chance, even in Preston's car. Nathan might drive right past me. On a county two-lane highway, he wouldn't be able to miss me.

The main thing, the huge thing: I have to come up with a diversion. It has to be substantial enough to get the attention of the dirtbags, half a mile away. That's a substantial diversion. And it has to draw *all* the dirtbags away from the main house, not just *some*. If one of the dirtbags stays behind, it's a problem.

I yank on my boots and pin the sheriff's badge to my vest. Salvador isn't working tonight and a couple of new hires didn't show for their first shift, so I have to make do without a deputy. I deliver the first group of guests to the Townfolk Ghouls. While the Townfolk Ghouls moan and claw, I imagine I'm a dirtbag. I'm sitting in my double-wide. What rouses me? What gets me off my ass to go raging through the woods?

A car horn honking? No. Dirtbag in his trailer wouldn't hear a horn honking, or he'd just think it was coming from the county highway. Blasting music? Maybe. Some Jimmy Page, in honor of Eleanor's grandma. The music would have to be *loud,* though, to reach that far. I wish I knew how the dirtbags were alerted to the teenage paintballers. I'd text Tracy back and ask if she knows, but I'm once again under strict instructions. Do not text. Do not call.

The night's fourth group of guests is small but extra obnoxious: three sunburned and swole frat dudes who think it's hilarious when they try to scare the scarers, bellowing and making faces at them. Waste of time. Nothing scares us. We work at Haunted Frontier. Our doom has already been sealed.

When did I start to hate this job? When did I start to realize that the life I've been living isn't enough *life* for me? I guess I know when, and why. Less clear is how I proceed from here. Once I drop Tracy and the kids off in Arizona, what then? Come back to . . . this? To bong rips and reruns of *The Office* and never being really sure, or really caring, what day of the week it is, what month of the year, what year of the decade? I don't think I can come back to this. Figuratively, I mean. Maybe literally too. Arizona is close to California. Head west, young man! It's not an original idea, but I've never seen the Pacific Ocean. What used to make me content won't do the trick anymore. I'm pretty sure about that.

Going back to college is a possibility. Preston is so obsessed about that. But I'm still paying off my first onerous debt. Do I want to pile on even more, and that on top of the four thousand I'm going to owe Salvador?

I wonder what it takes to get licensed as a private investigator. Don't laugh. Obviously I wouldn't be some brilliant detective who solves baffling murders, but I could grind, pay attention, listen closely to people when I talk to them. The private investigators I called before I met Felice charge crazy rates. I could charge half that and still, like, double my income. More importantly, I'd be doing something interesting and challenging that, you could argue, I'm not half bad at. Maybe I could specialize in cases that CPS can't handle.

Two of my frat dudes are now trying to wrestle Justin's squished eyeball out of his hand and/or hump him, apparently. The third dude snaps photos of them with, you guessed it, a flash.

"Please don't harass the ghouls," I tell them. "And no flash photography, please."

The frat dudes, you guessed it, ignore me. Justin manages to break free and escape with his eyeball. High fives all around.

"This way, pardners," I say, after the last of the Townfolk Ghouls have dispersed. Next up: Boot Hill.

Instead I lead the frat dudes down Main Street to the Old Town Jail. I usher them inside the empty, dark shell that has never, no matter what that aggravated guy last week insisted, been a part of the Haunted Frontier tour.

"Nobody ever lasts long in here," I say. "This is the most terrifying place on the frontier. You've been warned. Only yellow-bellied cowards try to escape."

They whoop and howl and nudge-wink each other about lasting all night. They call each other pussies. I back out, shut the door, and head to the old tinker shop. I don't know how long those idiots will stay inside an empty, dark shell of a building. Five minutes? Ten? It took me twenty-three years to walk out.

I change into my street clothes and pin the sheriff's badge to the HR corkboard. I'm crossing back past the split-rail entrance to Haunted Frontier, on my way to the parking lot, when Duttweiler spots me.

"Hardly!" he says.

"Hey."

"Where are you going? What's happening? Where's your group? Why—"

He keeps talking but I can't hear him—the first barrage of Let Freedom Ring explodes above Colonial America. The guests lined up for Haunted Frontier break away and go streaming toward the central hub. What's so irresistible about fireworks? You can watch them just fine from over here. You can hear them just fine. The instant the sky lights up in the distance, though, all the moths go flapping toward it.

Oh, wow, I realize. *Fireworks.* That's it, that easy.

41

The next morning I call Salvador to ask if he's withdrawn his robot cash from the bank.

"You got fired!" he says, aghast.

"No, I didn't. How did you hear about that already? I quit."

"Duttweiler had security remove you!"

"I quit very politely, Salvador. Duttweiler and I shook hands. Did you get the cash?"

"Yes!"

I drive over to his house. He and his mom live not too far from Eleanor and her grandma, but in a neighborhood that's up and coming, scruffy in a cool way as opposed to scruffy in a depressing way. From out front I text Salvador that I'm here. While I'm waiting, I call Eleanor.

"Can't talk," she says.

"When can you? We need to. How's your grandma? When's her next appointment?"

"Can't talk."

Salvador's mom, Mrs. Velasco, steps out of the house and heads to her car in the driveway. I've met her a couple of times when she had to pick up Salvador at work for one reason or another. I doubt she remembers me. She doesn't have any reason to. I give her a wave anyway.

She walks over. "You're Hardly?"

So she does remember me. Which might mean, I realize . . . uh-oh. Did Salvador talk to her? Did he tell her about the four thousand dollars he's loaning me? He's smarter than that, right? If Salvador told his mom about the four thousand dollars, this could be a very short, tense, and disastrous conversation.

"That's me," I say. "Hi. Hey."

Mrs. Velasco is around Felice's age, but nothing like Felice. She's tall, gangly, and uses her hands a lot, very enthusiastically. She laughs quickly and easily and noisily. You can see from where Salvador inherits his goofiness. On her, though, it works. It puts you at ease. I bet she sells the shit out of real estate.

"Well, well, well," she says, then laughs.

"Well, well, well," I agree nervously.

"I have something to say to you, buddy."

"Okay."

She punches me lightly in the shoulder. "Thank you for being cool to Salvador. I love that guy with the heat of a thousand suns, but I know he can be a little extra. He says you always pick him to be your deputy."

I nod, even though that's not exactly the truth. Close enough. "It's no big deal," I say.

"And you're helping him with his robot club idea?" She laughs again. "You know how you can really help him with his robot club idea? Talk him out of it, buddy. Salvador needs to be in a club with more than one member."

I laugh too. I relax—he didn't tell his mom about the four thousand dollars. But I also don't feel great about the kudos she's showering me with. They are fully undeserved. I remind myself I'm just borrowing the money and will pay it back somehow. I remind myself what the money is for and what's at stake.

She punches me again, invites me over to have dinner anytime I want, and drives off. Salvador, who must have been waiting for her to bounce, comes outside. He's sneakier than I give him credit for.

He hands me a fat envelope. I look inside. Forty one-hundred-dollar bills. Wow. Safe to say I never envisioned a moment in my life when I would hold an envelope full of hundred-dollar bills. I have never envisioned a moment when I would stuff that envelope in a cargo pocket of my shorts.

Salvador wants to know the plan. I give him the short version of what I've come up with. Wait till Nathan Shaw is away from the farm. Create a fireworks diversion to draw off the remaining dirtbags. Grab Tracy and the kids at the pickup point. Go, go, go.

"It's perfect!" he says.

I wish. Ha! But it's not terrible. I honestly think I can pull this off. I still have a lot to do, though, and I don't know how much time I have.

He frowns. "But how do we get into the pyro shed?"

The pyro shed at Beautiful America is where the park fireworks are stored, locked up twenty-four/seven. But we don't need the artillery shells the Freedom Ring crew blasts the sky with every night. We don't need to wow a whole crowd of spectators, just a few dirtbags.

"I'm not stealing the fireworks," I say. "I'm buying them. There's a stand out on the highway. I looked it up."

"Am I in charge of the diversion?"

"We'll see."

The real answer is that Salvador will *absolutely not* be in charge of the diversion. And I mean that with the heat of a thousand suns. Eleanor will handle the fireworks. I'll have to find some job again to keep Salvador far from the action. But I let him come with me to get the fireworks. It's a long drive and his SUV is much more comfortable than my clunker.

The fireworks stand sits just over the county line, on the edge of a vast, flat field of some crop that's been mowed down to brown stubble. The stand is an old cargo container painted bright yellow, with FAMILY FIREWORKS! in huge red letters across the front. Smaller red letters spell out BANG FOR YOU'RE BUCK! Three windows have been cut from the cargo container, with the metal flaps propped up like droopy eyelids.

A teenage girl around Salvador's age lounges in a lawn chair shoved up against the side of the container, in the only slice of shade for miles around.

"Hello, hello, hello," she says. "Step right up. Blah blah blah."

She's got long dirty blond hair or blond dirty hair and wears jean shorts over a one-piece bathing suit. She lights a Black Cat firecracker with a disposable lighter and chunks it toward the vicinity of a rabbit about fifteen feet away. *Bam!* Salvador and I jump, but the rabbit barely twitches.

"It's called operant conditioning," the chick says. "Are you not entertained?"

"Hi," Salvador says shyly. He's smitten.

"We need something loud and dazzling," I tell the chick. "Like something you'd see at a theme park, but we can afford it."

"Well, my friends, you've come to the right place." She chunks another Black Cat at the rabbit. *Bang.* The rabbit twitches and resumes eating weeds. The scene reminds me of a short story I read in college. I don't remember much about the story, but one image has stuck with me. A family driving to Florida during the Depression stops at a roadside stand and sees a pet monkey in a tree, picking fleas off itself and cracking them between its teeth.

"Wait here," the chick says.

She scoots her lawn chair out of the way and drags open the door of the cargo container. She has to squeeze inside because the space is packed so tightly, floor to ceiling, with colorful boxes. When she squeezes back out, a few seconds later, she's carrying a box about the size of a cinder block. On the label there's a photo of a snarling dog and the name of the product: Bite Your Tushy. She places the box at our feet. Both Salvador and I take a step back.

"This is my all-around favorite aerial cake," she says. "Two hundred grams of gunpowder, twenty-four shots and screaming tails. Six colors, lasts almost a full minute."

Sounds good to me. But I want to make sure Bite Your Tushy will do what we need it to do. "So our friends will be watching from, like, half a mile away. Is that too far?"

"Oohs and aahs are guaranteed. How many do you want? Fifty apiece or three for a hundred thirty-five."

I buy six. That should be enough. The more fireworks that Eleanor can fire off, and the longer she can keep the show going, the better—it's more likely the dirtbags will take notice and come running. At the same time, though, she'll need to bolt as quickly as possible. She can't just sit around popping off unlimited Bite Your Tushies or the dirtbags will catch her.

The chick licks her thumb and counts the money twice. She goes back into the cargo container and carries out five more boxes, plus a rubber-banded bundle of what looks like incense.

"Do you need punk sticks?" she says. "Five dollars. I don't recommend using an open flame for cakes. I speak on behalf of your extremities. Are you going to stake and tape?"

"Am I?"

She goes back inside and returns with six wooden stakes and a roll of electrical tape. "So the cakes don't tip over. Drive the stake into the ground, tape the cake to it. Another ten dollarinis, please and thank you."

"Okay. How far apart should they be spaced? The cakes?"

"Up to you, good sir. Two feet or twenty. Blast away."

I hand over the money and she returns to her lawn chair. She scissors a piece of her dirty blond dirty hair between two fingers and runs the flame of the lighter across the tips of it.

As Salvador and I load our purchases into the back of the SUV, as I'm wondering if aerial firework cakes ever spontaneously explode when your car hits a bump, he tugs on my sleeve.

"Do you think I should ask for her telephone number?" he whispers.

I look at him. He's not joking. It's hard to believe how dangerously clueless he is. Is Salvador who Felice sees when she looks at me? How accurate is the comparison? I try not to think about it.

"Maybe next time," I tell him.

"Right," he says, nodding. "Excellent idea. Exactly."

42

What am I missing? My approach, while I wait for Tracy's call, is to assume my plan has holes. That way I can find them and fix them. I study the satellite image of the farm. I pinch into the compound of buildings, then zoom back out and scroll around the edges. What detail have I overlooked? It's hard to see for sure, but there might be a gate where the private road becomes a driveway. Another good reason to have Tracy and the kids meet me there.

I'm focused mostly on the diversion. Tracy and the kids need—and I need—as much time as possible. How long will it take the dirtbags to run from the compound out to the farthest spot in the woods, where Eleanor will set off the fireworks? There's a small clearing not far from the county highway that should be perfect. I search "how to measure distance Google Maps." The exact distance from the compound to the clearing is six-tenths of a mile. The top result for "how fast can an average person run a mile" is nine to twelve minutes. Six-tenths of that is approximately five to seven minutes. So that's a total, round-trip, of ten to fourteen minutes, not counting how long the dirtbags spend hunting for the trespassers.

That should be enough time. It's not like any of the dirtbags, especially Big Beard, are world-class athletes. But how can I add some padding? Every minute counts. The longer I can keep the dirtbags hunting for the trespassers the better. What if Eleanor, before she sets off the fireworks, creates a trail for the dirtbags to follow. That will keep them busy for a while. Empty beer cans? A shoe. A flip-flop! A brightly colored flip-flop on a path leading in the wrong direction. *Look! They must've gone that way! C'mon!*

As luck would have it, there's a 7-Eleven just about a mile from Burke's house. I set the time on my phone and take off, sprinting for a while until I'm about to collapse, then shuffle-jogging the rest of the way. Eleven minutes and nine seconds. I buy a twelve-pack of the cheapest beer, Old Milwaukee. I buy a pair of cheap sunglasses for the dirtbags to find too. *Look! Sunglasses! This way!* I walk slowly back home.

Monday I try Eleanor again. "Why haven't you texted me back?" I say. "It's important."

"I told you. I'm working, then I have to work tonight too."

"What time do you get off?"

"Late. After ten, usually. I'll call you tomorrow."

Tomorrow won't work. Tracy could call at any time. I need to talk to Eleanor *now*. But I don't argue with her. A little before ten I just drive over to the municipal building. My idea is to wait in the parking lot and catch her on the way out. But there are only a couple of other cars in the lot and her beater isn't one of them.

I text her. Outside muni bldg where r u

A second later my phone rings. I hear her sigh. "I'm at home."

"Already?"

She sighs again. "Come over."

We sit on her front porch. I fire up a joint and pass it to her. The porch is old-fashioned and deep, wrapping around three sides of the house. I can picture a family sitting out here fifty or even maybe a hundred years ago. Would they be able to even imagine us, Eleanor and me? Would they even be able to imagine how the world has changed?

"So you got off early tonight?" I say.

"I didn't have to work tonight. I haven't had to work any nights."

"You were lying about that?" I'm baffled. "Why?"

She shrugs. From above us, the second floor, drums begin to pound and then a guitar solo screams out into the night.

"Headphones!" Eleanor yells up. A few second later the screaming guitar cuts off just as it reaches its crescendo.

"What do you mean you haven't had to work any nights?"

"Let's go for a walk. It's too hot and stuffy here."

We walk a few blocks to a park by her house. We sit on a bench by the fountain. I know this park and I know this fountain—it's usually out of order and bone dry. Tonight, for once, the water cascades and sparkles. The breeze here is cool and pleasant.

"So, okay, first," I say. "I came up with a diversion, to get the dirtbags away from the compound. Fireworks. You'll set them off, on the edge of the property, while I slide in from the main road."

I take her through the full plan, all the details. When I finish, she's quiet. I have no idea why she's in a mood, or why she lied about dodging me. I'm not seriously concerned, though, that she's not on board. Eleanor isn't scared. This is a chick who vaults eight-foot fences in the middle of the night and pepper-sprays bad dudes. And she's not Felice. Deep in that black goth heart of hers, Eleanor actually cares about Pearl and Jack. She's been through, with her mom, what I've been through. She understands why I'm doing this, why those kids need us.

"Give me some constructive criticism," I say. "This is a work in progress. Any ideas you have, I'm all ears."

"Hardly," she says. "I need you to really listen to me."

"Okay. I'm really listening."

"It's too dangerous."

"It's not. I promise. The clearing is like a hundred yards from the highway. You'll be back to your car and long gone before anyone shows up. Are you a candy-ass now?"

"That's not what I mean. I mean all of it's too dangerous. So many things could go wrong. *Everything* could go wrong. And if that happens . . ."

Is she really telling me what I think she's telling me? "So you want me to . . . do nothing?"

"You should try CPS again."

I can't believe this. "And, like, hope they've gotten their shit together in the last few weeks? Hope Pearl and Jack get lucky and stay alive until they do?"

"Just give it another try."

I can't fucking believe this! First Felice, now Eleanor. *Eleanor*? Felice, I can understand why she cut me loose. Who am I to her? She doesn't need the complication in her life. But *Eleanor*?

"I honestly thought we were legit friends," I say.

"A legit friend points out when the other legit friend is batshit crazy."

I get up and move from the bench to the edge of the fountain. Eleanor follows me over. She sits down, her feet drawn up so she doesn't get her sneakers wet, her chin resting on a knee.

"Don't be mad," she says.

I feel light-headed, but I'm not mad. I just keep turning it over and over and over in my mind, trying to make sense of it. How can Eleanor let me down like this, and now?

She reaches out and scoops her hand through the water. And then, before I realize what's happening, the big scoop of water is arcing toward me. I try to jump out of the way but it still nails a lot of me—the full left side of my body, practically, from my cracked rib down to my flip-flop, is soaked.

"Sorry," she says. "Oops."

"You're not going to help me?"

"I'm trying to help. Are you listening to me?"

I remember a very specific shade of green. The grass that time of year, the trees. May. Tornado season. But it was a beautiful, calm day. The last day of school, or maybe just my last day. Recess. A teacher came walking across the playground. Was recess already over? She led me inside, to the principal's office. The principal must have used the same shampoo as my mom, because that's what her office smelled like. Or maybe I'm just making that up.

Sit down, Hardy. I have something very important to talk to you about.

"Hardly," Eleanor says. "I don't, like, despise you. You may have noticed."

"Okay. Thank you."

"Which is rare for me. And, in this instance, inexplicable."

"Okay."

"So please, please, please trust me. Don't do this. There are better ways."

"So you're saying no, you're not going to help me."

"CPS. Give them another try. Okay? I know they're fucked up. But why not give them one more chance? What will it hurt? Talk to them and see what happens this time."

Exactly the bullshit argument that Felice made. "I don't have time to take one more shot. And suppose they do listen? They'll take Tracy's kids away from her. You know they will. How can you, of all people, want that to happen?"

She doesn't say anything. She scoops more water at me. This time I'm ready. I hop out of the way.

"Eleanor," I say. "I'm not delusional. I know this is kind of crazy. I do. But look me in the eye and tell me it's not worth the risk. How many times in a lifetime do you get an opportunity to actually make a real difference. Like, a true life-changing difference. This might be the one point in my entire life that *is* the entire point of my life."

"Hardly . . ."

"It's okay," I say. "Thanks for everything. I mean it. I'll see you around, maybe."

I do mean it. And then that's it, we're done, no big dramatic drawn-out scene. I'm back on my feet and walking to my car, my left flip-flop squishing.

43

On the drive home I don't see another car on the road, not a single one. Which isn't weird, exactly, since it's almost midnight, but also quite weird because my city is a fairly large city and midnight isn't really that late. Finally I spot a sign of life, a pedestrian striding very purposefully down the center median of a major boulevard. He's exceptionally tall and thin, wearing a shiny trench coat and—what!—old-fashioned aviator goggles. He ignores me as I pass. He has critical business to attend to, in this or some other dimension. I roll down the window to let the wind pummel me, to make sure this isn't a dream.

When I get to Burke's house, after I pull up to the curb and shut down my engine, I'm suddenly so exhausted, so cashed, so flattened—like the world has been flipped upside down and now it's all on top of my body, crushing me. I lack even the will to trek the short distance from my car to the front door to my room.

I crank my seat back and close my eyes. It feels like I've been awake forever. I've been awake since the first time I saw Pearl and Jack. I open my eyes. The mysterious dude in the trench coat and old-fashioned aviator glasses is striding purposefully toward me. What is he doing here? He grabs my shoulder and shakes it. He's trying to tell me something. The message is urgent. He's pointing at the sign in the alley. *DO NOT* . . . In the dream I know exactly what the sign means. *DO NOT GIVE UP ON THESE KIDS.*

"I won't," I tell the mysterious dude. "I won't."

"Won't what? Wakey, wakey. Rise and shine."

I open my eyes. The glare of sunshine off my windshield makes me squint. Morning. Burke is shaking my shoulder. Birds trill and toot. It's warm but not too hot yet. The crushing weight from last night is gone and I couldn't feel more certain, absolutely clear, about what happens next.

I don't need Eleanor. I don't need Felice. This is that moment in every movie where the main character realizes it's all on them—realizes, specifically, that's the way it has to be.

"I can fucking do this," I say.

"By all means," Burke says.

"I'm going to do this."

"What exactly is that?"

I look up at him. I see my reflection in his mirrored tactical sunglasses and for a second I don't recognize myself. "Burke," I say. "You're right. I should have a gun, right? Just to be safe."

He smiles. "Shall we confer in the kitchen? Meet me in three minutes."

In the kitchen I drink two tall glasses of tap water. My shelf in the fridge is bare, my part of the cabinet too—just a can of black olives I don't remember buying and one old packet of microwave popcorn. I nuke the popcorn. Now that Eleanor is out, Salvador will have to set off the fireworks. Am I really going to make him—*Salvador?*—responsible for the most critical part of the plan? But it's just a ripple of doubt, faint, gone almost before I notice it. I can do this. I can get Salvador ready. I can make sure he pulls it off.

I get a text from Eleanor: plz plz consider CPS again

I text back: no

what can it hurt???

I put my phone away. Just as the popcorn stops popping and starts burning, Burke enters with a lot of pomp and circumstance, holding a molded plastic case in front of him like it contains precious jewels or treasure or a glowing human soul.

He sets the case on the table and pops the latches. "I've given this some considerable thought," he says. "Every job requires the right tool. Your thoughts?"

The gun nestled in the foam cutout is . . . a gun. That's the beginning and end of my thoughts. I've never touched a real gun in my life. I've never even been this close to one. This gun is small, black, stubby. It looks heavier and much more ominous than the fake six-shooter the Dead Sheriff carries at Haunted Frontier.

"I trust your opinion, Burke."

"A sensible decision."

He removes the gun from the case—again, with much pomp and circumstance—and snaps the top of it open. He peers down and around, checking to make sure the gun isn't loaded. That's what I assume he's doing. What I hope he's doing.

"The Glock 19 isn't the prettiest girl at the discotheque, but it's reliable and easy to use. Adequate stopping power when you use hollow points. Am I correct to say that you have limited experience with firearms?"

"Correct. Yes."

He offers the gun to me, handle first. "The Glock doesn't have a safety, so be careful at all times. You don't want to shoot yourself."

I stare at the gun in Burke's hand. *No, thanks,* I want to say, *changed my mind.* But I have to be prepared for anything and everything. And I'm not going to actually *use* the gun. Worst-case scenario, I'll just wave it around to get some dirtbag to back off, back down, and let us—me and Tracy, Pearl and Jack—go on our way.

"Go ahead," Burke says. "It won't bite."

It won't bite? I glance up to see if he's serious or joking. Hard to tell. "How much does it cost?" I say.

"You get the friends and family discount. I'll throw in a box of hollow points. And don't worry about that pesky serial number. I've taken care of that. Six hundred."

"Six hundred dollars?"

"This is your most affordable option. Resale value is solid. You'll have no trouble getting your investment back. Six hundred."

Six hundred dollars is a lot more than I expected, a sizable chunk of the money I'm planning to give Tracy. If anyone knows about the resale value of guns, though, it's probably Burke. I can sell the Glock once this is all over and send Tracy the proceeds.

"Go ahead," Burke says, nudging the gun closer to me. "Try it on for size."

My phone buzzes, a call coming in. *Unknown.* I tell Burke I'll be back in a minute and race off to my room. I tap the green button.

"Hello?" I say.

Silence. I almost say her name, Tracy, but stop myself in time. For all I know Nathan found her stashed phone and hit redial on the number she called last. For all I know Tracy is lying dead on the floor right now, next to Pearl, next to Jack.

"It's me," Tracy says.

"I'm ready."

"Thursday. Day after tomorrow. He'll be gone all afternoon and most of the evening. I heard him say he'll be back around ten."

My mind works on that. The safest time is right in the middle, between when he leaves and when he comes back. Say six o'clock? But the fireworks will be a better diversion after dark, or at least at dusk.

"Make it eight-thirty," I say. "Meet me with Pearl and Jack at the end of the driveway. I'll be there with the car, waiting for you. Eight-thirty exactly."

"How am I going to do that?" Tracy says. "I told you. When he's gone, there are always people around. He always has someone watching us. If we just start walking down the driveway . . ."

"It's okay. I'm going to distract them. I'll get them away from the main house."

"How?"

"Fireworks. Off on the edge of the property, to the west."

"Fireworks? What?" But then I think she remembers the paintballers. I think she gets it. She sighs. "Fuck."

"Eight-thirty exactly."

Hold on. No. Having Tracy and the kids meet me at eight-thirty *exactly* won't work. I can't really know how long it will take Salvador to do his thing. If he's running even a few minutes behind, if Tracy and the kids try to leave the house *before* the fireworks go off and the dirtbags get distracted, we're screwed. I realize I've just dodged a major potential disaster.

If Salvador is running a few minutes *early,* that could be a problem too. I don't want the dirtbags to get back from chasing the fireworks too soon.

"Not eight-thirty exactly," I say. "Wait till you hear the fireworks. It should be eight-thirty, but it might be a little earlier or a little later. When you hear the fireworks, wait until everyone clears out. Probably like five or ten minutes. Will you be able to tell when everyone's gone?"

"I don't know. Yes. I think so."

"Take off and move as fast as you can." I worry about Pearl and Jack, if they'll be scared out of their minds by all this. Maybe. But they'll be with their mom, they'll be leaving behind Nathan. They'll understand, I'm hoping, that good things are happening. "Don't bring anything with you. Suitcases or boxes, anything like that."

"What if everyone's *not* gone," she says. "Have you thought about that?"

It's all I've been thinking about. It's why Burke is in the kitchen, about to sell me a Glock 19 and throw in hollow points for free. "Yes," I say.

"And?"

"Everyone should be gone. If they're not, call me and I'll come to the house. I'll meet you there. I'll be ready."

She's quiet for a long time. She doesn't ask what I mean by *ready*. I get the sense, again, that answers don't matter now. She's made the leap, she's soaring into the future. Where she lands is out of her hands.

"Anything else?" she says finally.

"Eight-thirty," I say. "Day after tomorrow. Wait till you hear the fireworks. Wait till it's clear, then meet me at the end of the driveway. If—"

"I have to go now."

"Okay, but . . ."

"Right now."

The call *beep-beep-beeps*. Dead.

When I get back to the kitchen, Burke is making coffee. He's returned the Glock to its nest of gray foam. I hesitate, then pick it up. The gun is even heavier than I expected, and much warmer. I keep my finger as far from the trigger as possible. I feel my palm start to sweat.

Jutta, who usually zeroes in on me for an ear rub whenever I enter a room, stays right where she is, on the other side of the kitchen.

"You can't decide if a gun is right for you until you fire it," Burke says. "I can give you a few pointers tomorrow afternoon. No charge."

I carefully place the gun back in the case and wipe my palm on my jeans. "Let's do it," I say.

44

I call Salvador. As I listen to the phone ring, I wonder again if I'm out of my mind to put him in charge of the diversion. Everything—*everything*—depends on the diversion, which means *everything* will depend on . . . Salvador. But I don't have time to wonder. The time for wondering has come to an end.

He drives over. Burke is locked up in his room, so I avoid the awkwardness of introducing the two of them. Burke and Salvador. This is my team? No. This *is* my team. I can do this. I *will* do this.

Salvador is dazed that he's been allowed into my inner sanctum. He floats reverently around my room, gaping in awe at the non-awe-inspiring items, such as the futon, the brick-and-board bookshelves, the Xbox, the *Flight of Icarus* poster.

"Sit down," I say. "Just stay still, okay? Do you remember the plan?"

He takes a seat on the edge of the futon. "Yes!"

"You're going to be in charge of the diversion." I nod at the cakes of fireworks stacked against the wall. "You're going to set those off."

I wait for the whoop and the fist pump. Instead, for maybe the first time ever, I see Salvador stop and think before he speaks. "I am?" he says finally.

It's a good sign, right? That he's stopping and thinking, that he's maturing, that he recognizes how important his role will be.

I sit next to him, open the MacBook Air, and bring up the satellite view of the farm. We hunch around the screen as I zoom in on the northwestern edge of the property.

"See this clearing in the woods here?" I say. "That's where you'll do it. You'll park your car here, on the shoulder of the highway. Drop a pin there."

"Okay."

"Drop a pin now."

"Oh." He takes out his phone and drops a pin. I make sure he gets it right.

He should be taking notes. I find him a pen and a flattened sack from Sonic.

"Write all this down," I say. "You'll get there and park on the shoulder of the highway at eight o'clock the day after tomorrow. Eight o'clock in the evening. When you get there, before you set off the fireworks, you're going to create a diversion within the diversion."

I explain—slowly, so he can write down every word—how he'll scatter empty beer cans, a couple of flip-flops, and the pair of sunglasses. The point is to lead the dirtbags away from the clearing and deeper into the woods. There's a term for this kind of fake-out. What is it? Red herring. That's it. After he plants the red herrings, he'll set up the firework cakes, in a row. Stake and tape.

"Got it?"

He nods. I explain how, at eight-thirty, he'll light the first fuse. When the first cake finishes popping off, a minute later according to the chick at the fireworks stand, he'll light the next one. And so on. Then he'll bust ass back to his car and get out of there.

He nods. I explain everything again, top to bottom.

"Fill your tank today," I say. "Stick to the speed limit, coming and going. You don't have to worry about rain. I checked the forecast."

Together we go over the instructions printed on the fireworks. Each cake has a primary fuse and a reserve fuse, in case the primary fizzles. It's not complicated. Light the punk, light the fuse, step back fifteen feet.

I'm reading over Salvador's shoulder. He's taking good and careful and legible notes. But it's just *notes*. I wish, again, I could drive by the property, check out the clearing in the woods in person, the shoulder of the highway. Too risky, I know. What about the fireworks, though? There's no reason we can't do a practice run. We'll go buy a test cake. While we're at it, we can ask the psycho fireworks chick if she has any tips. Maybe there's a way to, like, connect all six of the cakes so that Salvador only has to light the first fuse. He'll be able to get back to his car faster.

"Let's go for a ride," I tell Salvador.

He nods. Still no fist pump. It's a good sign. He's taking this seriously.

When we get out to the fireworks stand, we discover it's not open. The metal flaps over the windows are shut and the psycho chick is nowhere to be found. The side door is locked. Is the stand closed for the day? The week? There's no sign, no way to tell.

Salvador slumps. I assume he's disappointed about the psycho chick, love of his life, but then he says, loudly even for him, so loudly a rabbit bolts away into the stubble, "But I need to practice!"

I check Google for other fireworks stands. The nearest one is thirty minutes away. I call the number listed to see if it's open. No answer.

"But I need to practice," Salvador says again, less loudly but more panicky.

I'm not sure it's a great idea to dip into our stash. We only have six boxes of fireworks—six total minutes of diversion. In a perfect world, Salvador gets to use a box for practice, for his peace of mind and for mine too, definitely. But you never know, that one extra minute of Bite Your Tushy might make all the difference tomorrow evening.

It's not that complicated. It's lighting a punk, then using the punk to light a fuse. "You'll be fine," I tell Salvador.

We drive back to my place. I tell Salvador to meet me Thursday in the Haunted Frontier parking lot, seven-fifteen p.m. *Sharp.*

He nods. "Sharp."

"You're going to kick ass, Salvador. You're the master of the fireworks. You have to believe in yourself. Copy that?"

He nods more energetically. "Copy that."

I spend Wednesday morning running errands. I gas up my car, check the oil, check the tire pressure. The new old tires are holding up. Home Depot next. I've made a list of items Salvador will need: a flashlight; batteries for the flashlight; three disposable lighters, plus a foot-long flexible fireplace lighter in case something goes wrong with the punks or the disposables. At Best Buy, next door, I buy a prepaid phone as a backup in case something goes wrong with Salvador's phone.

What am I forgetting? Before I check out at Best Buy, I close my eyes and clear my mind. I go back and grab a second prepaid phone in case something goes wrong with my phone. I walk back to Home Depot and buy a flashlight for me too.

Eleanor texts three times and calls once. I ignore her. It's not me being petty or pissy. There's just still a lot to do, and I have to stay focused.

That afternoon, I head to the address Burke gave me. It's a gun shop and shooting range out in the warehouse wastelands past Tipple and Pickle, not far from the alley where Nathan ambushed me. Burke is waiting for me at the door.

"Nervous?" he says, smiling.

"Yes," I say, because if I lie, he'll know it. He'll be extra delighted.

"Just relax, have fun, and aim for the center mass." He taps my center mass. "Knock, knock."

"Who's there?"

"Ka-pow."

We go inside. I do relax, moderately. The gun shop isn't sketchy and smoky and menacing like I expected. It's clean, carpeted, well lit—like a Barnes & Noble but with guns instead of books and the taxidermied heads of various dead creatures mounted on the walls. The customers I see browsing the racks and shelves seem like normal people, men and women both, only one twitchy furtive guy who's possibly mulling a workplace shooting spree. Oh, and the two salesclerks carry big-ass pistols on their hips. So that's not exactly Barnes & Noble either.

The clerks greet Burke like an old buddy. At the counter by the range area, one of them gives me plastic goggles and a pair of padded headphones. Burke zips open his daypack. He's brought his own eye and ear protection, much swaggier than mine.

"Take your pick," the clerk says. He turns to the wall behind him, where the paper targets are displayed. Along with the wide array of basic bull's-eye circles and silhouettes of human figures, all different sizes and colors, there's also a cartoon Osama Bin Laden, a cartoon robber holding a cartoon hostage, and an X-ray man with his internal organs highlighted in red.

"Let's do Hunter today," Burke says before I can point to one of the bull's-eye circles.

The counter dude pulls out two big sheets of a blue silhouette—a man from the knees up with target lines superimposed over him—and smooths them onto the counter. For a blue silhouette with no features at all, the figure is strangely lifelike. It's the body language—he looks like he's got his hands in his pockets, like he's standing around while his girlfriend uses the restroom at the food court.

"Lane four. Happy hunting."

We go through a door and enter the range area. Low ceiling, bare concrete walls, bare concrete floor. *Bang bang bang.* A guy in the first lane is firing at the cartoon robber and hostage, punching holes in both of their heads. *Bang bang bang.* Wow, it's loud. Even with the headphones on, my ears ring. Gunshots on TV, in video games, are not nearly this loud. I feel like I've been lied to my whole life.

Burke is smiling again. "You'll get used to it."

I nod. I just want to get this over with, as quickly as possible. He clips up the first paper target and pushes a button to send it ten yards down the lane—the poor dude, Hunter, with his hands in his pockets, waiting for his girlfriend to finish trying on blouses.

Burke shows me how to load the Glock's magazine. It's a magazine, he emphasizes, not a clip. Fifteen rounds. He shows me how to snap the magazine into the gun. He shows me how to charge a round into the chamber—I learn what it's called—and how to hold the gun with both hands. He shows me how to stand, feet squared, finger not on the trigger yet.

"First rule of firearms," he says. "Never point your gun at someone you don't intend to shoot."

Bang bang bang. The guy in the other occupied lane blasts away in unpredictable bursts. Just when I think he might be finished, another *bang bang, bang bang* makes me jump.

"Breathe," Burke says. "Relax. Line up your sights, front sight on the middle of his chest. Center mass. Finger on the trigger. Breathe. Squeeze, don't yank."

I just want to get this over with. I squeeze the trigger. The Glock explodes. That's what it seems like. A flash of fire, orange and yellow, right in my face, way too close to my face than an explosion should ever be. Smoke, the smell of burning hell. When I lower the gun, I see a hole in the upper right corner of the target, nowhere close to the silhouette itself.

Burke adjusts my grip so that both of my thumbs are pointing forward, then waits for me to fire again. I'm even less eager to take a second shot than I was a first one, now that I know about the explosion in my face.

"Concentrate on the front sight," he says. "Breathe and squeeze."

I grit my teeth and squinch my eyes and fire again. At least it's not quite as loud this time, since I've already gone partially deaf. I know I probably flinch as I'm squeezing the trigger, and I'm not sure I even have my eyes open, so afterward I'm shocked to see a hole in the silhouette's left thigh.

"Hmm," Burke says.

"Burke," I say.

"Yes?"

"Do you want to help me with this whole thing? You could be in charge of the diversion. You could set off the fireworks."

"Fireworks?"

"You could be in charge of that."

He smiles. "No, thank you."

"You're sure?"

He turns me gently back toward the target. "Again, please."

I lower the Glock. Why do I need a gun? I don't need a gun. I definitely don't want to point a weapon at anyone with the intention to shoot them. My hands are trembling so I squeeze the handle of the Glock tighter. I remind myself what's at stake, why I'm here. Think about it: tomorrow might be the last day, ever, that Pearl and Jack will have to be afraid of their father. In Arizona, they'll be normal kids, happy kids, and Tracy can be a mom like Salvador's mom, Mrs. Velasco, always there for them when they need it.

I'm so close. I haven't come this far, I haven't changed this much, to abandon Pearl and Jack now. And if I'm going to do this, if I'm going to take this as seriously as I should, I have to be prepared for anything. I raise the Glock back up.

"I don't think I understand about the sights," I tell Burke.

"I would have to agree."

"The front sight should be . . . ?"

"Centered in the notch of the rear sight."

I line up my sights. Center mass. I think about the cigarette burns on Pearl's ankle. I think about the double deadbolt on the HVAC closet door. That blue silhouette could be Nathan. That blue silhouette *is* Nathan.

"Breathe and squeeze," Burke says.

I squeeze the trigger and fire.

"Better," he says. "Not bad. Now, do it again. Practice makes perfect."

45

When we get back to the house, Burke sits me down at the kitchen table and has me load and unload the Glock until he's satisfied with my basic competence. I pay him the six hundred dollars for the gun and the box of bullets.

"One more thing," he says.

"Okay."

"If anyone should ever ask..."

"Ask what?"

"Where you bought this firearm."

It takes me a second, then I get what he's getting at. "I don't know the person who sold it to me."

"Perhaps you were at the gun shop, chatting with a fellow browser. And he—you don't know his name, but he seemed nice—mentioned that he had a Glock he wanted to sell."

"That's what happened."

"What luck!"

Burke locks himself away in his bedroom. It's eight-thirty. Exactly twenty-four hours to go. Eleanor sends another text: trust me plz

Then: if i have to drag you to CPS i will

I text back: no

can we just talk???

no

I make a detailed checklist of everything I need to do, then start checking off boxes. I load the firework cakes, punks, stakes, and duct tape into the trunk of my car. I put minutes on the two burner phones and batteries in the flashlights. I pour out the twelve cans of Old Milwaukee, into the kitchen sink, then dump the empties, plus a couple of mismatched flip-flops and the cheap sunglasses, into a Trader Joe's grocery sack. That goes in my trunk too, along with the Home Depot bag.

I stuff clothes into my backpack, a couple of books, a manila envelope filled with old photos, birthday cards, and important documents like my social security card. Everything else that I can't live without—not very much, honestly—I box up in a single small box. If I decide to keep heading west after I deliver Tracy and the kids to Arizona, I'll have Burke ship it to me.

The unloaded Glock goes in the small front compartment of my backpack. The magazine and box of bullets go in the even smaller side pocket. That's where I zip up the cash too, a roll of hundred-dollar bills secured with multiple rubber bands. Three thousand, two hundred dollars for Tracy. In my wallet I have a hundred bucks for the road, for gas and food.

It's fourteen hours from here to Phoenix, then either fourteen hours back or another six to Los Angeles. I'll wait to decide until I'm there, at the fork in the road. Though honestly, at this point, my mind is probably made up already.

Jutta, who's been observing all my packing, comes over to get her ears rubbed. She presses against me with all her weight and I almost lose my balance.

"I wish I could," I tell her.

I lie on my futon and go over the plan again and again and again. What am I forgetting? What am I missing? I'm too wired to eat anything. I don't even try to sleep. I smoke a bowl, but the weed has minimal effect.

The wind picks up. It beats and thumps against the fiberglass double-car garage door that's one of my walls. If it's this windy tomorrow evening, Salvador might have a tough time lighting the fireworks. I wash my hands for the fifth or sixth time. I can't get the smell of what I guess is gunpowder off my hands. When was that satellite image of the farm taken? What if the woods are no longer there? What if Salvador gets there and is totally exposed, with no cover at all? I think about his mom, Mrs. Velasco, punching me lightly on the shoulder and thanking me for being so good to her son.

I drive over to Nguyen and Mallory's apartment. They're doing bong rips and—hold on to your hats—watching reruns of *Parks and Rec* instead of re-runs of *The Office*. I ask Nguyen, the connoisseur I'm not, what indica he rec-ommends for maximum relaxation and couch lock. He ponders, then goes into his room and brings me some Skywalker OG.

"Where are you going?" Mallory says when I start to leave.

I go over and give her a hug. I give Nguyen a hug. They're too stoned to be surprised.

I call Preston.

"What now?" he says.

"You're going to do it," I say.

"Do what?"

"Design beautiful and elegantly efficient cities."

"Shut up."

"I mean it. You're going to do it, Preston."

He's quiet for a second, then says "I know" and hangs up.

Back at my place, I smoke some of the Skywalker OG and study *The Fall of Icarus*. Who is Icarus anyway? I know it's a Greek myth. With a minotaur, maybe? I've never actually read up on it. I take out my phone. Wikipedia tells me that Icarus put on a pair of wings his father made and tried to es-cape Crete. That's where I got the minotaur. Icarus escaped, but then he flew too close to the sun and the heat melted the wax. He fell from the sky and drowned.

That's not an inspiring story, given my current circumstances. Am *I* Icarus here? Am *I* the one flying too close to the sun in some rickety-ass wings?

No. Incorrect. In my version of the story, Pearl and Jack are in the wa-ter, the ones who need saving. Because, look, just because Icarus fell into the ocean doesn't mean he has to drown. In my version of the story, the farmer or the fisherman or the shepherd will dive into the water and pull him to safety.

Eleanor texts again: are you going to ignore me forever? seriously?

Then: can we not just talk for two minutes?

I wonder if maybe, just possibly, I should take her advice, Felice's advice, and do it—give Child Protective Services one last chance. I could stop by tomorrow morning. Maybe there's a caseworker there, one good caseworker, on the ball and ferocious, who will take the evidence I have and . . .

No. Remember? The time for wondering is over. Tracy trusts me. She trusts me with *everything*. I can't let her down. I can't let Pearl and Jack down. I can't doubt myself or be scared right now. This is the point in my life that is the point of my life. How many people get that chance? How many people get to choose it? Very few. Very, very few.

The Skywalker OG does the trick. I start to chill out. It's one o'clock in the morning. This time tomorrow night all this will be over.

46

I get to Haunted Frontier early. I park in the far, deserted corner of the lot and smoke one last bowl of the Skywalker OG I've saved for this moment. Dark clouds are stacking up in the west, above the jagged peak of Abandoned Mine Train Mountain. Half an hour ago, last time I checked, the forecast called for ten percent precipitation. I don't check again. If it rains, it rains. There's nothing I can do about it.

Trees border this side of the parking lot. The cicadas are deafening, the pitch rising and falling, rising and falling, the same song but a million different screaming guitar solos. I'm glad I have the Skywalker OG, but I don't *need* it. I'm already calm. I sync up the rhythm of my heart to the beat of the cicadas. I know the plan. I'm ready.

At seven-fifteen sharp Salvador drives up. He parks his SUV next to me and hops out. He walks around and gives my car a saucy slap on the hood.

"I'm going to kick ass," he says. "I'm the master of the fireworks."

"What's that?" I say. He's holding a paper sack. I pick up an enticing whiff of garlic and fried meat.

"Pastelitos. My mom made them. They're delicious. When I told her I had to work tonight, she gave me extras to share with you. We can save them for afterward, or eat them now, or eat three of them now and save the other three for later. Whatever you decide."

"Salvador."

"What?"

"Nothing."

I pop the trunk of my car. I know exactly what we need to transfer to Salvador's SUV: the box of six Bite Your Tushy firework cakes; the first

Trader Joe's grocery bag with stakes, duct tape, punks, and lighters; the second Trader Joe's grocery bag with one flashlight, one prepaid phone, twelve empty beer cans, two mismatched flip-flops, cheap sunglasses. I also have the MacBook Air to give back to him. It's all neatly arranged, in the left half of my trunk, so I won't forget anything.

So why am I just standing here, staring down into the eyes of a snarling Bite Your Tushy dog? Maybe it's those stupid pastelitos that Salvador brought, the smell of his mom's home cooking. I glance over. He's opened the sack and is peeking inside. To count the pastelitos again, I'm guessing, and confirm that he's given me correct information.

He'll be fine. He'll be long gone from the clearing before any of the dirtbags get there. The plan will go off without a hitch and Salvador will have a great story to tell his kids one day.

But he's only sixteen years old. He wants to start his own robot club. He's *Salvador*. I'm choosing to do this. I don't know if Salvador really is. No, that's false. I do know. He's not choosing. I'm choosing for him.

But he'll be fine. And how will I be able to pull off the diversion without him? It's too late to postpone. Tracy, getting Pearl and Jack ready, may have already crossed the point of no return. She's betting their lives on me.

"What's wrong?" Salvador says. "There are six pastelitos. Like I thought. Do you think we should eat three of them now? One and a half each?"

Before I can go back and forth another hundred times, I grab the MacBook Air, the MacBook Air only, and slam the lid of the trunk shut. I hand him the laptop. I can't put Salvador in this kind of danger.

"Guess what?" I say. "Tracy had to reschedule. Nathan won't be gone till tomorrow. We'll have to do this tomorrow."

"Oh."

"I found out a couple of hours ago. I should have called you."

Salvador moves through the five stages of Salvador processing big news, four of which involve being flummoxed to some degree. "Oh," he says, finally grasping the situation.

"It sucks. I was all stoked."

"Me too."

It's hard to tell if he's disappointed or relieved. Both, possibly? I think that might be how I'd feel if suddenly Tracy texted with the news that she and the kids were safe and sound in Arizona.

Salvador takes a deep, deep breath and pants it back out. "Tomorrow. Copy that."

"Okay? We'll meet here again. Seven-fifteen."

And then I'm back in my car, driving away, not looking back. I don't have to. Salvador is still standing there, holding those stupid pastelitos. I take my own deep, deep breath as I turn out of the Haunted Frontier lot. I remember reading one time that skydivers reach a point of perfect equilibrium where they can't really tell if they're floating motionless, peacefully in space, or are plunging at max velocity toward earth.

Wow. What have I just done? Without Salvador, I'll now have to set off the fireworks myself, then haul ass to pick up Tracy and the kids. I never even bothered to measure the distance from the clearing, all the way around the property, down the private road, to the end of the driveway. A mile, maybe? A two-minute drive, plus a minute to get from the clearing back to my car? That's not a big deal, right? Three extra minutes. Or it might be a big deal.

But I believe in myself. I can do this. There's less chance of a screwup if I do the fireworks myself. I believe that.

The city drops off behind me. The two-lane highway I'm on begins to swell and dip—not very much, but what passes for hilly on the southern plains of America. I pass wooded acreages for sale and cattle grazing in pastures. I'm right on schedule. I wish the fireworks place had been open. If I knew how to connect the six cakes of fireworks, I'd get back the three minutes I'm losing, plus a couple of extras. Maybe when I get to the clearing I can find a tutorial on YouTube. No. I remember my YouTube search for surveillance tips, long ago, and how well that ended. I won't let myself get distracted this time.

A big, fat raindrop hits my windshield, then a few more, each *splat* like the sound effect from a slasher movie. A second later the sky splits open and my wipers can barely keep up. I have to turn my headlights on, even though it's half an hour until sunset. Darkness is fine, rain is not. I make a bargain with myself. Whatever happens, from this moment forward, I won't freak out, I'll keep my cool. Okay? Deal. It's the only way I'll be able to pull this off. Felice doesn't think I have it in me. Eleanor doesn't. Let's find out.

The rain slackens, then sputters out. The wind carries most of the clouds away, like a hand swiped across a fogged-up mirror. Deep pink streaks light up the horizon.

I hit a stop sign—the intersection of County Highway 44 and Post Road. This is it, the northwest corner of the property. There aren't any cars behind me, so I take a second to check my bearings on my maps app. I'm reassured. Everything in real life seems to match up to the app. Straight ahead on 44, about five hundred yards into a wooded stretch, is where I'll park on the shoulder. I'll trek from there to the clearing. To my right, down Post past about a thousand yards of field and pasture, is the left turn onto the private road that leads to the driveway. That's the way I'll go after I set off the fireworks.

It's just now seven forty-five. I'm ahead of schedule, with plenty of time. I could make a quick run down Post to find and pinpoint the turnoff. It should be safe. Nathan is already gone. Tracy told me he'd be gone all afternoon, and she hasn't called or texted with any updates. A run down Post is a lot safer than missing the turnoff when every second counts.

So I hang a right onto Post. After a minute or so the road dips, then rises. I slow down. From the top of the rise I can see the compound in the distance. The main house, the barn, a couple of sheds. The layout is just how Tracy described it, just how it showed on Google satellite view. The double-wide is a little bit separate from the cluster of other buildings.

And then Post Road dips again and bends away. I'd love to take a longer look at the compound, but it's too risky to stop or go any slower. The turnoff should be up ahead. I study the slumping fence posts and sagging wire. I'm really hoping the turnoff is easy to spot. It will be darker when I come back, and I'll be hauling ass.

There it is, and totally easy to spot. The private road is dirt instead of asphalt, nice and wide, marked with a rusty NO TRESPASSING sign. I couldn't miss it if I tried.

I make a U at the next lonely intersection, then head back to Highway 44. I take another quick look at the compound, at the woods behind it. I can't confirm from this distance or angle, but I'm still almost one hundred percent certain you can't see the clearing from the compound.

Right on 44. I drive for a minute until my GPS lady tells me I'm one hundred yards from my destination. I slow down. Heavy woods on both sides of 44. My destination is really just a guess. I look for a promising place to pull over. The gravel shoulder between highway and trees is barely wide enough for a car. I creep along and find a spot where I can tuck in a few extra feet. According to my maps app, I am now a direct shot south to the clearing.

I turn off my engine, pop the hood, and make sure my headlights are off. I make sure I have my keys when I climb out. I prop the hood open. If anyone drives by and notices my car, if anyone happens to give a shit, I'm hoping they'll think I broke down and started walking back up 44 toward civilization. The cicadas out here are going crazy. They're deafening. They make the roar of cicadas at Haunted Frontier seem like soft whispers at church.

It's five after eight. I have twenty-five minutes. I'll need to make two trips, so first I grab the box of firework cakes. I don't think I'll need the flashlight yet, but I throw it in with the cakes just in case.

I make my way into the woods. The going isn't too tough. This is just the scraggly undeveloped fringe of a metropolitan area, not the Alaskan wilderness or some enchanted fairy-tale forest. The trees are spaced fairly widely, with plenty of room to maneuver, and the underbrush is easy to kick through. I'm not afraid I'll get turned around or lost. What I'm afraid of: the Google satellite image was taken a few years ago and the clearing has been swallowed up. If there's not enough clearing for me to shoot off the fireworks, I'm fucked.

The remains of the rain drip off the leaves. Sweat drips off me. The rain didn't cool things down much, and the humidity has spiked. The ground is a little muddy, but not slippery. It's getting darker, fast, and I'm glad I brought the flashlight. You see? I'm so much better at thinking ahead than I used to be. I remember previous me, standing in line at the parking window, too oblivious to extend all his parking tickets at once.

The clearing is right where it should be, nice and spacious, fully circled by trees. I walk over to the far edge of the clearing, to find out if I can glimpse the compound half a mile away. Nothing at all. Perfect.

I drop the box of firework cakes and jog back to my car. I time myself.

It takes me a minute and forty-three seconds, about what I'd estimated. I'll probably shave a good chunk of that off when the fireworks are popping and my adrenaline is pumping.

I carry the two Trader Joe's bags back to the clearing. A quarter after eight, fifteen minutes to go. First thing, I set up the diversion within the diversion, the red herrings, scattering Old Milwaukee empties into the woods away from the compound and away from the highway. I plant one mismatched flip-flop at the start of the trail, the cheap sunglasses at the end.

Now: the wooden stakes to anchor the firework cakes. I grab the first stake and realize . . . I forgot to buy a hammer or a mallet, something to drive the stakes into the ground. Shit. *Shit.* How could I forget to buy a hammer or a mallet? I feel the first bump of panic, testing my balance. I ignore it. I'm okay. Without any trees in the way, the rain earlier soaked the clearing. The dirt here is wet and soft. I stab a stake into the ground, then stand on it. I'm wearing Vans, not flip-flops. The stake sinks in. I give it a shake. Stable. I'm okay.

I duct-tape the first cake to the first stake—top facing up, fuse not blocked. *Warning: Shoots Flaming Balls.* Five more stakes, a couple of feet apart, five more cakes. My adrenaline is already pumping. I test the lighters. All three work fine. I untie the string around the bundle of punks. Five minutes to go, I'm done, right on schedule. I didn't want more extra time than this. The longer my car sits on the shoulder, the better the chances someone—a highway patrolman—might stop to scope it out.

What am I missing? What else, besides a hammer or a mallet, have I forgotten? This is the last time I'll have a moment to stop, to think, so I better take advantage of it. I jog back to my car. I hesitate, then take the Glock and the magazine full of bullets out of my backpack. I snap the magazine into place and draw the slide back the way Burke taught me. The gun is now loaded. I hesitate again, then place it in the right pocket of my cargo shorts. The gun fits snugly. I button the flap. I won't have to use the Glock, I remind myself. Worst-case scenario, *super* worst-case scenario, I'll have to fire a warning shot into the air. That's it, if that.

I stuff the envelope with all the cash into my left pocket. It's highly unlikely that someone steals my car, but I can't take the chance. What if those teenage paintballers come back and take my car for a joy ride? I have to think of everything.

I jog back to the clearing. I try to keep a smooth, steady pace. Burke assured me that the Glock won't go off by accident. I have to trust him on that, even though that's kind of the definition of an accident, isn't it? Something that happens when you're sure it won't.

It's full-on dusk now, the sky above a soft pale blue marbled with purple and gray. I check my phone for any last-minute texts from Tracy. Nothing, but I notice that the cell signal dips in and out. One bar, two bars, no bars. One bar, no bars, no bars.

I try to think of something funny, to help me keep my cool. What's something funny? Who knows how I remember it, since I was so doped up from the ER, but I remember Eleanor coming out of Walgreens and tossing me the box of lice shampoo. *Vamousse.* That makes me smile, but not for long. Eleanor should be here. We should be doing this together. Or I should have listened to her and Felice. I shouldn't be doing this at all.

I light the punk. I touch the punk to the first fuse. The fuse spits and sparks instantly, burning down faster than I expected. I barely have time to stumble backward a few feet before the first flaming ball whooshes drunkenly into the sky.

47

I haul ass. Light from the last cake of Bite Your Tushy flashes down through the tree branches and the earsplitting cracks sound like they're just inches away, chasing me. It's shockingly beautiful to stand right beneath a canopy of fireworks. Remember that time I stood right beneath a canopy of fireworks? That's my keep-cool tactic at the moment: imagine this has already happened and already ended happily and I'm looking back from, like, a comfortable chair, a tranquil view out the window.

I'm flying so fast I almost can't stop myself in time and almost skid into the side of my own car. It's taken me less than a minute to get back from the clearing. I know for a fact it's less than a minute because as I'm slamming the hood shut one final bright blue star explodes high above the trees. High, *high* above the trees. The psycho fireworks chick provided good information. This display should be easy to see, and hear, from the compound. Everything, so far, is going as planned.

I don't fumble my keys. My car starts on the first try. Highway 44 is clear, both ways. I swing smoothly out and around. I smoothly hit the gas.

The asphalt is still wet from the rain, shimmering in my headlights and probably slick, so I stick to the speed limit, fifty. I also stick to the speed limit in case of any potential highway patrolman who might be passing by.

At the intersection I make a full and complete stop, then turn left onto Post. When I check my speedometer, I see I've crept up to sixty. I ease back down. I'm maybe two minutes away from the turnoff to the private road. Tracy has already hurried the kids out of the main house. She's holding one of Jack's hands and one of Pearl's. *C'mon, guys, we're going to take a walk up the driveway.* Tracy will tell me all the details during the drive to Arizona. She's telling me now. We're already on our way there, miles from here.

The road dips and rises. I see the compound. Behind it, above the woods, I see a smudge of smoke, all that's left of the fireworks. And I see two small figures moving toward the smoke and the woods. The dirtbags— the diversion worked. It worked! But . . . how have the two figures already covered so much ground? They're running too fast, they're almost to the edge of the woods. They shouldn't be that far already. I slow down before I hit the curve and lose the view. I realize the two figures are driving, not running. They're driving three-wheelers, ATVs.

I lose the view. I hit the gas. It's okay. It's okay. Tracy never mentioned ATVs and I never considered the possibility. How fast can ATVs go? For sure a lot faster than a dirtbag can run. Tracy and the kids and I—we're going to have less time. But it's okay. We still have enough time. The dirtbags probably can't drive the ATVs into the woods, right? They'll have to climb off and start walking. And they'll still follow the trail of crumpled beer cans and search everywhere for the rogue teenagers. What matters most: the diversion worked.

The NO TRESPASSING sign pops up as I round a curve. I turn onto the private road—a little too sharply, a little too fast. I feel the back of my car levitate and swish. My stomach levitates and swishes too. But it's just a minor fishtail and I straighten the car out. The narrow road is wet red clay, even slicker than the asphalt, with a shallow ditch on the passenger side and an even deeper ditch on my side. I can't go any faster than fifteen miles an hour. We still have enough time. I hope there's a place to turn around when I get to the top of the driveway. Otherwise I'll have to back all the way out.

The private road snakes and winds. I'm expecting that, from the satellite view. The compound is screened by shade trees, so I catch only a glimpse here and there of lights from the main house.

I must be getting close to the end of the driveway, where Tracy and the kids will be waiting for me. Should I kill my headlights? I kill my headlights. It's not completely dark yet. I snake around and I see the spot, up ahead, where the red clay turns to gravel. I ease to a stop on the lip of the driveway. It's wide enough for a three-point turnaround. Huge relief.

But Tracy and the kids . . . they're not here. I look left, right. It's possible they're just lying low, out of sight, until they're sure it's me. Except there's really nowhere *to* lie low, no nearby trees and just a few patches of tall weeds. The deepest ditch on the side of the road is only a couple of feet deep.

I take a chance and flash my headlights. I can't honk, obviously. How long can I wait? They should be here by now. They should have been here five minutes ago.

I try to recall exactly every single word of the conversation I had with Tracy. I told her to *walk* to the end of the driveway and meet me there, right? Or did I just tell her to *meet* me at the end of the driveway? In which case . . . did she think I meant the *other* end of the driveway, a few hundred yards from here, that butts up against the main house?

No. I'm one hundred percent certain I told her to *walk* to the end of the driveway. I'm ninety-nine percent certain. This end of the driveway is what makes sense. So Tracy and the kids could slip away, so my car wouldn't draw any attention.

Pearl and Jack . . . what's happened to them? What's happened to Tracy? Did Nathan find out what she was planning?

But I stay calm. I keep my cool. I'm somewhat amazed, honestly, that I'm able to do it. I shift from park back to drive and head toward the compound. Because I'm calm, it's an easy call. Tracy and the kids are waiting for me at the other end of the driveway, or they've been delayed for some reason. Either way, I have to go get them. We don't have time for them to come to me.

Gravel strafes the bottom of my car. The driveway is more or less straight, so I can go faster now—thirty miles an hour, then forty. My new old front tires endure. So far. In the trunk I have a jack and a tire tool, but, once again, no spare. Why didn't I think to buy a spare? Though if one of my tires blows now, I won't have time to change it anyway.

I whip past the cluster of shade trees and hit my brakes and skid to a stop in the center of the compound. Main house directly ahead, barn to my left with a car out front, junky double-wide to my right with a red pickup truck out front. I know that red truck.

The whole place is a shithole. The main house is falling down—rotted wood and buckled roof and busted panes of glass. The barn has already fallen down, the back half of it at least, like a dog struggling to get up on its hind legs. A heap of rusted junk on one side of the RV. A filthy, waterlogged sofa on the other side.

No sign at all of Tracy, Jack, Pearl. Be calm. Keep cool. *Fuck.* They must be inside the main house. That's my best and only guess. Why hasn't Tracy texted me? I leave my car running and get out. It's okay. The two dirtbags have located the clearing by now. By now they're stomping through the woods, following the trail of beer cans, searching for the rogue teenagers. I have at least five minutes to find Tracy and the kids, probably more than that, right?

A guy steps out of the barn. I recognize him from the late-night party—the sketchy dude with the short bangs and mullet about to slide off the back of his head. He lifts his arm halfway. He's holding a gun. It's bigger than the Glock, and silver, a real version of the fake six-shooter I carry in my holster at Haunted Frontier.

"Who the fuck are you?" he says. His grip on the gun is loose. The barrel droops. It's still pointed in my general direction, though.

I don't turn to face him. I stay angled away so he can't see my right hand. With my right hand I reach down and unbutton the flap of my cargo pocket. I touch the handle of the Glock. My senses shut down, one by one. First the sound cuts out, the cicadas and the unsteady sputter of my engine, and all I hear is the suffocating sound of my own breath. Next my peripheral vision goes black and I can't move my eyes off that silver pistol. Every nerve ending in my body is concentrated in the tip of my right index finger, resting against the cool plastic of the Glock's handle.

"I said *who* the *fuck* are *you*?" he says again, giving the pistol a jiggle to emphasize certain words.

I've never really believed in God or a supreme being or anything like that, not since my mom died. Right now, though, I say a silent and fervent prayer. *Please, please, let me once in my life tell a good lie.*

"Who the fuck am I?" I say. "We met at that party at Nathan's old place the other night."

He hard-eyes me and doesn't lower the gun. But he doesn't lift it the rest of the way up either, so that's good. "I don't remember."

"You don't remember the party? How much of that vodka did you drink?"

"I don't remember *you*," he says.

"Where is he? Nathan? I'm supposed to meet him here."

"He's gone to the city. I'm not his fucking secretary."

"I'll wait inside for him," I say.

"I'm not his fucking secretary."

He lowers the gun, wheels around, disappears into the barn. My vision swims, then shapes back up. I can hear again. What almost happened? I know what almost happened. I'm shaking. I hear my mom's voice.

But it didn't!

I have to find Tracy and the kids. *Now*. I shut off my engine—too suspicious if I leave it running now—and hurry up the porch steps. The front door is open, the screen door unlocked.

48

A hallway. Stairs on the left. Living room on the right. A lamp on, but no-body there. The living room isn't as trashed as I expected. A few pieces of nice, solid, farmhouse furniture, some framed old-time family photos on the ledge above a fireplace. The place, though, is eroding on the edges: a gal-lon paint can filled with cigarette butts on the coffee table, a half-eaten pizza upside-down on the rug. I smell stale smoke and cat piss.

I take out the Glock. Finger off the trigger, finger laid flat above it, the way Burke showed me. Down the hallway to the kitchen. Lights on, deserted. The smell of cat piss is sharper here, plus burnt meat. I don't know if I should call out for Tracy. Who else might be in the house? I'd rather surprise them than vice versa. I should have asked the guy in the barn if anybody was in the house. But maybe not. I would have been pressing my luck.

The dining room, next to the kitchen, is deserted too. I return to the stairs and creep up as quietly as I can. Not much light in the upstairs hallway. I let my eyes adjust while I wait for some stupid cat to jump out of nowhere and scare me to death.

Two bedrooms at the front of the house, both empty. I can tell somebody's been sleeping here, though. Clothes piled on the floor, rumpled sheets, the smell of fresher smoke. Big Beard and Scrawny Drunk, I'm guessing. That's their red truck outside. It's them on the ATVs.

Down the hallway, to the rear of the house. I'm moving faster now. I've lost all track of time. I can't even guess how long I've been in the house. I sneak a quick peek at my phone. Eight forty-two. It's okay. That's not terrible. It's okay.

Bathroom. Nobody. Two more closed doors, two more bedrooms. A thin blade of light below the first door. I ease it open. *Tracy.* She's standing in front of a big antique wardrobe, frantically but silently trying to yank the door open. What is she doing?

"Tracy!" I whisper-shout.

She whirls, her eyes wild. "Why are you here?"

I don't understand. "For you. For the kids. We have to—"

"Why didn't you wait for us at the end of the driveway?"

"We have to go. Right *now.* Where are Pearl and Jack?"

She laughs, or sobs, or something in between. I finally notice the padlock on the door of the wardrobe. I see gouges in the wood around the hasp. I see, on the floor, the pair of scissors and the bent steak knife that did the gouging.

"He locked them in," Tracy says, "before he left. The motherfucker. I can't get it open. The motherfucker. He took my phone yesterday. I couldn't text you."

Pearl and Jack locked in the wardrobe—they must be terrified. There's even less room in the wardrobe, with the two of them, than in the HVAC closet. And Tracy gouging at the wood, sobbing . . .

"It's okay," I tell Tracy. I don't know what else to say. I have to keep my cool for both of us. I put the gun back in my pocket. I can't shoot the padlock since the kids are inside the wardrobe. "We'll sort it out. Okay?"

Miraculously, she nods. "Okay. Okay. Please."

The scissors won't work. The bent steak knife won't. The padlock is heavy duty. I need a screwdriver to pry the padlock off, to pry off the hasp or latch or whatever it's called.

"Is there a toolbox anywhere?" I say. "Is there like a drawer somewhere with tools in it?"

The wildness flares again in her eyes. "No!"

If she knew where to find a screwdriver, she'd be using it. Right. A screwdriver might not even be strong enough. My new old tires, I remember. The tire tool with one half a lug wrench and the other . . . a pry bar.

"I've got it," I say. "I'll be right back. Two seconds. Tell them it's going to be okay. Tell Pearl and Jack it's going to be okay. Okay?"

"Yes. Okay. Yes."

"Stay here. I'll be right back."

I fly downstairs. I crash through the screen door, hit the porch, and freeze. A car has pulled in next to mine, an SUV. Nathan? No. It's Salvador's SUV. It's *Salvador's* SUV? What! It's Salvador. He's frozen too, halfway out of the SUV, the driver's door open, one of his feet still on the running board. He peers through the glass of the driver's door window at the guy from the barn.

The guy from the barn, ten feet from the SUV. His arm raised, his big silver pistol pointed at Salvador.

"What the fuck is going on here?" the guy from the barn says.

"Salvador!" I say.

The guy from the barn whips the pistol over to me, then whips it back to Salvador and fires, a sonic boom so heavy it flattens my heart in my chest. The driver's-side window shatters and collapses in the frame. Salvador collapses. Suddenly I have the Glock in my hand. I don't remember pulling it from my pocket. I don't remember pulling the trigger. The barrel of the Glock flashes. One shot. The guy from the barn grunts and drops to his knees. I close my eyes, or have they been closed this whole time? When I open my eyes, the guy from the barn has toppled face-first into the gravel. He's not moving.

I run to the SUV. Salvador lies on his back. All I can make out is the white of one eye. The rest of his face is covered with blood. Blood bubbles from his mouth when he breathes out.

"You're okay," I say. "Fuck. Fuck."

I don't know where the bullet hit him. There's too much blood on his face. I finally find a cut across his temple where a shard of glass grazed him. That's where all the blood seems to be coming from. Was it a shard of glass or the bullet? Is it possible—did the bullet mostly miss him?

"I'm fine," he says. "I'm sorry."

He can talk. That's a good sign. That has to be a good sign. "You're fine," I say. "You're going to be fine."

"My head hurts. I came here. I knew you were here. I wanted to help."

I'm squeezing the handle of the Glock so tightly I'm about to crush it, like Superman in the comics squeezing a lump of coal until it turns into a diamond. I put the gun away and fumble for my phone, to call 911. *No. No, no, no.* I have to get Salvador out of here. I have to get Tracy and the kids out of here. If I don't get Salvador and Tracy and the kids out of here before the other dirtbags get back from the clearing . . . the dirtbags will be back way before the cops or an ambulance.

"Can you sit up?" I say.

I help him sit up. The bullet just grazed him, but there's so much blood. I help him stand.

"My head hurts. I'm sorry. I can't see very well."

"That's just blood in your eyes. Don't wipe your face. There might be glass. Don't touch your face. Just be quiet and relax." I load him into the backseat of the SUV. He still has the keys in his hand. I twist them free. "I'll be right back. Tracy will take my car, we'll go in yours. Just lie down, out of sight. You're okay. Lie down and relax."

I'm absurdly, miraculously calm. I wonder if I'm in shock. I open the trunk of my car and flip back the liner and grab the tire iron from the well. Then I'm running back to the house. I don't look at the guy from the barn lying facedown in the gravel. I can't. That's not real. That didn't really happen. I don't know how long shock lasts. I hope it lasts long enough.

Tracy is gouging at the wood around the padlock with the scissors again. She must know it won't work, but maybe she's in shock too.

"Look out," I say.

She sees the tire iron and steps away from the wardrobe. "Hurry!"

I try to work the pry end of the tire iron under the plate attached to the door. The plate is bolted too tight. What now? I slip the pry into the U of the padlock itself and throw all my weight against the tire iron. For an instant, nothing—I just hang there, floating on my toes. Then *crack*. The padlock snaps open. I lose my balance and stumble backward.

"Oh, my God," Tracy says. She unhooks the padlock and flings open the door of the wardrobe. Inside, Pearl and Jack are jammed together. There's barely enough room for one of them. You'd never guess from their faces, though, that they've been locked up so nightmarishly, that they've been listening to gunshots, scissors gouging, their mom sobbing. Their expressions are exactly the same as the day I first saw them on the bench: empty and impassive, just before or just after a yawn, riding the usual bus to work for the millionth or so time.

"We have to go," I tell Tracy.

She reaches for the kids. I hear the growl of engines—thin at first, then getting louder. Tracy hears it too. She looks over at me. I go to the window that faces the woods. Two separate, single headlights bounce and splash. The ATVs. Big Beard and Scrawny Drunk speeding back to the compound.

What will happen next isn't a big mystery. In the next minute or two Big Beard and Scrawny Drunk will come tearing into the compound and see Salvador's SUV. They'll see my car. They'll see the guy from the barn, lying facedown in the gravel. I didn't have time to drag his body into the barn. I don't think I could have brought myself to do that anyway. Do Big Beard and Scrawny Drunk have guns? They've been trying to chase down teenage trespassers. Definitely they have guns.

I grab Tracy's arm. "Wait here. Okay? Don't move. Keep the kids safe."

She nods. She's calmer now. She's definitely in shock too, I think.

"Here." I give her my keys. "Just in case. Take my car. There's a boy in the back of the SUV. Put him in my car before you go. He's hurt. Drop him off at a hospital on your way out of town. Do you promise you will?"

"I promise. Yes."

I give her the envelope with all the money too, then take the Glock out of my pocket and go down the stairs. I wait just inside the living room, peeking around the corner and down the hallway to the open front door. Aim for center mass. Don't rush. Aim for center mass. Don't rush. This is me now. This is not the previous me.

The engines growl, closer and closer. I hear someone yell, *Fuck!* The growling shuts off. More cussing and yelling. *What the fuck? Get over here! He's not. I can't. What the fuck?* I hear a name. Gerwin or Gerbler? The name of the man I killed. I fight back a wave of dizziness. I didn't kill a man. I didn't take a human life. That's not real. That didn't really happen.

The cussing and yelling abruptly goes quiet. Just a murmur of voices now. I can't make out anything. I can't see anything either. Through the frame of the front door I can only see a slice of Salvador's SUV. I hope he's holding his breath, making no noise whatsoever.

Boots thump up the porch steps. I duck my head back into the living room. I hear the screen door slap open.

"Stop!" I yell. "Drop your guns!"

"I know who the fuck you are." It's Big Beard yelling back, I think. "That's your car. Who else is in there with you? Come on out and let's all of us have a chat."

"Drop your guns! Both of you."

"Done. I'm setting it down, nice and easy."

"Drop it, please. So I can hear."

"It's already down. Come on out so you can see for yourself."

Shadows shift and I dive to my left as the living room window behind me explodes. My ears ring. Searing pain slashes diagonally across me, from shoulder to opposite hip. I feel the thud of boots in the hallway and drag myself over to the wall next to the window. I still have the Glock.

Scrawny Drunk sticks his head through the window, his profile silhouetted against the lamp. "I got him!" he yells.

I pull the trigger three times and the lamp blinks out. Through the smoke I see Scrawny Drunk slumped over the windowsill, a flap of his head touching the floor. I slip on blood as I try to stand up. His blood, but maybe mine too. The slash of pain has tightened to a knot, all of it concentrated in my side. Something smells like it's burning.

Big Beard wraps his arm around the doorframe and fires blindly into the living room. The sofa coughs out gray stuffing. The paint can full of cigarette butts detonates. I stay low. I don't know if I could get up if I wanted. I aim at the wall by the doorway and pull the trigger. Big Beard steps into the doorway and fires at me. I fire back. It's dark, smoke everywhere, a roar so loud it's like the earth is cracking open. My left shoulder splinters. The pain is unimaginable, a secret you can't know ahead of time because you'd die of despair. I still have the gun somehow, in my right hand. I fire once more, twice more, three times, then my finger goes numb and the silence swallows me.

49

Hardwood floor. Edge of rug dark and wet. Tufts of pale gray sofa stuffing. Ash. Snow. Snowfall in August. No two snowflakes are alike. That's what they teach you. How do they know? I'm dubious.

I look at a hand holding a gun. My hand. My gun. There are still bullets left in the magazine. One bullet left at least. I can tell. Burke taught me that the slide snaps open when the magazine is empty. I witnessed it with my own eyes at the gun range. The slide of my gun hasn't snapped open yet.

Pocket. Gun. I put the gun back. I need my right hand. I can't lift my left arm. My shoulder hurts less now. The pain has ducked out for a quick minute, not for long. *I'll be back in a jiffy.* I grab the next-to-bottom shelf of a bookcase with my right hand and pull myself up to my knees. *Encyclopedia Britannica VIII Piranha–Scurfy. Encyclopedia Britannica IX Scurlock–Tirah.* I climb to the next shelf, then the next, then I'm standing. What does *scurfy* mean? Is that maybe how I feel right now? Do I feel scurfy? If I wasn't in shock before, I am now.

Big Beard lies motionless on the floor, in the doorway, his eyes open and his mouth open and his cheek and ear pressed against the floor. Like he's listening to underground rumblings. Like . . . remember that one old movie? The outlaw listening to the iron rails, hearing the train approach. I don't know if I watched the whole movie, but I remember that one scene.

I walk across the room. Slowly, but I can walk. I'm not dying. I grip the doorframe with my right hand and step over Big Beard. I don't look down at him, at his open eyes or his beard, wet with blood. I'm shaking again. Remember that other old movie? When the elevator doors open and blood gushes out? My mom liked scary movies and the Bangles and her favorite member of Van Halen wasn't David Lee Roth or Eddie Van Halen or even the other Van Halen who played drums. Her favorite member was . . . I can't remember his name. The one with the beard. I think my mom felt sorry for him because no one ever remembered his name.

Stairs. One foot after another. If I'm dying, it's a little like dreaming. I'm both panicked and relaxed. I notice odd details. There's a thin brass rod at the base of every stair, to secure the strip of carpet that cascades down from the top. Ingenious. In the upstairs hallway, on the inside of a doorframe, I see faded marks and names and heights and dates. What? Oh! Long-ago kids, measured as they grew. Where are you now, Patrick 1983? How has life treated you?

Tracy hugs me. She tries to keep me upright. No good. I sink to the floor anyway.

"I need to lie down a second," I say.

"Oh, God."

I hear a car door slam. I hear gravel clatter as a car pulls up outside. Maybe not in that order. Maybe vice versa.

Tracy feels around gently. Trying to see where I'm hurt.

"Everywhere," I say.

"What?"

"Go."

I lie on my back and stare at the ceiling. Downstairs, the screen door squeaks. I have supernatural hearing suddenly. I turn my head. Tracy is closing the door of the wardrobe.

"Be very, very quiet," she tells Pearl and Jack, still inside. She fits the padlock back on the latch so you can't tell it was broken open, not if you don't look closely. She sits down with her back against the wardrobe and hugs her knees. She kicks. She's kicking away the tire tool. Under the bed.

No, no, no. What is she doing? It's not too late. She has to go, she has to get away, she has to try at least. The stairs creak. I stare at the ceiling again. I weigh a thousand pounds. I can't lift my hand. I can barely lift my pinkie finger. I have to lift my hand. I have to reach the gun in my pocket.

"I don't know where the fuck he came from," Tracy says. "He must have followed me from my meeting. I swear. You know I'm telling the truth."

Nathan stands over me. He moves his face into the square of ceiling I'm staring at. "Hi, there."

"Did he kill Billy?" Tracy says.

"He killed all three of those motherfuckers," Nathan says. Then, to me, "You killed all three of those motherfuckers. What do you have to say for yourself, young fella?"

My finger touches the button on the flap of my cargo short. I slip my hand into my cargo pocket, but the pocket is empty. The gun is gone. *Shit.* I thought I put the gun in my pocket. I thought I did. I see the gun. There it is: still downstairs, in the living room. Hardwood floor, edge of rug, puffs of snow. I could have sworn I put it back in my pocket.

Nathan sets his foot on my chest, on my heart. He presses gently, rhythmically. "You're leaking," he says.

"He must have followed me," Tracy says. "You have to believe me."

He looks over at her. "Do I?"

I grab Nathan's ankle. Both hands. I'm too weak to push his foot off my chest.

"He wanted Pearl and Jack," Tracy says. "He's insane. Or he must be some kind of pervert. I'm telling you the truth."

I understand why she's doing this. I understand. She's smart. She wants to keep herself and her kids alive. But how long will she be able to keep her kids alive? Oh, Tracy, make a break for it. Try, at least. This might be your last chance. You and the kids might make it downstairs.

"I believe you," Nathan says.

"I swear," she says.

He looks back down at me. He's still pumping his foot against my heart, a nice, even rhythm. He smiles. "Hurry up," he says. "I don't have all night."

I turn my head away. I won't let Nathan's face be the last thing I see in life. I'm watching Tracy now. I want her to understand . . . what? I'm not sure. I did my best? Oh, sure. That won't matter to her. It won't matter to anybody.

But Tracy isn't even looking at me. She's looking up at Nathan. She's raising the Glock, my gun, and pointing it at him. He doesn't see her do it. He's still smiling down at me, his foot pumping slowly away.

My gun. How did she . . . ? Oh. *Oh*. When she was feeling around. She wasn't checking to see where I was hurt. She was searching for my gun. *Oh*.

Her hands are steady. The Glock is steady.

"Look at me," Nathan says to me.

I don't. I keep my eyes on Tracy. I watch her pull the trigger, see the flash, feel Nathan thud to the floor next to me.

50

I'm calling 911," Tracy says.

I'm not dead. How is that possible? I manage somehow to lever myself up onto my right elbow. I still can't use my left arm. I use the wall behind me, my back and butt doing most of the work, and maneuver myself into a sitting position. Mostly a slumped position. How am I not dead? It shouldn't be possible.

"I'm getting you help." Tracy dials 911 on a phone I don't recognize. Nathan's phone. She puts it to her ear.

"Wait," I say. "Stop. You have to go. You can't be here."

She glances over at Nathan's body, then lowers the phone. She ends the call. I don't need to explain it to her. If she's still here when the cops and the EMTs arrive, if she's anywhere near, she's fucked. Maybe they won't arrest her for murder, but they'll take her kids. One way or another.

"It's fine," I say. "Go. Don't worry about me. I'm not dead."

"But—"

"The kids. Go."

She hesitates, then nods. "I'll call when we're on the highway. I'll call 911 from there."

"Then get rid of his phone. Throw away his phone."

"I'll send help."

"Perfect."

Now that I'm slumped up against the wall, I weigh a thousand pounds again. No, two thousand pounds. I can't even move my pinkie finger now. As the blood leaves my body, my body gets heavier. That doesn't seem like solid science. It doesn't seem fair.

"Don't forget Salvador. The hospital. Drop him there, please."

"I promise."

Tracy drags a blanket off the bed and covers Nathan's body. She doesn't want to see what she's done. Or she doesn't want the kids to see. She unlatches the padlock and opens the door of the wardrobe.

"Let's go, guys," she says. "We have to hurry. We're going for a ride. Just the three of us. We're not coming back here."

She takes Pearl's hand and helps her out of the wardrobe. Jack next. Their faces—still empty, still impassive. They are so deep inside themselves. This world is just a shadow to them, a vague outline, the loudest gunshot is probably just a whisper.

But then . . . what's happening? They see me sitting slumped against the wall and this time I catch a flicker of genuine surprise in their eyes. They recognize me. They do. They recognize me from the municipal building and they realize I never gave up on them. That flicker of surprise in their eyes, that flicker of *life*—it's honestly the most amazing thing I've ever personally experienced.

Tracy hurries Pearl and Jack across the room. She pauses at the door. Why is she pausing? She needs to go. They need to go *now*. Tracy puts a hand on Pearl's shoulder and turns her so she's facing me. Jack duplicates his sister's move. He's facing me too now.

"This is Hardly," Tracy says. "Hardly, this is Pearl and Jack."

"Hi," I say.

Then they're gone. I hear them on the stairs. I hear the front screen door slam shut. I hear car doors slam shut. I hear the engine of my car start. The transmission always shrieks, when you shift into reverse, like it's seen a spider.

One minute later, maybe less than that, the clunk and growl of my engine has faded completely away. All I can hear now are the cicadas and my own breathing. It's getting darker, but not darker like dusk giving way to night—more like darker from the edges in, like the light is being pulled down a drain.

I'm not dead, but I'm dying. I already knew this, but now I have to face facts. Even if Tracy had called 911, no way would the EMTs have been here in time. We're in the middle of nowhere. Fact.

But Tracy and the kids are gone. Free. Safe. I can relax now. I can't, though. I'm a candy-ass after all, suddenly scared of dying. I wish I believed in heaven, my mom waiting for me there. Yeah, no. I try to believe. Nope. But there's no rule against *imagining* it, right? That makes me feel a little less scared.

Tracy and the kids are gone and free and safe. That makes me feel a little less scared too.

My phone buzzes in my pocket. I weigh ten thousand pounds now, but miraculously I'm able to pull out my hand and tap the green button with a bloody finger.

"You can't elude me forever," Eleanor says. "I am relentless."

"I surrender."

"Where are you? Did you just wake up? You sound weird. Or are you just really stoned?"

I remember the toy cowboy I found in the HVAC closet. It's in the glove compartment of my car. I was supposed to give it back to Pearl and Jack. The big finish to my story! I completely forgot about it. Maybe they'll look in the glove compartment at some point and find the toy cowboy. No worries if they don't. Pearl and Jack are gone and safe and free. That's the only important part of the story.

"Hello?" Eleanor says. "I swear, if you're blowing me off again I will rip out your heart and eat it."

"No."

"No, you aren't blowing me off again, or no, don't eat my heart?"

"It was hard."

"What was?"

"When you bailed. On me."

"I didn't bail on you. You idiot, I'm going to help you. Whatever lunatic thing you decide to do, I'll be there. I just wanted to discuss all reasonable alternatives first."

The phone slips through my fingers and falls to my lap. It's much more challenging this time to pick it up, lift it back to my ear. Last time, I'm afraid, that's happening.

"Seriously?" I say.

It makes me happy that Eleanor wasn't actually going to bail on me. But she was right. I should have listened to her. I'm an idiot. Look at me. Look at all this. Felice was right. I got myself killed. I could have gotten Pearl and Jack and Tracy killed too—very, very easily. Thank God for Tracy, who shot Nathan and saved the day. Otherwise I would have fucked everything up.

"Maybe I helped," I say.

"What are you talking about?"

"Maybe I fucked up but also helped a little. It's complicated."

Eleanor is quiet for a few seconds. "Are you okay?"

"Scared."

"Scared?"

But talking to Eleanor makes me less scared too. It's just what I need at the moment. "Remember?" I say.

"Remember what?"

"That fence. You went all ninja."

"What's wrong? Hardly, are you okay? Where are you?"

"You are."

"What?"

"A fundamentally likable person."

"Tell me where you are. I'll come get you. Right now."

Is she crying? Why would she be crying? The phone slips from my hand. I weigh ten thousand pounds now. I am as heavy as an entire planet. No more moving. I have made my last move.

What will dying be like? And when exactly will it happen? I don't love the suspense. I decide I get to decide what dying will be like: smoke from a snuffed flame, one last curl of life rising into the sky, and in that moment I'll glimpse the future.

Arizona. A nice little house. Cactus in the front yard? Yes. And flowers. Swing set in the backyard. Tracy sipping coffee on the deck, watching Pearl and Jack play with the dog. I see Pearl and Jack laughing and running, falling down and popping right back up, laughing and running some more. Sunrise in the desert is unbelievably beautiful.

ACKNOWLEDGMENTS

I honestly can't express how grateful I am to have Shane Salerno as my agent and friend. Having Shane in my corner makes all the difference, every single day, and I don't know where I'd be without him. Thanks also to everyone else at the Story Factory, especially Don Winslow.

Thanks to Emily Krump, my editor, and Liate Stehlik, my publisher. Their belief in me as a writer is deeply, deeply appreciated.

I'm indebted to everyone at William Morrow and HarperCollins. Special thanks to Brian Murray, Jennifer Hart, Kelly Rudolph, Ed Spade, Andy LeCount, Kaitlin Harri, Tessa James, Julianna Wojcik, Mark Meneses, Sabrina Annoni, and Guillermo Chico. Extra-special thanks to Danielle Bartlett and Carla Parker, who have been with me, and behind me, from the very beginning.

There are so many excellent people in my life. I don't deserve them. To name just a few: Ellen, Adam, Jake, Sam, Sarah, Kayla, Lauren, Thomas Cooney, Terrence Cooney, Trish Daly, Misa Shuford, Rene Sanchez and Kerri Westenberg, Martha Sanchez, Laura Moon, Scott and Jennifer Booker, Alicia and Chris Milum, Chris and Elizabeth Borders, Titi Nguyen, Janice Dillon Himegarner, Kristen Cole, Thy Nguyen, Erin Redfearn, Susanna Rodriguez Lezaun, Carlos Bassas del Rey, Eduardo Nanclares, Ann and Joel Guthals, Dotty Baker, Theresa Lee and Sheila Prosser.

And I won't forget those who have passed away in the last few years: Chris McGinn, Sam Silvas, Peggy Hageman, Barbie Steelman, Mike Berney, and (that handsome devil with the world's best laugh) Evan Klingenberg.

I had help with the research for this book. Thank you to Aubrey McDermid, Rachel Holt, Kaden Cook, and Steve Hill.

The best part about being a crime writer is that you become part of the crime-writing community. I've met some of my absolute favorite people in the world here (they know who they are, I hope), and I'm so grateful for all the writers, readers, reviewers, bloggers, marketers, and booksellers I've had the good fortune to know.

My wife, Christine, is the best thing that ever happened to me. I've been playing with house money ever since.

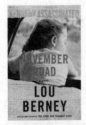